THEN AND NOW

Twenty years ago an unknown wrote the following opening to the dust jacket copy:

> **"A QUEER KIND OF DEATH** is a funny, far-out, malicious mystery novel."

Some things don't change.

GEORGE BAXT

A QUEER KIND OF DEATH

INTERNATIONAL POLYGONICS, LTD.
New York

A QUEER KIND OF DEATH

Printed and manufactured in the United States of America by
Guinn Printing.
First IPL printing September 1986.
10 9 8 7 6 5 4 3 2 1

A PREFACE TO THE TWENTIETH ANNIVERSARY EDITION OF A QUEER KIND OF DEATH

My birth pangs began in London approximately six or seven years before I actually began writing this book, which was to be my first novel. The seed of the idea came to me when I was taken to what I thought was a somewhat bizarre party given by a celebrated theatrical set designer. He was to be the inspiration for the character I later called Jameson Hurst. Years later, 1965 to be precise, I was back in New York and had been back for three years, and to paraphrase a line from ALL ABOUT EVE, the wolves were at my rear and nipping. I was flat broke and there wasn't a TV or movie script job in sight.

On June 11th of that year, which was my forty second birthday, I awoke at the crack of dawn, there not having been much sleep that night anyway, and stared at the ceiling where I hoped to find a solution to my financial problems, short of committing a burglary. That party reappeared, and I began to think of a very hip black man I occasionally had a drink with at Elaine's famous celebrity hangout on New York's upper East side. He soon evolved into Pharoah Love. (I deliberately misspelled Pharoah. Nobody has ever mentioned it!! If they ever do, I'll tell them his mother couldn't spell, although she took the name from the Bible). Seth Piro, like me at the time, was a failed writer. The psychiatrist I based on my own. Veronica was inspired by a close girlfriend who happily still remains close. And I knew my first novel had to be a shocker, demand attention, and I decided to utilize the New York homosexual otherworld that I knew so well.

That day, in a dead heat of inspiration, I wrote the first four chapters. I remember working from about eight in the morning until very late that night. It was easy because I knew how the book would end and when you know where you're going, it's a cinch getting there. I wrote with all the innocent assuredness of the first novelist. I was having a ball writing it and I let the juices flow freely. I wrote what came to mind and didn't give a damn about shocking or offending, I simply let myself go. But actually, there was no controlling the creative flow, the book had taken over by itself. One line led to another just as one incident dovetailed into another. Midway into the book I had to set it aside for a few weeks because, hallelujah and thank you God, David Susskind purchased an idea I had for a half-hour sitcom, "Penelope Beware!," which CBS bought with me to write the pilot script.

In the meantime, I let my agent, the wonderful Jay Sanford, read what I had written of my first novel which I intended to call DEAD CAT. He called me with what for him was restrained excitement. "For God's sake," I recall him saying, "where's the rest of this?" That was all the incentive I needed. After turning in the sitcom script (it now rests in sitcom heaven along with all other dead pilot films) I went back to DEAD CAT and about five days later, it was a Thursday, I brought it to Jay. The following Tuesday morning, he phoned me greeting me with his usually solemn "Good morning." There was a pause. He said, "Simon and Schuster". "Simon and Schuster what?" "They've bought DEAD CAT." I couldn't believe it! Within four business days? Unheard of. I later learned that on Monday morning it was rejected by Lee Wright at Random House who was afraid of it (she later published A PARADE OF COCKEYED CREATURES and its sequel, "I!", SAID THE DEMON, (soon to be reissued by International Polygonics) and Jay rushed it over to Bob Gottlieb at S&S who turned it over to his new mystery editor, Barbara Norville, who read it immediately and wanted it for her first book. It was she who came up with the title, A QUEER KIND OF DEATH (I still prefer DEAD CAT). After committing to the book, Gottlieb began expressing apprehensions. Publish it as a mystery or as a "straight" (no pun intended) novel? I insisted it was not a gay book and I still do. It is a murder mystery that happens to involve some homosexuals. (If you care to count the number of homosexuals in the book, you'll find they are still a minority!) At any rate, it was published under the Inner Sanctum label, and issued on June 11, 1966 (again my birthday), and then the fun began. Anthony Boucher in the Sunday *New York Times* gave it a dazzling rave notice. The book found its audience, small, but a beginning of faithful followers. Popular Library, despite equal amounts of raves and condemnations (someone name Richard Schickel writing in the now defunct *Herald Tribune* headlined his review "A Queer Bowl of Fruit" and was absolutely brutal. I tended to think at the time I must have struck a nerve), requested sequels. I wrote two, TOPSY AND EVIL preceded by SWING LOW, SWEET HARRIET (both to be reissued in proper order by International Polygonics).

Amusingly enough, while Hollywood and TV shied away from A QUEER KIND OF DEATH, they were attracted to SWING LOW, SWEET HARRIET. It was optioned for films over the years by producer Gabriel Katzka and director Barry Shear. It was Shear's untimely death and later the death of Walter Wanger who was to produce the film for Gabe that sounded the death knell to a film version of HARRIET.

A QUEER KIND OF DEATH, bless its heart, outlives it partisans and its detractors, and along the way over the past two decades, has acquired fresh armies of admirers. Even my dentist's daughter (he told me) said, after reading and admiring the book, "You mean to say that you put *your* hand in *his* mouth?." Bless her and bless all of you.

New York City
April 1986   George Baxt

For Jacqueline Babbin
My foul-weather friend

1

Seth Piro was constantly bored by cab drivers, the check-out girls at Daitch's Shopwell, and the social activities of Sybil Burton. He had never met Mrs. Burton; he resisted intimate conversations with the check-out girls, and he wished the cab driver hunched over the wheel in front would be struck dumb. The identification on the dashboard said his name was Salvatore Lopella and Salvatore had turned heart-attack white when Seth had given him the address in Brooklyn. But now, as he headed downtown toward Brooklyn Bridge, color had returned to Salvatore's cheeks and strength emanated from his vocal cords. Salvatore had a lot to say about the mayor, a union for cab drivers, Salvatore's brother-in-law who was a fink, and what to do about a water shortage. Seth prayed for a Salvatore shortage, but God was tuned out.

Seth tuned out. Salvatore's words dissolved into a hum like a dentist's drill, and Seth stared out the window and thought about the funeral. Goodbye to Ben Bentley whose twenty-six years had been summed up by the *Daily News* two days ago, in three paragraphs.

Ben Bentley, actor and model, was found dead this morning by his cleaning woman, Eliza Griffin. His body was submerged in a bathtub full of water. In the bathtub was a radio, still plugged into the socket. The coroner's report stated death was by electrocution.

Seth lit a cigarette. Death by electrocution. A radio accidentally falls into a bathtub and Ben Bentley is dead. Ben sitting and soaping his muscular body, singing along with Johnny Mathis, playfully flicking soapsuds at Seth sitting on the stool and staring at him dolefully.

"Snap out of it." Ben had laughed. "It's not the end of the world! We'll see each other when I get back from Mexico."

How soon after he silently left the bathroom, left the apartment, did Ben die? Was it quick, Seth wondered, as he had wondered for the past two days, was it painless, was Ben really dead? Ben was really dead. The funeral was at twelve noon and loquacious Salvatore would get him there on time. "What's the rush?" Salvatore had asked after a few anxious minutes stuck in traffic. "The stiff ain't goin' anyplace." The stiff is, thought Seth, to his own private corner of the world somewhere out on Long Island.

Traveling swiftly over Brooklyn Bridge, Seth thought about Pharoah Love. "That's a hell of a name for a detective, ain't it, man?" He smiled across his desk at Seth, whose face was etched with the aftereffects of too much Scotch and too little sleep. The handsome Negro shifted in his chair. "Did he always have the radio going when he took a bath?"

"He and the radio were attached at the hip," Seth replied. "Ben couldn't cope with silence." Pharoah smiled. This was something he understood about that dead cat. He didn't like silence either. Silence makes you think and a blaring radio deadens the thought process.

8

"I guess you were pretty good friends."

Seth stared into the inquisitive brown eyes for a few seconds while he measured his words and then spoke. "We shared an apartment for about a year until a few months ago."

"How long did you know this Bentley cat?"

What's it any of your damn business, thought Seth, but he quelled his rising gorge and spoke evenly. "About two years."

"Guess you get to meet lots of actors in your business."

You guess right, Buster. Sometimes you wonder if that's all you're going to meet in your business. Actors who wonder if you might introduce them to this director or that producer. Actors who wonder if there might be a part in your next television script. Actors who wonder if you expect them to go to bed with you and probably will if necessary. Sometimes if it's not necessary.

"Ben and I used to work out at the same gymnasium," Seth heard himself saying. "That's how we met. When my wife and I separated, Ben suggested we take a place together. What's all this got to do with his death?"

Pharoah lit a cigarette. "Just that you were the last to see him alive. Your statement winds it up as far as the department's concerned. He always keep the radio on the shelf with the toilet articles?"

"I think so." On the shelf, just above the bathtub. He sat patiently awaiting Pharoah's next question.

"Did you know he's been on the books?"

Seth felt his temples begin to throb, and Pharoah sent a smoke ring into orbit.

"Three times. The first time for petty theft, case dismissed. The second time for soliciting, twenty-five-dollar fine. The

9

third time for attempted extortion. The charges were dropped. This last one was just a few months ago."

I know about this last one, you bastard, and you probably know I know. It was my wife he was trying to shake down.

"The lady in case number three was Veronica Urquist." Pharoah's eyes never left Seth's face, and Seth wondered if a muscle was twitching, betraying any emotion.

"That's no lady," said Seth with a trace of a smile, "that's my wife." Pharoah grinned and it pleased Seth that it was such a warm grin. The detective could be likable if he tried.

"What'd he have on her?"

"What difference does it make now?" asked Seth. "Ben's dead."

"But your wife ain't."

And the reason behind this interview began to engulf Seth. His hands held tight to his knees to keep himself from trembling.

"You've written enough thrillers yourself, Mr. Piro. What's the odds on a guy taking a bath and pulling a radio down into the tub from a shelf two feet above his head and electrocuting himself?"

"I don't know." His voice was hoarse and crackled like static. "Freak accidents always happen."

"Only to freaks." Pharoah stubbed out his cigarette and sighed. "Did you know your friend had a record?"

"No," Seth answered truthfully. "I didn't know he was a thief and I didn't . . ." And he stopped, unable to finish the statement.

Pharoah's ivories glistened again in the reflection of the desk lamp. "He was a hustler, Mr. Piro. A professional whore. Since the age of at least sixteen, when we picked him up for lifting a wrist watch and a wallet from a buyer's room at the Hotel Astor." He read from a report on his desk. "Case dismissed on plea of youthful indiscretion by the defendant's sister, Ada Bergheim, who made full restitution to the et cetera et cetera et cetera." He looked up. "Four years later he was picked up for soliciting in a subway john. I was the arresting officer."

If I screamed, Seth thought, would he lock me up for a maniac?

"He's also been brought in for questioning about half a dozen times during the past five years." Pharoah settled back in his chair. "You didn't know any of this while you were living with him?" Seth shook his head. If he said No his voice might crack and he'd burst into tears the way he often did with his analyst. And Pharoah Love was no analyst, though Seth was beginning to believe he could qualify.

"I guess that's possible," said Pharoah as he jotted a note on the pad. "Now let's see if I've got this straight. Bentley was taking the bath and you were sitting on a stool chatting with him."

Seth nodded.

"He was leaving for Mexico, presumably on a modeling job."

"Why 'presumably'?"

Pharoah looked up. "Because his agency has no record of any assignment in Mexico for him. And they handle all his bookings."

Seth said nothing. Pharoah continued.

"You brought him some cash he was borrowing and then left him while he was still bathing for an appointment with your analyst—which your analyst says you kept."

11

And I wish I could see the good doctor right now, thought Seth.

"The door was unlatched when the maid arrived an hour later. You remember if you pulled it shut when you left?"

Seth cleared his throat. "Ben had asked me to leave it open for her."

"Why? She has a key."

"I don't know why. He asked me to leave it open, so I left it open."

"Maybe he was expecting someone other than the maid."

"Maybe. I don't know."

"We found twelve dollars in his wallet. Is that all he borrowed from you?" The last was spoken with a satirical lilt, as though at any moment he might render Adele's Laughing Song.

"I never gave him the money." Pharoah's mouth formed an *O*. "When I got there, he said he didn't need it. He just wanted to see me, that was all."

"Tricksy little bugger, wasn't he?"

Very tricksy. And cutesy. And a liar. And a whore. And dead.

Seth heard Pharoah ask, "Did you have an argument?"

"There was no argument," said Seth, striking a match and lighting a cigarette. "I got angry at his pulling me from the typewriter when I'm fighting a deadline."

"You could have told him to drop by your place for the money." Score another for you, you bastard.

"It really didn't matter after all," said Seth, mustering a smile. "I was on my way to the analyst."

Tie score.

"I guess that does it," said the detective, adding "for now."

"But you think he might have been murdered?"

Pharoah shrugged. "We think a lot of things before we mark one of these cases 'closed.' Takes our minds off muggings and racial incidents."

The taxi swerved and avoided hitting a car pulling out of a parking space. Seth sat up with a start as Salvatore hurled curses out the window. They were heading down Flatbush Avenue toward Prospect Park, and Seth was trying to remember the last time he'd been to Brooklyn.

It was on the back of Ben's motorcycle last summer, heading for Coney Island and a hot dog at Nathan's. "I was born near here!" Ben shouted as he guided the motorcycle through the heavy traffic on the Brooklyn Expressway. "It's a stinking ghetto! I hate it!" That was when he first learned that Ben was Jewish, the second-born of an immigrant family that had settled in the Brownsville section of Brooklyn. Father dead. Mother ran a newsstand near a subway station. Sister, ten years older, a registered nurse. Benny Bergheim had played on the streets of Brownsville with other Jewish boys and Negro boys and Puerto Rican boys and had hated enough and learned enough to become Ben Bentley and move to Manhattan and be fawned over by wealthy and not-so-wealthy admirers and live in a studio apartment on the East Side and there take a bath and die of electrocution by a traitorous radio that had given him so much pleasure.

Seth began to think about the funeral. There'd be the sorrowing mother and the spinster sister with the piercing eyes, possibly moist in memory of the sweet little kid brother she occasionally took on picnics to Prospect Park, the park through which Salvatore was now so professionally maneuvering his taxi. That sweet little kid brother was Benny Bergheim. Seth couldn't evoke an image of Ada crying over Ben

Bentley. Benny Bergheim used to cadge pennies from her to buy sweets. Ben Bentley tried to cadge morphine from her to sell at an outrageous price. An echo chamber in his brain began to reverberate with Pharoah's question: "You didn't know any of this while you were living with him?"

Not at first, Pharoah, not at first.

The memory of that interview with Pharoah Love was still too painful. He filed the detective away in a dark recess.

Who else would be at the funeral? Veronica? He almost chuckled. She'd be just perverse enough to be there. "Why not?" he could hear her saying. "After all, sweetie, until he showed his nasty streak, he was an absolute love." He was indeed. Seth didn't know how absolute a love Ben had been to Veronica until Ben's drunken confession he'd been to bed with her at least four times. But who hadn't, mused Seth, at least four times. Even Seth had been to bed with her at least four times.

Cool, controlled Veronica. The girl seemingly wise beyond her years who had read his first short story, which he had submitted to the agent for whom she worked, and promptly sold it to *Collier's*. Veronica Urquist, Hunter College's gift to the world of literature. The girl most likely to succeed, and did. "Why shouldn't we get married, darling?" she had asked that evening in Michael's Pub, one hand caressing his, the other hand caressing a glass of very dry martini. "We go well together. We have fun together. We underst nd each other. And people are beginning to wonder why we're both still single. If only to see all those jaws drop, we ought to get married."

Seth fought a tiny shudder and unconsciously began to hum "Seven Years with the Wrong Woman." It wasn't that

Veronica was so wrong, it was that she was always so right. She told him often enough. She rose rapidly from secretary to Ruthelma Kross, lady literary agent extraordinaire, to the seat of editor at Saber House. Didn't Saber House publish his first two novels, unacclaimed and unprofitable, but published? Life with Veronica had been compatible enough. A man couldn't ask for a better roommate.

Seth stared out the window after filing Veronica away alongside Pharoah Love. They just might get to like each other. His eye caught a street sign. Eastern Parkway. They must be nearing the funeral parlor. What would he say to Ada—"I'm sorry?" And Mrs. Bergheim? What does one say to a heartbroken mother who had looked at her son through rose-colored glasses? He had met her that night on their way back from Nathan's.

"Come on. Let's go say 'hello' to my old lady!" And Ben bore down on the gas. It was after midnight when they reached her newsstand, an island of printed matter on a busy intersection. The stand was piled high with the evening papers and business was brisk. She wore an apron over a faded print dress, and the apron pockets bulged with coins. "Evening papers! Getcha evening papers!" she hawked with a thick accent. And then her happy cry of "Benny!" as they pulled up alongside her and Ben cried, "Hey, Mama!"

They had stayed with her for about half an hour as Seth marveled at the amount of business she did. How much of her money, Seth mused, went to Ben? What had he had on her? Seth hated himself for thinking that.

Salvatore cut through his thoughts. "Hey, Bud. I t'ink dat's it up ahead."

Seth looked through the windshield and saw the funeral

parlor up ahead. There was a hearse parked at the curb and, behind it, two limousines. There were a few people standing on the sidewalk and an old man vending pretzels to some of them. Seth couldn't imagine funerals rousing appetites. Salvatore pulled in ahead of the hearse. Seth paid him and got out of the cab. He didn't know a soul on the sidewalk. He passed the pretzel vender and entered the funeral home.

A tall young man in a black morning coat stepped from behind a desk and asked solemnly, "Can I help you?"

"The Bergheim funeral."

"Auditorium C. The services are in ten minutes."

Seth found Auditorium C and went in. There were about twenty rows of seats, almost half of them filled with mourners, to Seth's surprise. At the end of the auditorium was a dais and a lectern. Beneath the dais was the coffin. The lid was open. An usher approached him.

"Do you have a hat?" he asked Seth.

"No," came Seth's startled reply, "I don't," as he cursed himself silently for not having familiarized himself with the rituals of the Jewish funeral. The usher gave him a reassuring look and crossed to a table on which rested a carton of paper skullcaps. He gave one to Seth, who placed it on his head, wishing for a mirror.

"Take any seat behind the first two rows. Those are reserved for the family. If you wish to view the body, please do so now. The coffin will be closed when the services begin." Seth nodded and slowly walked down the side aisle. He wondered why he felt a fool. A few mourners turned to stare at him out of curiosity, and Seth wondered why he blushed.

"Hello there, cat." It was a whisper, but the voice was unmistakable. He looked down into the face of Pharoah Love

16

and the combination of the detective and the paper skullcap seemed incongruous. He stifled the urge to laugh. Pharoah seemed to read his mind and winked. Seth continued on to the coffin. There was a door a few feet beyond the coffin and he could hear the muffled sound of mourning.

Then he looked into the coffin.

Ben lay encased in a shroud, on his head a white satin skullcap. The thick black hair was neatly combed; the handsome face was carefully waxed; and for a chilling second Seth thought the eyelids had fluttered. How often had he seen this look of repose on Ben's face in the bed alongside his. How often had he stroked the cheek gently to awaken him. Oh my God, he thought, oh my God, I'm going to cry.

And Seth wept.

2

HE GROPED in his pocket for a handkerchief. As he pulled it out, he felt something coming out with it, and too late, his key chain clattered to the floor. He heard a gasp behind him as through his blur of tears he looked for the offending object. He scooped it up, returned the key chain to his pocket, and then swiftly wiped his eyes. He wanted to move to a seat, but he was too paralyzed with embarrassment. He didn't want to look at Ben again. A hand touched his arm. Veronica stood alongside him. He took her hand and held it tightly as she stared down at Ben. Then gently leading Seth, she headed up the center aisle and they found seats in the rear of the auditorium.

"Trust me to make a fool of myself," Seth whispered, jamming the handkerchief back into his pocket. Veronica patted his hand sympathetically.

She kept her voice modulated when she spoke. "Where have you been past two days? I left a dozen messages on your service. Why didn't you call me?"

"Later," he whispered.

"Later" was not a word to stop Veronica Urquist. "What's

18

that detective doing here? He doesn't look Jewish." Seth wanted to pinch her but thought better of the attention the resultant outcry might bring. Instead he said, "Shut up till we get this over with." But it would have been easier to have stopped a flow of lava.

"He questioned me for over an hour yesterday," she whispered. "Brought up that whole mess of Ben trying to blackmail me. He doesn't think Ben's death was accidental." Seth said nothing. He nudged Veronica as the door beyond the coffin opened and Mrs. Bergheim, weeping softly, was led in. Ada, her face betraying no sign of emotion, held Mrs. Bergheim's right arm. Holding Mrs. Bergheim's left arm was a middle-aged man wearing a skullcap, a prayer shawl around his shoulders, and carrying a Bible. The women wore pinned on their dresses a small tape of black cloth slit up the center. Seth thought this might be the equivalent of the black armband worn by gentiles in mourning. Two middle-aged couples, all weeping, followed the Bergheims and the rabbi, and behind them, six other mourners, four young men and two young women. "Cousins," hissed Veronica, and Seth nudged her again.

The rabbi led the Bergheims to their seats in the front row and took his place behind the lectern as the usher shut the lid on the coffin and then moved away. Seth's eyes followed the usher's progress up the side aisle until he passed a heavily veiled woman sitting alone, digging around in a huge purse. Seth stared in fascination at the woman as she extracted a filmy lace handkerchief from the purse and held it to her mouth. Seth whispered to Veronica, "Don't look now, but Ella Hurst is here." Veronica's head swiveled immediately to the left as the rabbi began the services.

19

"Well I'll be damned!" whispered Veronica. "Where's that shit of a brother of hers?" Seth squeezed her hand for silence. The service was conducted in Hebrew and Mrs. Bergheim's weeping was becoming more audible.

Seth closed his eyes, but he could not shield his ears. Others were now weeping too, and even Ada's head was bowed. It's got to end soon, it's got to end soon, he repeated to himself. It's got to end and I'll find a bar and . . . what the hell's Ella Hurst doing here? Ella the recluse, who has claimed never to have budged from her Gramercy Square apartment in over fifteen years. Ella the strange. Ella the weird, with her face forever swathed in veils, even within the boundary of her own apartment. And where indeed was her brother? If Ella could make the touching sacrifice of crossing the threshold of her self-made sanctuary, where was Jameson? Fat Ella and lean Jameson, as unlikely a pair to be cast in the roles of brother and sister.

Jameson the debonair. Jameson the chic. Jameson the wit. Jameson the man of sixty—maybe less, maybe more—with the body of a man in his twenties, lean, taut, and muscular, face miraculously unlined by age, as he strutted along the poolside of his country home in Westport. "He's had his face lifted twice," Ben confided as they lay side by side sunning themselves that weekend. "Ella told me."

And Ella the veiled. Ella the fat. Ella the enigma, whose loathing of her brother was vocalized at every possible occasion. "That simpering pederast!" she said with deadly simplicity the first time Ben had taken Seth to meet her, and Ben had chuckled with delight. How much had Ben gotten from the Hursts?

The services were over and two ushers were wheeling the coffin out the side door. The rabbi joined Ada and together they helped the sobbing Mrs. Bergheim to her feet. "Benny!" she cried. "My Benny!" And Ada softly whispered in her ear. Veronica whispered to Seth, "Let's get out of here. I'm starved." Seth was peering about, looking for Ella Hurst, but the hulking enigma was gone. He looked at his wrist watch. Twelve-fifteen. He rose and followed Veronica out of Auditorium C.

They found the combination delicatessen and bar directly across the street from the funeral parlor. Drinks were ordered and Veronica sat with her arms folded on the table, searching Seth's face.

He sat back in the chair and tapped his fingers nervously against a glass of water. "What do you see?"

There was a trace of affection in Veronica's voice when she spoke. "It's not what I see, it's what I'm looking for. I'm looking for a sign of what I once saw in you ten years ago."

Seth mustered a laugh.

"I'm serious," she continued, "and I'm worried about you. Ruthelma tells me you haven't written a line in months. What are you living on?"

"I'll get back to it soon."

"But what are you *living* on?"

"Lay off."

"Do you want to get back together again?"

"And do what?"

"I thought you might be finished with all that when you bounced Ben."

"He bounced me."

"You wanted to be rid of him. Don't jazz me."

"I wanted to be rid of the relationship."

The waiter set the drinks in front of them and then stood

patiently with pad and pencil poised to take their food orders.

"Two pastramis on rye," commanded Veronica without looking up.

"You want pickles?" the waiter asked innocently.

Veronica glared at him. "Just the sandwiches."

"Tea, coffee, Pepsi-Cola, celery tonic . . ."

Veronica's eyes narrowed as she snapped, "Hemlock."

"That we don't carry," and he moved to the counter to give their orders.

"What about that detective?"

Seth's eyes met hers. "What about him?"

"If he doesn't buy Ben's death as accidental, then we're suspects in a murder case, and I don't like *that* one bit." She leaned back sharply in her seat for emphasis and then fiddled in her purse for a cigarette. "It could reopen that whole mess when Ben tried to shake me down."

Seth didn't want to talk about Ben or murder or shakedown, but he knew that wherever Veronica's conversation would lead, he would follow. That's how it always was with Veronica. He said, "Nobody forced you to go to bed with him."

"I was mad at you!" she snapped, clicking a lighter.

"Why'd you come to the funeral?"

"I was looking for you!" She plunked the lighter into her purse where it connected sharply with her compact. "I'm frightened. I don't know how to deal with police interrogations. It's not like negotiating with an author for publication. I thought you were finished with Ben. What were you doing in his bathroom?"

"Taking a leak. Next question."

Veronica burst out laughing and the waiter brought their

sandwiches. Seth sipped his drink while Veronica blew her nose, staring at him over the border of her handkerchief. Then she stared down at the sandwich and knew she could never eat it. "I still love you." She did not take her eyes off the sandwich. Seth put his drink down and took Veronica's hand.

"I'll always love you, but we can never get back together again. I just couldn't face it, that's all." Veronica squeezed his hand tightly and then reached for her drink.

"What the hell," she murmured. "I thought you'd agreed to what it would be like when I proposed to you. I guess it never works when you can't figure out who's wearing the pants in the family. Maybe neither one of us was ever meant for marriage."

"I'm planning a new book," he said suddenly. She looked up, eyes wide with delight, her face beaming with pleasure.

"If I was a composer I'd set a melody to that line and sing it over and over to myself. You're not kidding now. Yourself, that is."

"Nope." He smiled.

Veronica was immediately all business. "Saber House gets first crack at it. We still think you can come through. Maybe I can get you an advance. Try to get me a brief outline on about five sheets of paper and . . ." The "and" hung in mid-air as Seth turned around to see what Veronica was staring at.

Pharoah Love had entered and was striding toward them. "Greetings, cats! Can I sit for a minute?" He was sitting before anyone could reply. "Not interrupting anything?"

Seth smiled pleasantly. "Would you like a drink?"

"No, thanks, cat. Just spotted you through the window and thought I'd save myself a phone call. I'd like to get together with you again." He gave a friendly smile. "Your convenience, this time." Veronica began stirring her drink with her index finger.

"Can I phone you around five?" Seth asked.

"Five . . . five . . ." Pharoah was staring at the ceiling and thinking. "Yeah, cat, five'll be fine." Then he stared down at their sandwiches. "How you've got a stomach for that after what we've just been through. I hate funerals."

"Then why'd you come?" Veronica couldn't disguise the edge to her voice. Pharoah beamed his grin in her direction.

"Better yet, why did you?" He rose, placed his hat on his head, and sauntered out without waiting for a reply. With an exhale of disgust, Veronica pushed her sandwich aside.

"How can you *sit* there so calmly?"

Seth's voice was an octave higher when he spoke. "How the hell do you expect me to sit?"

"But he's after something."

"Any ideas how I can avoid him?"

"None. But just be careful what you tell him about yourself and Ben."

"Or do you mean you and Ben? Why was Ben shaking you down? What was it all about? What *was* it all about? Why'd you bring the police into it and then why did you just as suddenly drop the charges?"

"I can't tell you."

"Why not?" Faces turned as Seth's voice rose.

"Keep your voice down, for God's sake!" She shifted about in the chair and crossed her knees, puffing thoughtfully on the cigarette. "Oh, what the hell," she said suddenly, dropping the cigarette on the floor and grinding it with her shoe. "Ella Hurst took care of it."

"Ella!"

Veronica sipped her drink and then smiled. "She'd been writing her memoirs and thought Saber House might be interested in publishing them. So I went up to her inner sanctum and had tea with her a few times. And one day she turned to me and said, 'Dear girl, is someone shaking your tree?' You've met Ella. Half the time she talks you wish subtitles would flash across her chest. But I got her message. She knew Ben was giving me trouble. She never told me how she knew, but I spilled it all to her and two days later she phoned me and told me to drop the charges. There'd be no further trouble."

Seth chewed on this for a moment and, after sufficiently digesting it, asked her pointedly, "Why'd you call in the police at all if Ben's information was so devastating?"

"On my lawyer's advice." Her face hardened. "We hired a private detective to look into Mr. Bentley-Bergheim's background and found he had a police record. So we decided to play tit for tat."

"Was that before or after you laid him?"

"Oh, thanks a lot!" she stormed, jumping to her feet. Seth grabbed her arm and pulled her back into the chair. The waiter came rushing over.

"Something's wrong with the pastrami?"

"It's just dandy!" snapped Veronica, and the waiter retreated. Then, face red with rage, she leaned across the table to Seth. "The first time I slept with that bastard was a week after you walked out on me. And I deliberately set out to get him. And as you damn well know, he was never hard to get! The next three times were because the first one was so good. A statement I could never attribute to you!" She tore a dollar

25

bill from her purse and flung it on the table. "My share! We always go halfies, remember?" She stormed out of the place in a trail of Russia Leather, leaving Seth staring down into his drink. He kept his hands clenched under the table as he waited for the fire in his face to abate.

Seth Piro. Age, thirty-six. Height, just under six feet. Weight, one hundred and sixty-five pounds. Born, Atlantic City, New Jersey. Color of hair, light brown. Eyes, brown-green. Race, Caucasian. Religion, agnostic. Religion at birth, Greek Orthodox. Parents, dead. Profession, writer.

He could feel his pulse beat coming back to normal.

He looked up and the waiter was smiling down at him. He placed the check on the table and clucked his tongue sympathetically. Seth thought again about reading some Sholem Aleichem and smiled. "Sorry," he muttered. The waiter's shrug was a friendly one, and his sigh as he walked back to his station was the sigh of a man who understood the pain of the weight of emotional burdens.

Seth didn't know how many miles he walked or in which direction. He walked along a street heavily populated with pushcarts and voices with Jewish and Spanish accents crying their wares and haggling over prices. He smelled herring, pickles, halvah, freshly killed chickens, coffee roasting, and pizza pies. Then body odors and excrement and somehow, not remembering making the purchase, he was holding a cardboard cup of shaved ices and the tangy lemon flavor sharpened his taste buds and cleared his head. He flung the cup into a wastepaper basket and looked around for a taxi. Dear God, he murmured, dear God, it shouldn't be Salvatore.

It wasn't. Sitting behind the wheel of the red Jaguar that pulled up at the curb was Pharoah Love.

3

Hı, THERE, cat! Want a lift?"

Seth stared down at the quixotic smile on the detective's face. "You've been following me."

"That a statement, cat, or an accusation? Either way, you're right."

"Why?"

"I'm a slave to my impulses. Felt like it. Come on. Hop in."

Seth shook his head. "If it's not compulsory, I'd just as soon get a cab."

"You won't get a cab around here, cat, and the nearest subway is eight blocks. Come on." The trace of seductiveness in Pharoah's voice didn't escape Seth. Pharoah's face was beginning to take on an identity of its own. The eyes were no longer just a pair of inquisitive bulbs set in an inquisitor's face. They seemed to be asking for understanding, perhaps friendship. He can't be much older than myself, Seth thought. "Get with it, cat—" Pharoah laughed—"before I get a ticket for illegal parking. I got no pull with these Brooklyn cats."

Seth got in.

They drove in silence for a few minutes and then Pharoah finally spoke. "You kind of reached me back there at the funeral."

Seth stared straight ahead.

"I mean, the way you weren't ashamed to show your emotions. Some guys would rather choke to death than let a few tears run down their cheeks." He stole a glance at Seth when there was no reply. "Listen, cat, I'm *sincere*."

Without looking at him, Seth spoke. "I know you are. Why were you there?"

"I'm a cat like all the other cats, baby. Curiosity."

"About what?"

"About who'd be there besides the family. I figured you'd be there, but I didn't figure on your wife. Did you know the fat broad with the veils?"

"Ella Hurst."

"Who she?"

"Sort of a friend of Ben's."

"Just 'sort of'? Didn't know 'sort of' was enough to drag anybody to a funeral. Me, I have to have liked them a heap."

"I don't know Ella too well. I only met her a few times. Don't ask me to explain her reasons. Except . . ."

"I hear you, cat. Except what?"

Seth shifted uneasily and couldn't understand why he felt uneasy, but told him what he knew about Ella anyway. "She's been a recluse for at least fifteen years, or at least that's what she claims. Says she never leaves her apartment."

"Even in case of fire?"

"I haven't heard of anyone attempting to apply a match to her."

Pharoah chuckled.

"Her brother is Jameson Hurst."

"I figured that."

"You know him?"

"I seen him around."

Seth didn't ask where.

"Always has three or four handsome young numbers trailing him and always, but always, picks up the tab. Saw him one night in a crib in the village. He was having a fit. I don't mean angry, but I mean a fit."

"He's epileptic."

"Aha. Recognized it. Had a kid brother who went in for that. He's dead now." He honked his horn twice at a jaywalker. "That was the last time I cried."

Seth said nothing.

"Got knifed in a fight. Right in the middle of the fight he took this fit. One stupid bastard didn't know what it was all about. You know what I mean? Like superstitious. So he knifed him. I found the bugger. He's dead now." Seth was chilled by the matter-of-fact way Pharoah recited the incident. "No one harms mine," he said flatly.

Seth didn't recognize the bridge they were crossing.

"Williamsburg," said Pharoah. "Lived in it most of my life. Williamsburg, that is. Back there in Brooklyn. That's why in a way I understood the dead cat."

Ben Bentley. Dead cat.

Seth turned to look at Pharoah. "Why were you following me?"

Pharoah's face betrayed nothing. "I don't really know, if you want the truth. You see, later—and don't you forget to call me later. Right now's pleasure, later is business . . .

more questions." He interjected a sigh. "And they are necessary, I'm afraid, and . . ." He was searching for words that Seth began to understand did not come easily to him. "I guess it's only because you just touched me back there. And nothing reaches me like that too often. Where can I drop you? I'm heading for the station."

"Anywhere. I'll get a cab."

They found one on Third Avenue and Pharoah pulled up alongside it. "Five o'clock, right?"

"Five o'clock."

Pharoah pulled away and Seth entered the cab, giving the driver an address on West End Avenue. Seth sank back against the seat and lit a cigarette apprehensively. Then he exhaled with a sigh of relief. The driver wasn't a talker.

The funeral. Ben. Veronica. Ella. Pharoah Love. They had joined hands to dance a minuet in his brain. Ben and Seth. Seth and Veronica. Veronica and Ben. Ella and Veronica. Pharoah and Seth. The dance continued, but who was choreographing?

Think of the book, Seth said to himself, think of the book. You haven't written a line in months and what have you been living on?

"You kind of reached me back there at the funeral."

Think of the book.

"We always go halfies, remember?"

Veronica and Ben.

"Why, Ben, why?" Ben was stretched out on the sofa, puffing a cigarette and watching "Wagon Train."

"Because she asked me, that's why." He smiled contentedly as gunfire echoed from the set and a rustler dropped.

"It's so sick."

Ben had turned his head slightly and focused on Seth. "We agreed no questions, didn't we? You do yours and I do mine. Nobody set up any restrictions. Nothing was put off limits. You know how I am. It didn't mean anything. Why get into a shit snit about it? I did it for pleasure and she did it for spite. If you don't let her know you're mad, then she didn't gain any points. You want to go to a movie?"

It seemed as though the lights would never change. Then the driver shifted gears and the cab shot ahead. Seth hoped the letter had reached the New York *Times* in time for this Sunday's *Book Review*. I'm going to write a book. I'm going to write a book. I wonder if I will ever finish it. He lowered the window and flipped the cigarette out. They were crossing a Central Park transverse to the West Side when a motorcycle whizzed by. Seth leaned forward when he caught a glimpse of the driver. But it can't be. Ben's dead.

His effects. The stuff in his apartment. Seth clenched the armrest. What did Ben have locked in his desk drawers? Snapshots. Letters. What else? Ben saved everything. Ben never threw anything away.

"Why don't you throw some of that junk away?"

Ben was rummaging in the top drawer of his desk looking for book matches. "What do you want from me? You never can tell when some of this stuff will come in handy."

Handy for what, thought Seth as the cab turned into West End Avenue. For a shakedown? That sweet, handsome face. That strong, healthy body. Who could ask for a better façade to mask so perverse a mind? Why didn't I ever guess? Or did I suspect and wouldn't admit it to myself?

The cab driver was staring at him. "We're here."

"Oh!" Startled, Seth roused himself, paid the fare, and got

31

out of the cab. He entered the lobby of the building which he had described to the doctor as being decorated in early Samuel Goldwyn, and in a minute the elevator delivered him to the fifteenth floor.

The waiting room was empty when Seth entered the doctor's office, but the door to the doctor's room was open. Seth poked his head in. Dr. Walter Shlacher sat in the black leather armchair staring at him. His eyes peered owlishly from behind a pair of thick horn-rimmed glasses. His hands were folded over his ample stomach. His fly, as usual, was half open, and the legs were crossed, ankle over ankle. Seth had once described him to Veronica as an Austrian cherub with a mind like a steel trap.

"Ziddown," said Shlacher, moving his head slightly to indicate the couch. Seth shut the door and crossed to the couch. He fumbled for a cigarette and lit it, then reached over to an end table for an ash tray. Shlacher's eyes never left Seth. Seth cleared his throat.

"I went to Ben's funeral."

Shlacher uncrossed his legs.

"Veronica was there."

Shlacher took off his glasses and cleaned the lens with the end of his tie.

"So was the detective. You know, the one who questioned me. Pharoah Love."

Shlacher held the glasses up to the light as he examined the lens for any remaining specks.

"And Ella Hurst was there. You remember, I told you about her once. Jameson Hurst's sister. That was a surprise. You remember I told you. She's a recluse."

Shlacher cleared his throat, brought up some phlegm, pulled a handkerchief from the back pocket of his pants, and married handkerchief to phlegm, replacing the handkerchief in back pocket and readjusting himself in the chair.

"I'm afraid I cried."

"Vod's to be afraid of?"

Seth stared at the burning tip of his cigarette. "He's dead and I'm still emotionally involved with him."

Shlacher shifted his right arm so the elbow rested on one arm of the chair and opened the palm of his hand to prop his chin.

"I've started a new book."

Shlacher nodded.

"It's about Ben." He looked at Shlacher and all he could see in the glasses was the reflection of his burning cigarette. He placed the cigarette in the ash tray and then leaned forward, interlacing his fingers. "Actually I'd been thinking about it for weeks." He unlaced his fingers and sat back. "The book started to take over by itself—in my mind, that is." He unloosened his tie, the fingers fumbling at the knot. "Anyway, I haven't been this enthusiastic about writing something in months."

"Becawz you dink id will be a good book"—pronounced "bewk"—"or to eggzpiate your feelinks of guilt?"

"Guilt about what?" snapped Seth angrily.

"Aboud whad we alwayz dizcuzz."

Seth rubbed his forehead, wishing he hadn't asked for this extra hour, and knowing the doctor was reading his mind.

"Maybe," said Seth. "I'm not sure." Then he smiled. "But at least this time I know what I'm writing about."

Shlacher nodded approvingly. "Kud be very profidable. Emozzionally." Then he smiled his owl's smile. "Und finandjully."

Seth retrieved the cigarette from the ash tray and puffed on it thoughtfully. "A lot of people are going to be upset when they find out I'm doing this book on Ben."

"Ve are not indrezted in people, ve are indrezted in you. Vill you write fact or vill you write fiction?"

"I'm going to write the truth. I'm going to tell it all!"

"But vot is the truth? The boy was zuch a liar. And yourself? Vill you have the courage nod to abandon ziss project?"

"I had the courage to get rid of him!"

"He got rid of you. You told me zo." Seth started to remonstrate and then thought better of it. "You have been in treatment how long now? Five monz? You still cannot aggzept that redjection." Seth felt his eyes beginning to smart. Why did he always find himself trying to prove something to the doctor instead of to himself? "Id iz not zo terrible to be redjected. Iz often a blessing in disguise." Seth fought the tears with another puff of the cigarette and then squashed the butt to a pulp in the ash tray.

"Veronica wants me back."

There was a trace of a nod from Shlacher.

"That disturbs me."

"Vy?"

"Because Veronica never forgives."

"Perhaps she forgives ven it iss someone she loves. Can you not aggzept that?"

"But I don't want to go back to her!"

"Zo you redject her. Zere will be zomeone elze—ven you are ready."

Don't cry, darling, Seth could hear his mother saying, when you miss a streetcar, there'll be another one along in a little while. But, Mother, I don't like any of the other girls in school. Now, now, dear, just remember—there's a cover for

34

every pot. Seth smiled, and it proved contagious. The doctor smiled too. It was like having a gold star placed alongside his name when he'd been a good boy at school.

"The police aren't so sure Ben's death was an accident."

"Zo?"

"I guess—" Seth tried to muster a chuckle, but it stuck in his throat—"that makes me their number-one suspect. I was the last to see Ben alive."

"To your knowledj."

"Pharoah Love trailed me for about an hour after the funeral." The doctor cleared his throat. "I finally accepted a lift from him." The doctor scratched his cheek. "I dreamt about him last night."

"Zo?"

Seth lit another cigarette. "It wasn't much of a dream. I was on the motorcycle with Ben. I think we were going out to a beach—you know, the way we often did when we first met. Except, when we got to the beach, it was Pharoah Love driving the motorcycle."

Shlacher nodded.

"That woke me up."

"And vod duz thiz reprezent to you?"

"I'm not sure. Maybe it's because Ben represented a threat to me, and now it's the same with Pharoah." He could see the doctor wasn't buying.

"Iz ziss detectiff young?"

"About my age, I think."

"He haz zpoken to me, you know."

"Yes, he told me yesterday. To corroborate my alibi." And "alibi" brought Seth up short. Alibi!

"He haz zpoken to me again."

There was no hiding the startled expression on Seth's face. "About what?"

"He vished to know vod zort of cat you are." Seth burst out laughing. "I told ziz man that ziz treatment iz confeedendjul."

"And did he accept that?"

Shlacher shrugged. "Wiz me, he haz no choice."

"I have to call him at five. He wants to question me further."

"Yez."

"I suppose I can expect that to go on for a while."

"Perhapz."

"I don't know how to handle him."

"Perhapz vod is more important iz how he handlez you." What's going on in that mind of yours, Seth wondered. What do you really know about me? What opinions have you formed? Give me a clue. Give me a hint. Where do I stand?

Pharoah Love sat behind his desk finishing his paper work. He glanced at his wrist watch and then up at the wall clock for a second opinion. Five P.M.

The phone rang. Pharoah picked it up. "Detective Love." He smiled. "Hello, cat." He listened while the smile remained stationary. "That's right. Five on the dot. You free tonight?"

Seth sat in an easy chair by the window, staring at a tug pulling a barge down the Hudson. "Tonight?"

Pharoah was trying to balance a paper cutter on his index finger. "Be more relaxed away from the office. Police stations make people nervous."

You're making me nervous, thought Seth. He spoke matter-of-factly. "I was planning to do some work on my book."

"Nothing like work to take your mind off the late unpleasantness. Tell you what—I ain't free until about nine anyway. Got a few errands to do. Why don't we meet around nine. That'll give you a couple of hours in which to unwind."

How'd you guess I was taut, thought Seth.

"Place up in your neighborhood called Ida's. You know it?"

You probably know I know it, inscrutable one. It was a home away from home for Ben and me.

"Why don't you meet me there at nine?"

"I'll be there," said Seth, and hung up abruptly.

Pharoah heard the click and gently placed his phone in its cradle. "Very cool cat indeed," he whispered to himself. "Very cool."

Seth was drenched with perspiration. He fought a desperate urge to phone Dr. Shlacher.

"I don't know how to handle him."

"Perhapz vod iz more important iz how he handlez you."

Perhapz, Doctor, perhapz. Seth crossed to the bathroom and ran the tub. He stripped and then checked the contents of his wallet. Thirty-two dollars. Who picks up the check on an occasion like this? Pharoah? Does he have an expense account? He tossed the wallet back onto the desk, went back to the bathroom, and climbed into the tub. He closed the taps and began soaping himself. The soap slipped from his fingers, and as he lunged for it, his arm hit a container of Kleenex which plopped into the water.

Seth yelled. He knew it wasn't a radio, but he yelled.

4

Jameson Hurst posed with one hand on the mantelpiece of the enormous fireplace imported from Italy, which showed no visible aftereffects from its long and tedious journey. He wore a dark plaid smoking jacket, orange slacks, and on his feet delicate black pumps, each decorated with a green velvet bow. Pharoah thought he was a technicolor delight. If there was a cherry on his head, he might have dug in with a spoon. In his left hand Jameson warmed a snifter of brandy with a sensuously delicate movement of his wrist.

"It was kind of you to conduct the interview here, Mr. Love." His voice was a mellifluous purr.

"Gave me an excuse to examine your pad, cat." Pharoah smiled with a wink. "I saw the layout in *House and Garden*. It's even better in wide screen." He had been walking around the forty-by-thirty living room of the Gramercy Park town house, giving minute attention to the minute detail of the wallpaper which required minute attention.

"You're sure you wouldn't like a drink?"

"No, thanks," said Pharoah with a wave of his hand. "I've

got a long night ahead of me." Through the fifteen-foot mirror on the wall opposite the fireplace he could see Hurst studying him and he felt like a smear on a slide under a microscope.

"Something to nibble on perhaps?" asked Hurst, crossing to a coffee table and lifting a cup of macadamia nuts.

"I'm fine. Don't fuss, cat." Pharoah settled into a huge easy chair, his weight causing the delicate pillows to sigh with exhaustion. Hurst sat on the couch opposite him, arranging himself with professional ease, one leg crossed over the other and swaying gently, though there was no breeze in the room. He's got to be over sixty, thought Pharoah, but if pressed, he'd have to make the guess at forty. There was a tiny Cheshire grin on Hurst's face, and Pharoah felt that if Hurst were to leave the room, the grin would remain behind to keep him company.

"Such a tragic way to die." Hurst sighed, anxious to get down to the interview. "Electrocution! And *just* when it's been outlawed in this state." He sighed again and shook his head sadly. "You don't suppose it was painful, do you? I mean, can electrical appliances *really* be lethal?"

"Yes, when you're sitting in a tub full of water with one and it's plugged in."

"Oh oh oh," agonized Hurst. "To think the one thing he loved the most would do him in. A radio!" He sipped the brandy, mmm'ing as the warm liquid trickled down his throat and warmed his cold, aged veins.

"How long had you known him?"

Hurst contemplated the ceiling for a moment as he mmm'd again. "Ohhh, almost four years, I think." He lowered his eyes and they zeroed in on Pharoah. "You intimated on the phone the death might not have been all that accidental. Now who would want to murder poor Benjamin?"

"A lot of people."

Hurst was about to stiffen but thought better of it. Instead he cocked his head like a flirtatious parakeet and asked, "Surely you don't consider me *one* of them?"

"That cat's never paid any income tax in his entire life, did you know that?"

"Not *ever?*"

"No, never." Pharoah hoped this wouldn't lead into a Gilbert and Sullivan duet. "But he still managed to live on a pretty grand scale."

"Well, there was his modeling . . . and his occasional walk-ons on television . . . and didn't he do some commercials or something?"

"All penny ante. I get the impression he might have been subsidized."

Hurst contemplated his brandy. "He did borrow sums of money from me from time to time."

"Borrow?"

"Borrow."

"And did your sister contribute to his welfare?"

"Probably. She doted on the boy."

Pharoah popped a macadamia nut in his mouth and chewed on it thoughtfully for a moment. "Mr. Hurst, I think Bentley was blackmailing you, your sister, and a few other cats."

Hurst's finger traced the oval around the lip of the snifter. "I would never submit to blackmail, Mr. Love. And there is no reason for anyone to attempt to blackmail me. Ben and I were extremely fond of each other."

"So I gather from some of the stuff we found in the cat's desk."

Hurst sat up sharply. "Stuff? What do you mean, stuff?"

"Letters. Some notes. A notebook with some entries."

"Like what?"

"Like a list of monies received over the past three years from Jameson Hurst. That's an awful lot of money to lend anybody, Mr. Hurst."

Hurst leaped to his feet angrily, sloshing some of the brandy over the sleeve of his jacket. "He did odd jobs for me from time to time. He ran errands. He was terribly amenable that way. Ben liked to *do* for people."

"He did, Mr. Hurst, and two days ago he got done. We examined and re-examined that bathroom and the shelf on which the radio rested. It was impossible for Ben Bentley to have pulled the damn thing down into the tub, unless the whole shelf collapsed. And that shelf didn't collapse."

Hurst segued swiftly from anger to hauteur. "If you knew me better, Mr. Love, you would realize I am totally incapable of murder or violence of any kind." He crossed to the fireplace and pressed a button on the wall. "This interview is concluded, and I assure you I shall consult my attorney about your—your—slanderous inferences!"

"Listen, cat," said Pharoah, rising slowly, "when you got it down in black and white, it ain't slander and it ain't an inference. Baby, it's just laying there."

Hurst pivoted around, his eyes narrowed into paper-thin slits. "How do I know anything *does* exist? Let me see for myself."

"In time, Mr. Hurst, in time."

Pharoah didn't realize the tall young man had entered the

room until he caught his reflection in the mirror. "Adam," Hurst snapped, "the gentleman is leaving." Adam crossed past Pharoah and opened the door to the hall. Pharoah picked up his hat and turned to Hurst.

"I'll be in touch." And he left.

Hurst waited until he heard the front door close, the lock snap into place, and then shouted, "Adam!"

The tall young man returned to the living room as Hurst slammed the snifter down on the coffee table and began pacing the room, left hand clutching his side, right hand clutching his forehead, an attitude Norma Shearer would have recognized as her very own. "Did you hear that blackamoor? Did you *hear* him?"

"Every word," said Adam with a pleasant drawl.

"They why didn't you grab him by the throat and throttle him?"

"Jamie," he said with great patience, "he's a policeman."

"Oh, you Indians!" raged Hurst. "From the moment you were placed on reservations, you lost your initiative!"

Adam crossed to Hurst, took his hand, and led him to the couch. "Sit down. You're working yourself into a state."

"Murder!" he shrieked, plopping onto the couch. "Blackmail! Publicity! Ruin! Why didn't you break into the little kike's apartment the way I told you to?"

"Because there was a cop on duty there. I told you."

"Who was stupid enough to do this? What idiot killed the little sheenie without having the sense to clean out his papers?"

"And then there'd be somebody else to pay," Adam said quietly, taking Hurst's right hand and rubbing the wrist gently.

42

"Oh, that does feel good." He stared at Adam in the moment they sat quietly. Was Sitting Bull ever that attractive, he wondered, or were they from different tribes? "Adam," he said softly, "you were out of the house most of that day."

"So?"

"You loathed him."

"So?"

"There could be trouble for you too, you know."

"You'll protect me," said Adam, his strong fingers working briskly, "won't you, Great White Father?"

"Do you suppose—do you think—Ben wrote down everything about Ella?"

"Ella can take care of herself. We both know that." And Hurst began giggling uncontrollably.

Ida's Place was jumping. Every table was filled and the bar was thirty deep. Ida Maruzzi was at the door telling a foursome there would be at least an hour's wait for a table, and they reluctantly departed.

"Squares," Ida muttered as she adjusted her girdle and popped her cigar back into her mouth. On a clear day she looked like forever. She weighed close to three hundred pounds and convinced herself that on her it looked good. She wore her red hair cut long and with bangs in front like Alice in Wonderland, and woe be unto any rabbit's hole she tried to crawl through. She waddled down the long narrow restaurant past the bar to a table for two well in the rear, where Seth sat nursing a Scotch and water, and settled into the chair opposite him. Seth wondered if she had modeled for one of the sequences in *Fantasia*. She came from California.

"What a night," she muttered, and he mustered a sympathetic grin. "I tell you, you never know who you're gonna see in this place again from one night to the next." She slammed her hand down on the table and the table groaned for mercy. "One night he's sitting here boozing it up at the bar, yakking with Ward, my crooked bartender. The next day he's frying in his bathtub. You never know, do you?"

She studied Seth's face carefully. "You were still hung on him? Well, I never liked him. He was a stinking cock teaser. With everybody. Big deal. Hey, you." Seth looked up. "When are you and me gonna make it? You better grab me before fifty, and that's any month now. After fifty I'm cutting down. Once a week. Enough." She adjusted herself for a better view of the bar. Someone had played the jukebox and the Beatles wanted to hold somebody's hand. "You can't tell the boys from the girls any more. Look at that number over there— the one with the Beethoven sweat shirt." Seth looked up and saw a boy in his twenties whose hair almost reached his shoulders. "Barbers must be going bankrupt all over the place. Uh huh. That dinge that just came through the door looks like trouble."

Seth had already seen Pharoah. "That's my date." Ida flashed him a look and simply said "Oh." She got up and waddled her way to Pharoah. She was all smiles as she pointed to Seth, and Pharoah looked and waved.

"Man," he said, sitting down, "what a cage full of peculiar cats tonight."

"I thought you'd been here before," said Seth. Pharoah grinned.

"No. But I knew you had. Hey, waiter!" A boy wearing a black leather apron sauntered over.

"What's your pleasure?"

"At the moment, a seven and seven." Then he turned to Seth. "Ready for another?" Seth nodded, the boy nodded, and Pharoah placed his hat under his chair. "Just had a dull half hour with a friend of yours. Mr. Hurst."

"Did he take a fit?"

"No, cat, he was too busy taking a dislike to me. Who's the Indian chick tippy-toeing around on little cat feet?"

"Adam Littlestorm, his—er—man of all work. What did you want with Hurst?"

"Cat—" Pharoah laughed—"I'm a detective. And I'm on a case. I got a long list of people I got to see before I'm anywhere finished. Most of them'll be duds, but it's a mighty long list. Cat, the deceased had himself a real going concern there. Whooeeee, was he collecting! There was a fine example of our acquisitive society. And I thought he was just a small-time hustler."

The waiter brought the drinks and said to Seth, "These are on Ida." He took Seth's empty glass and left as Seth raised the fresh drink in a silent toast to Ida, who held her hands over her head and waved them like a champion prize fighter in acknowledgment.

"If my daddy was alive," Pharoah began after a sip of his drink, "he'd wham that Ida into bed and keep her there a month. My daddy liked them big. Unfortunately my mama was small. Tell me about the Hurst cat. He always keep a number on the premises?"

Seth sighed. This was his fourth drink and he was beginning to feel amenable. "Ben worked for him for about a year. Adam moved in the day Ben moved out. That was when we agreed to take a place together."

"I dig."

45

"Adam was a professional masseur."

"Cat, he's built like one. With braves like that, how'd the Indians lose the country to us?"

"When did you pick Ben up for soliciting?"

"Couple of years ago."

"How well did you get to know him?"

Pharoah scratched his nose. "Not well enough, I guess. I was on the decoy patrol. You know—hang out in fag bars, fag toilets, fag movie houses and make an arrest every now and then. I'll admit the deceased was pretty drunk the night I pulled him in, but we were a little hungry for entries on the police blotter that week so I collared him."

"Who paid his fine?"

"Ella Hurst."

"In person?"

"Sent a lawyer. Hibbons—Dibbons—"

"Philip Cribbons."

"That's the cat."

"Did you ever see Ben again?"

"Not deliberately, cat. Just around. Here and there. With the Hurst cat every now and then. After I made detective, I did a lot of checking on the Village cribs. Your baby was in them cribs mighty often. Now how about me asking a few so I can keep my professional standing?"

Seth folded his arms on the table and leaned forward. "Shoot."

"How many have you had so far?"

"This is the fourth. Why?"

"Just want to make sure I'll be coming in loud and clear. When'd you and the deceased cut?"

"About four months ago."

"Seen him much since?"

"Not till the day he died."

"Uh huh. You split angry?"

"No. I just made up my mind never to see him again. Since you know I'm being analyzed, I'm trying to overcome some problems. And Ben was one of them."

"Well, that problem's been overcome for you. Didn't see him for four months, yet when he phoned with the cock-and-bull about borrowing some loot, you high-tailed it over to his place"—he snapped his fingers—"Just like that."

"Just like that."

"How come?"

"Because I was dying to see him, that's how come."

"Fair enough. I have had the experience myself." He took a healthy swig of his drink and then stared around Ida's Place for a few moments before resuming the interrogation.

"You ever chew buttons?"

Seth knew he was going to get very drunk.

"I said, 'You ever chew buttons?' " Pharoah had turned back to him. "Peyoti, cat. You chew the buttons for technicolor dreams."

"I tried it once." His eyes challenged Pharoah's. "I'll try anything once."

"I'm hip." Pharoah smiled. "Didn't you know the deceased conducted a heavy traffic in buttons?"

"So?"

"That was why the trip to Mexico. It was getting too risky getting it through the mails."

"Nobody gets hooked on buttons." Seth enunciated too clearly. By his fourth drink his words tended to slur.

"I know." Pharoah nodded, looking like a mechanical

gypsy fortuneteller in Coney Island. "But you can do dangerous things while under the influence. You know what I mean,
cat? It relaxes the inhibitions. Curtains drop. Courage rises.
Midgets grow ten feet tall."

"You're not telling me anything I don't know. My last
novel had a character that chewed peyoti. That's why I tried
it. Research."

"I think the deceased had been chewing some when he was
taking the bath. What do you think?"

"He might have been. He seemed a little high. I'm not
sure. It was hard to tell with Ben."

"You didn't chew any with him?"

Seth laughed. "You forget. I was on my way to see my
analyst. I'd hardly try to spend an hour with him in that
condition."

"Check."

Seth drained his drink and Pharoah motioned to the waiter
for a refill. "How'd you know I wanted another?"

"You got the look. I know it well. Got any ideas who might
have done the deceased in?"

"I don't know."

"But you've been giving it a lot of thought."

There was an edge to Seth's voice. "There's nothing
shrewd about that deduction."

"Cat, you better start offering some deductions of your
own. To our knowledge you were the last to see him alive,
and that ain't the catbird seat."

Seth snorted. "Innocent until proven guilty." He fished in
his pockets for some coins. "I'm going to play the jukebox.
You want something special?"

"I want something special, but it ain't in that jukebox." He watched Seth weaving his way through the crowded room to the machine that stood next to the entrance. Why do I like that cat, he wondered. Why does he need a head shrinker to help straighten himself out? If he's so smart, why'd he get mixed up with a Krazy Kat like Ben Bentley? Why not? Man does not live by bread alone. Pharoah lifted his drink and the ice cubes were sparkling like prisms.

Seth took a long time at the jukebox. He knew the selections by heart and he knew which he'd play, but he wanted some time to think. How to handle Pharoah Love. There's a clever brain encased in the black man's skull. There's a clever brain encased in mine. Pharoah's trying to use me. The trick is, how do I use Pharoah? Then he smiled to himself as he made his selections, filling the room with Gerry Mulligan and "The Wee Small Hours."

Ida waved him over to her corner of the bar.

"Who's the spook?" Ward, the bartender, was mixing manhattans.

Seth rested his head on Ida's ample bosom. "He's a detective," he whispered.

"Oy."

"He's on Ben's case." Seth straightened up and patted her cheek. "They think he was murdered." Ward overheard and stared at Ida. Ida caught his look and then took Seth's hand.

"You ain't in any trouble, are you, baby? Like you got an alibi any time you need one, see?"

"I'm clean, sweetheart. I'm very clean."

The fresh drink was waiting for Seth. He eased into his chair. "I'm beginning to like you, Pharoah Love."

"That's good, cat. I'm always in the market for friends."

"And I think I'm going to need you."

"That's part of joining the brotherhood."

"Because I'm starting a new book and it's going to be all about Ben Bentley."

"Well, how about them apples?"

Seth was becoming very pleased with himself.

"And I'm going to need to see all the stuff you cleaned out of Ben's desk."

He's coming on strong, Pharoah was thinking, he's coming on very strong. He barely spoke above a whisper. "We'll see."

"Because my book is going to be the only way to bring this case to a logical conclusion."

Pharoah chuckled. "Could be."

Seth took a healthy swig of the drink and continued the pursuit. "I mean, you'd like to be a part of this book, wouldn't you? I mean now—right now—you're part of the story. Like right now you're a part of my life. Even if we never see each other again after tonight, we are a part of each other's life and there's no erasing any of it. Am I coming in clear?"

"I'm getting your signals, cat."

"What I'm trying to tell you, Pharoah Love, is that you've had me scared shitless the past two days and I'm not any more. I mean, cops are the natural enemy and I don't see them as that any more now that I know you."

Pharoah lifted his glass, clinked it against Seth's, and drank.

"Like when last seen, Veronica was scared shitless of you because of something tacit and unspoken in her life. What is unspoken in my life is something I'm trying to tell an analyst at twenty-five bucks a throw, and unless you've got the price of the trip, I don't want you phoning him to find out what makes this cat tick. This cat's spending loot to find it out for himself."

"You are shouting," said Pharoah.

"Because I want to be heard." Seth looked like a little boy. "Now what is it you want to know? Because like any normal human being in this worst of all possible worlds, I lie."

Pharoah chuckled. "You know something, cat? You are lovable when you are drunk."

"I am lovable at *all* times, Pharoah Lovable, when given the opportunity to *be* lovable. Now about them buttons—and by the way, I am not drunk. When I am drunk, you will know it. My rich tenor will fill this room with 'Meet Me in St. Louis' and the applause will be deafening."

"Now about them buttons."

"What?"

"The buttons." Pharoah resisted the urge to push back the lock of hair that had fallen over Seth's forehead.

"Ah, the buttons. The peyoti. Well, sir, it's like this. I have taken them on more than one occasion. And not because I liked them. It was to please Ben. You had to do small things like that to please Ben. Like the time Ben was thinking of converting to Catholicism because it was cheaper than converting to oil. I *also* thought of converting to Catholicism! *That* kept peace in our ménage for about five days, when he came home with some Christian Science pamphlets. I tell you, there was no keeping up with our boy. And keeping up is what started to drag me down. Did you ever chew buttons, Pharoah Love?"

"Not my type of diet."

"It's wild." He waved his hands furiously and the waiter came running. "What do *you* want?"

"You were waving," said the waiter.

"Well, not at *you*."

"Bring us another round," said Pharoah, "so it shouldn't be a total loss."

After giving the bartender the order, the waiter said to Ida, "Seth's off and running." Ida turned and stared at the two men and wished she was wiser in the ways of the world.

"You get visions," Seth was telling Pharoah, "almost like hallucinations, but your mind is clear and lucid and you describe it all vividly. Where does that grab you?"

"Is that why you went to see the deceased that day?"

"You are very smart, Pharoah Love. That is why I went. And he said he didn't have any, and I got very upset because I was in the depths of a very deep depression. And he said to me, 'Snap out of it. It's not the end of the world. We'll see each other when I get back from Mexico.' So I went to see my analyst after all. I wasn't going to. I was going to play hooky all by myself in my apartment and chew a button and just get lost for a while."

"We found a box of six in the apartment."

Once again their eyes locked.

"Now why do you suppose he held out on me?" asked Seth. Pharoah said nothing.

"Strange little bastard." He stared down at the table. A fly was making a pilgrimage across the checkered tablecloth and Seth brought his fist down on it. Pharoah handed him a napkin and Seth wiped his hand. He was now the center of attention in his vicinity, but his mind was on betrayal and injustice.

"You want something to eat?" asked Pharoah. Seth shook his head no.

"You want to cut?"

No again.

"You want to split?"

Seth looked up, flinging the napkin aside. "You got better things to do?"

The waiter brought the round of drinks before Pharoah could reply. "These are from the lady at the bar," said the waiter. Seth squinted his eyes toward the bar and then smiled in recognition.

"It is our wife." He waved at Veronica who was perched on a stool alongside Ida, sipping a brandy and smoothing the green cloth sheath to the contour of her body. She took the wave as an invitation and joined the men.

"Take my chair," said Pharoah, rising. "I'll get another." He found one two tables away and returned in time to hear Veronica say, "I'm sorry about this afternoon."

"Forget it." Seth had pulled a dollar bill from his wallet and dropped it in front of Veronica. "You can have it back." She let it lay there. Since she detected no warning in Seth's glazed eyes, Veronica plunged right in.

"Has Mr. Love been giving you a hard time, darling?"

"Mr. Love has been a love."

"Oh," said Veronica, wondering why she was beginning to feel uncomfortable, "you mean this is a social party."

"It just happened to turn into one," said Pharoah.

Veronica turned to him. "Jameson Hurst phoned me. He screeched every word, so you must have upset him terribly."

"Murder is very upsetting to most people. I'm giving that cat time to cool down. Then he'll cooperate."

"I'm sure you understand, Mr. Love," said Veronica with her party smile, "that to be a murder suspect is highly unnerving."

The expression on Pharoah's face was placid. "Nobody said Jameson Hurst was a murder suspect. Nobody said you were a murder suspect. I can't form any suspicions until people cooperate and start giving me answers."

"It's not all that easy for people like us to go into a verbal strip tease."

"What makes you think you're so special?"

"It isn't that I think I'm so special . . ."

"Yes, you do," interjected Seth with an impish grin.

"It isn't that I think I'm so special," Veronica began again with an ominous look at Seth. "It's that murder is so special."

Pharoah moved his chair back and crossed his legs. "Has your husband told you he's going to write a book about the deceased?"

Veronica slammed her glass down on the table as she turned to Seth. "About *Ben?* But *why,* for Christ's sake? It's not as though he was Schweitzer."

"Ohhhhh," said Seth, almost whimsically, "I don't know. Ben was a bit of a humanitarian in his way. I mean, once you really start examining it." He trilled his next sentence. "There's good and bad in all of us."

"As the priest said to the sailor," snapped Veronica. Then she thought a moment and permitted them the pleasure of a smile. "Of course, who knows? Knowing the subject as well as you do, it just *might* be good." She aimed her mouth at Pharoah. "We've published two of his books, you know."

"I'd like to read them," said Pharoah.

"They're not bad," Veronica continued, overlapping Pharoah's words. "Short, swift, and to the point—except too many reviewers found the point pointless. I happen to know Seth has a good book in him."

"I've got a lot of good things in me," said Seth, wagging his thumb in emphasis.

"Yes, you do," agreed Veronica softly. "But a book about Ben Bentley—well, well, well." She shoved the dollar bill to the center of the table. "That says you'll never finish it."

"You're covered," said Pharoah, pulling a dollar bill from his pocket, and Seth looked at him in astonishment.

"Good God! The man believes in me!"

5

"You men," said Veronica, as she and Pharoah shook hands over the bet, "you're like a secret society."

"Trouble is," said Seth pointedly, "too many women have learned the password."

"I need another brandy. Shall I have it here or do I go back to the bar?"

"Please." Pharoah smiled. "Be my guest." He motioned to the waiter.

"Say," began Seth, after the waiter took the order, "is this party on you, Pharoah Love, or are we going dutch? I was wondering about it when I was getting dressed."

"This is my party," said Pharoah. Then he looked at Veronica. "And I'm just beginning to have a good time."

She was staring at the door. "You're going to have an even better time. Look what's making a grand entrance."

Jameson Hurst swept into the room, followed by Adam Littlestorm. He walked as though invisible handmaidens were preceding him, strewing rose petals on the floor. He wore a purple opera cape and a Tyrolean hat, and one felt that at any moment Ida might lift a baton and tap for silence. In direct contrast, Adam wore tight black pants and a black leather jacket and a black expression, and had someone approached him with hand raised and said "How!" he would have probably replied, "It ain't easy." Ida waddled over to greet her new guests.

"How are you, Mr. Hurst? Where you been keeping yourself?"

Jameson loathed the expression "keeping yourself." It was too synonymous with "well preserved."

Forlorn best described Jameson when he replied. "I've been much too *distrait* the past few days to mingle in public. Poor Ben. Do you have a table? *Must* the jukebox be *that* loud?" Ida signaled the bartender who reached under the bar and adjusted the volume on the machine. She led Jameson and Adam to a table in the center of the room, and Adam was the first to espy the three in the rear. Jameson followed his gaze and emitted a world-weary sigh.

"Oh, what the hell," said Jameson, and commanded Ida to bring them stingers on the rocks at once. Adam removed his leather jacket and most of the bar was riveted on his well-proportioned torso.

"Why don't you ask them to join us?" he said to Jameson with a twinkle.

Jameson fixed him with a deadly look. "I loathe jocular Indians." He swept the cape off his shoulders onto the back of his chair, then placed his elbows on the table, clasped his hands, placed his chin on his hands, and knew Theda Bara couldn't have done better. He thought for a moment and then smiled. "You know, it just might be amusing at that. Seth looks tight as a tick. Veronica's dislocating an arm trying to

57

catch my attention. And the detective person thinks he's hit the jackpot. Go get them."

Adam crossed the room like an ancestor stalking a deer.

"Hello, sweetie!" said Veronica gaily. "How'd you manage to get him out?"

"It was his own idea," said Adam, and he pecked her on the cheek. "He'd like you three to join us."

Pharoah's mind snapped to attention as Seth said, "Why, that might be most amusing. Mr. Love?"

"I'd be enchanted, cat." Pharoah smiled.

Ida added chairs to Jameson's table as Adam returned with the three.

"How marvelous to see you all here!" chirruped Jameson as they greeted him and took their seats. "Even you, Mr. Love."

The sarcasm didn't escape Pharoah. "Am I forgiven?"

"Forgiven? Let's say I'm giving you an amnesty." The waiter brought their drinks as Jameson delicately blew his nose and then commented sadly, "It's a bit like a wake, isn't it? I mean, here we are, caught up in a web spun by the late lamented, while he lies in his grave, cold, alone," and he couldn't resist adding, "without the comfort of a goddamned radio." Seth drummed on the table lightly with his fingers.

Veronica decided to be cheerful. "Now we aren't going to be morbid, are we, Jameson?"

"I shall try not to be, but it requires utter effort." He made "utter effort" sound like the name of a used-car dealer. He directed his attention to Pharoah Love. "Are you planning to cross-examine my sister?" Adam lifted his drink and sipped. Pharoah was lighting Veronica's cigarette.

"These aren't cross-examinations, Mr. Hurst. I'm merely conducting an investigation. Cross-examinations occur at trials."

"This entire nonsense is a trial. It's all too bizarre. I feel as though I've stepped through the looking glass!"

"Well, you've got one in your apartment big enough."

Seth's laugh was too loud and too forced and he knew it. Jameson ignored it. "You must be very gentle with my sister, should she consent to see you. She's a very old and a very sensitive lady. She has completely withdrawn from life. Perhaps you already know. She had a terrible accident to her face fifteen years ago and has kept it swathed in veils ever since. She lives across the park from me in a very cramped apartment and never sets foot from it."

"She was at Ben's funeral," said Seth. Adam's knuckles whitened as he clasped his glass tightly.

"Was she?" said Hurst, looking like the White Queen he would have found on the other side of his looking glass. "How terribly touching! She never once told me she planned to go. But there you are and there you have Ella! Contradiction, contradiction, contradiction! Well, then—" and he was speaking to Pharoah—"she might very well give you an audience."

"We must be grateful for small favors," murmured Pharoah.

"The tinge of sarcasm in your voice does not escape me. Adam, more stingers." Adam signaled and the bartender nodded.

"I'd like another brandy," said Veronica. "What about you, Mr. Love?"

"Fine. How you doing, pal?"

"You mean 'cat,' " said Seth. "I'll have another. This is all water."

Jameson's eyes swept the table, and from Adam's look he knew there would be a lot of questions later about Ella's appearance at Ben's funeral. He settled on Veronica.

"Did you attend the sad event?"

"I did," she replied, "and your absence was even sadder."

"I promised Adam I wouldn't go." Seth stared at Adam who said nothing. "He knows what emotional upsets do to my—condition."

"You could have gone with him, Adam," offered Seth.

Adam looked at him. "I hated the bastard's guts."

"And there," said Pharoah, "sits an honest man."

"Well," sniffed Hurst, "I'll wager you can't wait to get *him* on a hard chair under a hot light."

Pharoah couldn't resist. "Everything about you is so colorful, Mr. Hurst. Hard chair. Hot light. Hot damn." He leaned back in his chair to give the waiter room to place the drinks. There was silence until the waiter left, broken by Pharoah. "Mr. Hurst, since you appreciate the colorful, you ever chew peyoti?" Hurst's jaw dropped.

"We have all chewed peyoti," said Adam.

"I can speak for myself!" snapped Hurst. He glared from Adam to Pharoah. "Is that the extent of the revelations about me that you found in Benjamin's effects?"

"Why do you personalize so, Mr. Hurst?" asked Pharoah in a patronizing tone.

"Because I'm selfish and self-centered," Hurst shot back, winning a round of applause from Seth. "You're drunk!" he snapped at Seth, and snapped his head back to meet Pharoah's gaze. "I loathe the thought of my private life becoming public property."

"I'm not conducting a smear campaign," said Pharoah. "I'm just trying to find out what made the deceased tick. Once I hear tick, then maybe I'll hear tock, and then maybe I'll have figured out why he was murdered, and then maybe by whom."

"The use of peyoti is not illegal," said Hurst, bristling.

"I beg to differ, cat. The Food and Drug Administration has a law that says peyoti can be used only by a doctor's prescription. And it is illegal to bring peyoti across state lines for the use of non-Indians. And the deceased was bringing peyoti in from Mexico for use right here in New York. Cat, that means crossing an awful lot of state lines. And somebody was putting up the money for that dead cat's trips."

"My God!" cried Veronica, turning to Seth. "He's as good as got us. We've *admitted* we've used it. Oh my God!"

"Cool it," said Pharoah matter-of-factly. "You're small pickings."

"You damned fool!" cried Hurst to Adam. " 'We have all chewed peyoti' indeed!" He glared at Pharoah. "You haven't got a thing on me!"

Pharoah smiled. "I only want to know who killed Ben Bentley."

Veronica stared at Pharoah. Seth stared into his glass. Adam stared at Hurst, and Hurst was staring into a void. Suddenly his face twisted hideously and his hands began to tremble. A rasping groan issued from his lips as his head jerked back in convulsion. The table shook and Hurst's right hand shot out, spilling his drink. Adam leaped to his feet as he pulled a bottle cork from his pants pocket and jammed it between Hurst's teeth. He loosened his tie, and Pharoah and Veronica moved swiftly from their chairs as Adam lowered Hurst to the floor with an effort.

"Shit!" gasped Ida as sixty horrified faces stared at the epileptic fit.

"Seth," cried Veronica, "for God's sake do something."

"Meeeet me innnn Saint Louieeeeee Loueeeeeeee!" And Pharoah collapsed onto a chair, roaring with laughter, holding his stomach, and wondering if the rest of the world had also gone mad.

Ruthelma Kross sat behind the desk of her untidy office in the Sardi Building contemplating a tuna-fish sandwich for lunch. That was the day's calorie allotment, but she was getting fed up counting calories. She had been counting commissions all morning, and by rights the dim financial prospects they afforded should have caused her to lose her appetite. But adversity only increased her hunger.

One ray of hope, she thought. Seth Piro's planning a new book. She still believed in him and knew that one day he would deliver. He was finally on his way five years ago, she reminded herself. Where did it all go wrong? Was it Veronica? Had she so completely de-balled him? Why had Seth permitted her to edit his book? Ruthelma had insisted that she was cutting the heart out of it, but Seth trusted Veronica and overrode Ruthelma's protests. Maybe there's still hope of getting a paperback publisher to take them.

The failure of the first book was Veronica's fault and Ruthelma would never be convinced otherwise. But the second one—Ruthelma shook her head dolefully in memory of it. What a lot of tripe! Two hundred and fifty pages about a peyoti orgy. And all the time he was writing it she thought a peyoti was a wild animal. She knew Veronica got Saber House to take it out of her guilt for having ruined the first. It would have been better left unpublished, and Ruthelma long suspected Veronica had shared her opinion. She looked at her wrist watch. Seth was due in less than an hour. She couldn't stand it any longer. She bit into the sandwich.

Veronica sat in the brown leather armchair and stared at Daniel Saber who was sitting behind his huge walnut desk signing letters. It was a ritual with Saber at the beginning of an audience. Forty-five, Adolphe Menjou mustache, gray suit, gray tie, gray skin. Veronica uncrossed and recrossed her legs and stared at the family portrait on Saber's desk. Chubby gray wife, chubby gray son, chubby gray daughter, and chubby gray baby. It all matched Veronica's gray mood. Someday she'd write a treatise on which was worse, brandy hang-overs or champagne hang-overs. She hoped there was some aspirin left in her desk.

Saber lay the pen aside, sat back in his upholstered swivel chair, and cleared his throat. "I think another book by Piro is a chancy proposition."

Veronica selected friendly persuasion. "This one reeks with commercial possibilities." She wished she hadn't used "reeks." It was too synonymous with Seth's previous books. "It's the story of a young man found dead in his bathroom three days ago." She reached over and placed the clipping from the *Daily News* in front of Saber who picked it up and read it swiftly, his eyes darting back and forth like a spectator at a tennis match.

"So? What's so special?"

Veronica leaned forward, her breasts pushing up over her neckline, gasping for air. Saber gave her the courtesy of staring at them for a moment. He knew her breasts well. "There's much more to the story. The police think it was murder."

"Aha," said Saber.

"The facts behind the case are extremely lurid and sordid."

"Oho," said Saber. "Lurid" and "sordid" were musts in every Saber House ad.

"Ben Bentley was a blackmailer, a whore, and he trafficked in peyoti."

"And on the seventh day he rested." Saber beamed. "How did Piro get on to the story?"

Veronica settled back in the chair and her breasts sagged with exhaustion. "Seth and Bentley once shared an apartment. What he doesn't already know, he's digging out with the help of a detective assigned to the case."

"Uh-huh," said Saber. "Is there an outline I can look at?"

"I asked him to submit one to us."

"How soon can I see it?"

"I don't know. He wasn't too happy with the results on his first two books."

"Neither was I." Saber thought a moment. "Sounds like it might make an exploitation item no matter how badly it's written."

"That's what I thought."

"What about his agent—the pig with food stains on her dress? Can't she get an outline for us?"

"I wanted to speak to you first."

"Call her. Get us an outline. If it's any good, arrange a small advance. You ever give him that divorce?"

Ruthelma had the phone jammed between her shoulder and her ear as she licked the tip of her handkerchief with her tongue and began scrubbing the tuna-fish stains on her bosom.

64

"Well, I'll see what I can do, Veronica dear," she cooed, cooing being the only means she had of modulating her voice which was normally the volume of a brass band. "He hasn't told me a *thing* about it. He was due here in half an hour, but he just phoned to say he'd be late. Sounded *horr*-ible." She paused for a moment, rolling the handkerchief into a ball and flinging it onto the ·desk next to four balls of used Kleenex. "Well, dear, let's be honest with each other. What happened to his *first* book should happen to *Castro*. And the *second* one. *Both* of us know it should have remained *still*born. Of course—" the coo blended into a purr—"perhaps we'll be third time *lucky*." She giggled politely at something Veronica said. "I'll call you after I've spoken to him. Give *Daniel* a big fat *kiss* for me."

She hung up and contemplated the mess on her desk. Seth must have something hot to make that witch so overanxious. Maybe the horoscope was right for a change. "Brighter aspects in domestic scene. Hunches could pay off. Make someone close to you happy."

She decided to phone her mother.

Jameson Hurst was reclining on the beige chaise longue in his pink-and-white bedroom. He held an ice pack to his temple and occasionally lifted a bottle of cologne to his nose and sniffed delicately. The event of the night before was too humiliating to contemplate, but retrospection couldn't be avoided. This curse, this dreadful curse. Why did it have to happen at Ida's? They'd have been so much more sympathetic at the Persian Room. Didn't they know that epilepsy was an affliction of kings? His cheeks began to flame with hatred. It was that nigger's fault. That dinge. That black-amoor. Peyoti. Oh God. Adam.

"How do you feel?" Adam was bending over him. He hadn't heard him enter. *I never hear him enter.*

"The hell with how I feel!" he snapped, lowering the ice pack. "Is there much of an abrasion?"

"Just a small bruise. You can cover it with pancake." Adam sat opposite him and lit a cigarette, then he asked, "What was Ella doing at the funeral?"

"She had a compulsion to go."

"It could be dangerous."

"Ella's not afraid."

"I am."

"Of what?"

"That detective."

"Oh God." Hurst sighed. "Why doesn't he park himself in Benjamin's apartment and wait for the killer? Don't they always return to the scene of the crime?"

"Did Ella do it?"

Hurst sat up, eyes ablaze and nostrils flaring. "You trying to send me into another fit?" He screeched the word "fit." "Ella adored Benjamin. Adored him! He understood her! She enchanted him!" He sank back, trying to look spent, but he knew that Adam knew better.

"There's still not a line in the papers about Ben's being murdered."

"The police take their own sweet time about releasing that kind of information. They like to imbue the murderer with a sense of false security. *Then* they *pounce!*"

"That detective's no fool. He's already ass-hole buddies with Seth."

"Please, Adam. Not before lunch."

"We have to be careful."

Hurst sat up again. "Careful! Look who's talking about *careful*. The way you shot your mouth off about the *peyoti*." He flung his arms out dramatically. "Wouldn't you know *I'd* get mixed up with the only talkative Indian in America! Why didn't you smack that blackamoor when he burst out laughing last night?"

"He wasn't laughing at you. He was laughing at Seth. He helped me get you into the cab."

"That was mighty white of him." He giggled. Adam stifled the urge to grind the cigarette into Hurst's cheek. Hurst reached for the cologne, sniffed, and then reached for a cigarette.

"Seth could have done it. Veronica could have done it. Ben tried to bleed her, the damned fool. A good thing Ella stepped in."

"I wish Ella would die," said Adam.

Hurst exhaled into Adam's face. "Don't upset me too much, my dear. Benjamin used to do that and it hastened his departure from these premises."

"Any time you want me to go . . ."

"Don't say that."

"Don't threaten me."

"Don't bug me."

"Then look at this damn mess rationally. Once the newspapers get wind of this they'll have a field day."

"What can I do?"

"Be nice to Pharoah Love."

Hurst jumped to his feet. "He's beneath me!"

"Don't look now, Jamie. He's right on top of you."

Pharoah Love had spent most of the morning conferring with his chief. He returned to his office self-satisfied and confident. The chief liked the way the investigation was going. Slow but smooth. Easygoing but profitable. No rush. There were a lot of unsolved cases in the file the department was still working on. And the department knew most of them would be stamped "Closed" sooner or later. Sure, the chief had told him, cooperate with Piro. Help him with that book. He just might end up doing most of your work for you.

He started to reach for the phone and then thought better of it. Don't push. Let him come after you. He'll call. Could he really have been all that drunk last night when I was undressing him? Anybody else behaved the way he did last night, I'd have pulled them in for disorderly conduct. But there can be order in disorder. I'll have that cat just where I want him. "Meeeet meeee in Saint Loueeeee . . . Loueeeee. . . ." Pharoah chuckled.

I'll meet you anyplace you say, cat.

Ward, the bartender, was bored with taking inventory. It happened only once a month, but did it have to happen after a heavy night? And whatever Ida had on her mind, he wished she would say it.

She must have been reading his mind. "How mixed up were you with Ben Bentley?"

"What do you mean?" He hoped Ida could envision the blood in his injured tone of voice. Three days a week Madame Grabatkin (formerly of the Moscow Art Theater) pounded into his head "Yew muz make de haudience soffer weet yew." That was when his exercise was *Hamlet*. "Dey muz soffer weet *'Omelette'!*"

68

"You know what I mean. You've been peddling those buttons for him."

"Ah, come on!"

"Don't give me any crap. I don't miss a trick around here."

Ward shrugged. "Ah, so what difference does it make now? He's dead."

"Just dead wouldn't bother me. Murder is something else. And that means cops. And I can't afford to lose my liquor license."

"They got nothing on me."

"I had my radar tuned in to that dick last night." Nobody fought Ida's radar. It made the Navy's look obsolete. "They found a lot of stuff on a lot of people in Ben's apartment. That could mean you too." Ward's stomach did a flip-flop as Ida continued. "If they ever get around to you, I'm telling you right now, I didn't know from nothing. You hear me?"

"Yeah, yeah. . . . Ah! Nothing'll happen."

"From your mouth to God's ears. But just in case—I'm out of it. Or you'll never work in this town again. And I mean no place!"

Ward chewed on the pencil eraser.

"And another thing," she said, raising her voice and wagging a beefy index finger for emphasis, "stop getting so chummy with the customers. What you do on your own time is your own business. What you do behind that bar is mine."

"Ah, come on, Ida."

"Don't ah, come on me! A lot of Ben Bentleys hang out at this bar. I can smell them a mile away. Till this thing blows over, you cool it. I don't want the plain-clothes detail hanging around here looking for an arrest. All I need is a 'Raided

Premises' sign in my window. Oy, is that all I need! You hear me?"

"I heard. I heard." He hoped God heard too. "Please, God, don't make me have to lay her again. Please. I'll be good. I promise."

Why'd you get so drunk last night, stupid?

Seth waited for his reflection in the bathroom mirror to hang its head in shame. The Alka-Seltzers had dissolved and he drank them down in a gulp. He lathered his face and then decided to see if his hand would stop shaking before he applied the safety razor to his chin. He had been trying to reconstruct the events after Jameson Hurst's epileptic fit, but his subconscious was treating him kindly this morning. It was keeping the unpleasant under lock and key. Pandora's box. Sooner or later the furies would escape to wreak havoc upon his conscience.

His hand relaxed and he began to shave.

He tried playing the game with himself, the same game he played after every blackout. Now let me see, the cast of characters included Jameson, Adam, Ida, Veronica, and Pharoah Love.

He nicked himself.

"Damn." The styptic pencil was applied and he resumed shaving.

Jameson took a fit and I sang. Jameson must have loved that when Adam told him about it. No man appreciates a serenade when he's having a convulsion. Then Ida yelled "Shit!" which he often thought was the extent of her vocabulary, and Veronica slapped somebody. Who? Me. The door in his brain was unlocked and beginning to widen. Then what happened? Pharoah. Pharoah did something. He laughed. The razor was frozen in mid-air.

Seth walked into the bedroom and stared at his clothes neatly hung in the closet. I didn't do that. I fling them all over the place. Ben used to follow me around the room, picking them up, chanting, "He loves me, he loves me not." Who brought me home? Who undressed me? Who folded my clothes and hung them up so neatly? Who put up with my behavior? I know how I get when I'm drunk. Affectionate. Loving. All my subconscious needs go to bat when I'm drunk and occasionally score a homer. Who tucked me into bed and pulled the blanket up around my chin? Who said, "You're going to hate yourself in the morning, cat."

6

"ARE YOU *serious?*"

"That's what it's going to be."

Seth challenged Ruthelma's stupefied look.

"A book about *him?*"

She sounded like an organ recital coming over short wave.

"Well!" she exhaled, puffing up like a pouter pigeon. "It *must* be saleable. Veronica's *already* been on the phone asking for an outline."

"She's not getting one."

Ruthelma was grateful for a reason to beam with pleasure. She loathed Veronica and never dared admit it to Seth. "You mean I can give the early worm the *bird?*" Seth wondered if she had been born italicized. He sipped the lukewarm coffee in the cardboard container and nodded as he swallowed.

"Nobody's seeing it till I'm good and ready."

"Now listen," began Ruthelma, "I want you to promise me something and then I'll give you a surprise." He didn't react to "surprise" and it somewhat deflated her. "I want you to promise me it's going to be a serious treatment of a certain *type* of person. I mean, you must *divorce* yourself from the subject. I know how close you were for a while, and I know we can level with each other. I disapproved of him *thoroughly*. Of course you can't use real *names,* you know, because so many people he was involved with are still *alive.* Not that it was going to stop *him*."

"What do you mean, 'Not that it was going to stop him'?"

"Well, didn't you *know?*" When she screwed her face up, she looked like an irate Pekinese.

"Know what, for crying out loud?"

"Well!" She slammed her hand down on the desk, flattening some of the rolled-up balls of Kleenex with a squish. "He came to see me about a *year* ago. *He* was writing a *book.*"

Seth could feel the beads of sweat rolling down his spine.

"A *book! Him!* I read a few pages and it was *awww*-ful! All about his sordid adventures in and out of bed. I mean, he said if *City of Night* can sell, so can I. And he named *names,* and places—even hotel room *numbers!* I couldn't *believe* it! I thought he'd made it all *up,* but if he *had,* then he really was a *genius!* It was disgusting and I wouldn't touch it." She slammed the desk again. "And nobody in their right mind would *either!* You mean you didn't *know?*"

"No."

"Well!"

They sat in silence for a few moments. A few pages, thought Seth. Was that all there was? Had Ben destroyed them? But Ben never threw anything away. You never can tell when the stuff might come in handy. It's coming in handy to someone, Ben Bentley, wherever you are.

Seth tried to keep his voice normal. "Do you remember much of what you read?"

"Oh God, do I have to? It was so *ugly*." She thought a moment with lips pursed. "It was mostly about being arrested when he was sixteen or something. Something about rolling some traveling salesman in a hotel room. It was *very clinically detailed*. I thought you probably *knew* about it. Why else would he come to see *me*?"

"Ben was cute that way."

"Well, if that's the kind of material you're going to use in your book, I hope you're going to treat it more *journalistically*. You know what I mean. As if it was John Gunther going inside Ben Bentley." A tender look crossed her face.

"Seth."

"Yes?"

"Is all this the result of your psychoanalysis?"

"Some of it."

"Oh God." She sighed. "Analysis can be so *dangerous!*"

"I know what I'm doing, Ruthelma. I've thought this one out very carefully. This book isn't going to be like the other two bombs I've had published. I know my subject firsthand. And I'm going to show him for what he was. No fantasy. No romanticizing. The cold hard facts. Tough, brutal, and uncompromising. Weren't you the one who told me I should write about the things I know, the things I've experienced? Well, I knew Ben Bentley, and Christ, what an experience!"

"Isn't it *funny?*" She was cooing again. "I'm beginning to get one of my *tingles*." Seth knew her tingles well. "Now that we've had this talk, I think *this* one's *really* going to be *good*. Yes, I think it *just* might make a *big* difference in your life."

It just might, Seth agreed silently.

"Now for the surprise." She pulled open a drawer of her desk and handed him two checks. His face lit up with delight.

They were residual payments for television scripts he had written almost two years ago. "Wheee!" he cried with delight. "My chickens have come home to roost!" Then he sighed. "A blessing! Thank you, dear God. A blessing! These ought to keep me alive for the next few months. A very welcome transfusion for my anemic savings account."

Ruthelma had many clients, but there were few she regarded so fondly as Seth. She rarely overstepped the invisible boundary line separating business and friendship. She was a middle-aged woman who supported a near-senile mother of eighty and had turned her back on romance twenty years ago when the man she was engaged to marry, a playwright, disappeared to Europe with an actress. And now she had to fight desperately to keep from throwing her arms around Seth and kissing him.

Seth pocketed the checks and then leaned across the desk and kissed her on the cheek. "Don't worry about the book. My doctor thinks it can be a hell of a good one. Goodbye, sweetheart. I'll call you in a few days." And he left.

Ruthelma understood the tears in her eyes. She had lied about the tingle. She didn't for one minute believe in the book and she felt that he knew it. But Seth needed encouragement desperately. He hadn't had a job in television in almost two years. From the moment he became involved with the dreadful Bentley boy, the quality of his writing had severely diminished. Perhaps she was wrong about this book. She'd been wrong before and occasionally admitted it. Maybe when she'd read the first few chapters she'd feel the tingle. That had happened before too.

But should she have told him everything? Should she have told him that the chapter Ben had asked her to read was about Seth and himself? The chapter that had kept her in bed for three days with an illness no doctor could diagnose. Should she have told him about the portion involving Veronica? Veronica! She believed every word she had read about *her!* The dreadful creature worked for me, and if Daniel Saber hadn't hired her away, I would have fired her. Or killed her.

But Seth. Those dreadful things about Seth.

Perhaps that doctor is really helping him. I hope he is. He's a good writer. A good person. He deserves a decent break. She dialed.

"Luncheonette? Mrs. Kross. Send me a chocolate malted and a prune Danish."

The I.R.T.-New Lots Avenue Express was pulling into the Times Square station as Seth descended the steps two at a time. He leaped into the vestibule of the last car and found a seat. He hadn't brought anything to read for the long trip out to Brooklyn, but there was enough for him to think about. He felt the inside breast pocket of his jacket where the residual checks emanated a comforting warmth. Some day he would shower Ruthelma with lavish gifts. Her belief in his talents never faltered. If they had, she never let him know it. But he knew she wasn't sold on the book about Ben. She didn't even flinch when, shortly after he had arrived at her office, he told her the police believed Ben had been murdered.

There was so much for him to do, so little time in which to do it. He had to deal carefully with Veronica and even more carefully with Pharoah Love. He must get to know him better and do it subtly. He mustn't push, but he needed access to

Ben's papers. He shivered. Somebody just walked over my grave. Ben's papers. Ben's book. Ben's book! When did Ben work on it? How did he manage to keep it hidden from Seth that year they shared the apartment? Seth snorted and four passengers looked up. How did he manage to keep it hidden? He managed to keep an awful lot hidden. What's more important, Seth, how could you have been so naïve?

"You have ze tendenzy to belief only vod you vish to belief. Zat iz your childich nay-chur."

Dear Dr. Shlacher. Has a patient ever punched you in the nose?

Seth composed and filed a series of mental notes. Try to see Ella Hurst and find out why she helped Veronica when Ben tried to blackmail her. A long talk with Jameson Hurst, though the man repelled him. Try to see Adam Littlestorm alone. He rather liked Adam. He knew he could get Veronica's story sooner or later, even if it meant going to bed with her. And that idea didn't repel him as much as he thought it might. He hadn't been to bed with anyone in too long a time. Any port in a storm, and Veronica usually offered safe harbor to all the ships at sea. And Pharoah Love. He'd find a way to cope. He had to.

Now the Bergheims. Now how to cope with the Bergheims.

Mrs. Bergheim sat on a wooden crate. She wore a black babushka on her head tied in a solid knot under her chin. She wore a simple black dress with a black sweater thrown over her shoulders. She nervously twisted a black handkerchief. Soon it would be sundown, the Friday Sabbath, and there would be a twenty-four-hour respite for the grieving mother.

She could sit in a comfortable chair and cry her uncomfortable tears. Until sundown she was condemned to sit *shiva,* mourn her dead, on a wooden crate.

Ada sat in an easy chair looking at her mother. She was not Ada's ideal choice for a mother. At the age of ten, when Ada began to wish there had been a choice, she would have selected Irene Dunne or Eleanor Roosevelt. Too much attention was being paid to little Benny and not enough to Ada. And now, twenty-five years later, with the miserable little bastard cold in his grave, too much attention was still being paid to little Benny and not enough to Ada. She knew colored people made her mother uncomfortable, yet marveled at how affably she treated Detective Love.

Pharoah sat in a straight-backed chair waiting for the smoke to clear. He had dropped a bomb, and somehow it hadn't had the effect he expected. Only the sweet-faced neighbor, Mrs. Gabriel, had gasped, with her hand flying to her mouth.

Mrs. Bergheim spoke to Ada. "Do you believe him, Ada?" Ada knew how really distressed the old lady was. Her accent was thicker. "You really believe somebody killed Benny?"

"We have to, Mama. He's the police and they would know."

Her Mother turned to Mrs. Gabriel. "You heard, Mrs. Gabriel?"

"I heard. Terrible. Terrible."

"Could you believe someone would kill my Benny?"

"Terrible. Terrible." She rocked back and forth to prove she really meant it.

"But he only knew the best people," insisted Mrs. Bergheim. "When he came for dinner, he told me about all the wonderful people he met. Rich people. Actors. Writers. His friend Seth. Does he know?"

"He knows," said Pharoah.

"Ada said she saw him at the funeral. Why didn't he say a few words to me, Ada?"

"I don't know, Mama. Maybe he saw how upset you were."

"Yes. He's such a gentleman. Maybe it was a burglar?" Mrs. Bergheim occasionally read the papers she sold.

"Maybe," said Pharoah, tactfully refraining from adding, "But I don't think so."

There was a knock at the door. Mrs. Gabriel went to the door and admitted Seth.

"Come in," she said. His grip tightened on the dozen roses in his hand when he saw Pharoah. He nodded to him and Pharoah winked. Mrs. Bergheim burst into tears and Ada rose to greet Seth.

"Thank you for coming," she said as he handed her the flowers.

"I didn't know if these were appropriate."

"You didn't have to bring anything. It was kind of you just to come." Mrs. Gabriel took the flowers from Ada and went to the kitchen. Mrs. Bergheim wiped her eyes and looked up at Seth, took his hand, and held it to her cheek. He bit his lip and said very softly, "I'm so sorry." She nodded as she released his hand.

"Sit down. Would you like something?" Seth sat in Mrs. Gabriel's place. "A glass of tea? Some cookies? We got lots of cookies. Everybody brought cookies and cake and candy and, *guttenyoo,* what will we do with it all? Still, it was nice of everybody."

"Nothing, thank you."

"Seth," said Ada, standing and staring down at him, "Detective Love just told us Ben was murdered." Seth stared at Pharoah who sat with his arms folded.

"I thought they ought to know," he said quietly.

"I suppose you're right."

"Who would do a thing like this?" cried Mrs. Bergheim. "Who would want to kill Benny?" With an effort she rose from the wooden crate and crossed to a sideboard. Tenderly she lifted a photograph of a four-year-old boy with a Buster Brown haircut, eyes the size of saucers, and lips coquettishly pursed in a cupid's bow. She carried the picture to Pharoah. "Look how sweet he was." Ada sank into her chair. "Look at that face. Who could hurt that sweet face?" Pharoah managed a sympathetic "Tsk" and Mrs. Bergheim moved on to Seth. "You never saw this picture before, did you? Is that a sweet picture?"

"What do you mean, what kind of a kid was I? I was the most beautiful kid on the block. People used to stop my mother just to pinch my cheek."

"People used to stop me," said Mrs. Bergheim, "just to pinch his cheek. And sometimes they'd say, 'Would you like a nice new penny, sonny?' and he'd look up at me, and I would say, 'If you're a good boy, you can take the penny.' Sometimes—" and Ada was startled to hear her laugh—"he collected six—seven—even eight pennies in a day! Can you imagine?" She took the picture from Seth and sat down on the crate, clutching the photograph to her breasts with both hands.

Six, seven, and even eight pennies, thought Ada. Then the day he came back with a nice shiny quarter.

"Where'd you get the quarter, Benny?"

"A man gave it to me."

"What man?"

"In the park."

"Didn't I tell you you mustn't speak to strangers?"

"But he asked me to do something for him. He asked me to get him some hot dogs and he let me keep a quarter."

"That's a very nice man."

But there's no hot-dog stand open in the winter, Benny. But Ada had said nothing at the time. She never did. She never cared. That wasn't the kind of attention she wanted.

Mrs. Gabriel returned to the living room with a vase filled with the roses and set it on the sideboard. "I know we shouldn't, but they smell so good."

"Benny loved flowers," said Mrs. Bergheim. "He always brought me flowers." Mrs. Gabriel sighed and rocked her head back and forth.

"He had such a good heart, that Benny. If it wasn't for him, I'm positive my son, the bartender, would still be out of work." Seth and Pharoah looked at Mrs. Gabriel. Ada examined her fingernails. "Do you ever go to a place called Ida's? It's someplace on the west side."

"We know it well," said Pharoah.

"Behind the bar is my Moishe!" she cried elatedly. Then as an afterthought she said, "That is, I call him Moishe. To everybody else he's Ward." She eased into a chair next to Pharoah. He wasn't such a bad *schwartze* after all. "He's studying to be an actor like Benny." She caught herself. "I mean, they took classes together with that what's'ername from Russia." She smiled embarrassedly. "I can't pronounce her name."

"Madame Grabatkin," said Seth.

"You know her?" asked Mrs. Gabriel.

"No," said Seth, "but I knew Ben and Ward were taking the same acting class." He added Ward Gabriel to his list. He didn't know Pharoah had already beaten him to it.

"Do you know how long those two were friends?" continued Mrs. Gabriel, as Mrs. Bergheim sighed. "Since they were this high." She held her hand two inches from the floor and Pharoah wondered if they had met while crawling. "Cops and robbers they would play, cops and robbers."

"Bang! Bang! You're dead!"

"Whaddya mean I'm dead? I was dead the last time."

"I said 'Bang! Bang!' first, Moishe. You're dead!"

"Ah, come on, Benny! It's your turn to die."

"Ward knows Benny died?" asked Mrs. Bergheim.

"Certainly he knows," said Mrs. Gabriel. "Sunday he'll be to see you."

He heard Pharoah speaking. "Have you told Mrs. Bergheim?"

"About what?"

"The book."

"What book?" asked Ada.

"I'm going to write a book about Ben." Ada choked the urge to burst out laughing. Mrs. Bergheim rescued her.

"A book about *my* Benny? But what will you write?"

Seth struggled for words. "Well . . ." Pharoah was staring at the floor and Seth wished it would rise up and hit him. "I think . . . I think it'll be a book . . . about someone who . . . who died too soon."

"Didn't I tell you?" Mrs. Bergheim wept. "Didn't I tell you, Mrs. Gabriel? My Benny has such good friends."

Fifteen minutes later Seth and Pharoah stood in the hall with Ada.

"You're not serious?" she said to Seth.

"I meant every word."

"Damn it!" she hissed. "He's dead. Let him stay dead. Wherever he is, roasting in hell or stealing harps in heaven."

"Ada, for God's sake. Your mother'll hear you!"

"She's heard plenty from me. Nobody's kidding that old lady. She knew he was bum, she helped draw the blueprints."

Pharoah winced and knew she saw it.

"You heard me, Mr. Detective!" Her searchlight eyes gave Seth center stage again. "You tell him how Ben tried to get me to steal narcotics from the hospital? How he threatened me? His own sister!" Seth was positive this was the first she had wept since Benny's death.

"Get him to tell you the rotten story," she said to Pharoah. "He may as well as long as he's writing that rotten book. You misfits!" she shrieked at Seth. "They ought to kill the whole goddamn lot of you! And let me tell you this," she snapped at Pharoah. "Whoever did it deserves a medal. You hear? A medal! And I'll pay for it myself. From the little bastard's insurance." She stormed back into the apartment, slamming the door behind her, and they could hear Mrs. Bergheim shouting as a second door slammed, "Ada! Ada! What's the matter? Ada!"

Pharoah and Seth descended the three flights of stairs in silence.

"My Jag's parked near the corner." Seth followed him obediently. Seth noticed a plain carton on the back seat when he got into Pharoah's car. Ten minutes later they were headed up Atlantic Avenue toward Brooklyn Bridge.

"Sorry about the book, cat," said Pharoah. "I wasn't trying to be cute."

"It doesn't matter. I was going to tell them."

"I'm going to help you with the book, cat." Seth met his eyes in the rear-view mirror, and Pharoah winked. "The chief says it's okay. I asked this morning. Am I making your day?"

"I'm very grateful. When can I see Ben's stuff?"

"You can see some of it tomorrow. They haven't finished Photostating it. They been dusting them." Seth's brows furrowed quizzically. "For fingerprints. We been dusting the whole apartment. You won't find much about her."

"Who?"

"Sister cat."

"I know most of what there is to know."

"Fill me."

Seth stared ahead, deep in thought.

"Come on, cat, there's got to be a give and take in every relationship, or it ain't a marriage made in heaven. I'm going to help you. I give. You take. Now give back. What's with Sister cat?"

"Cigarette?" Seth held out the pack to him.

"Light me one."

Seth placed two cigarettes in his mouth and lit them. He held one out to Pharoah who leaned over and took it with his lips. "Now fill me."

"Little over a year ago Ada fell in love with an intern. She got pregnant. He wouldn't marry her. So she decided on an abortion. She didn't dare ask around the hospital, so she went to Ben. She figured he was bound to know a scraper."

"She figured right." Seth didn't comment on Pharoah's remark.

"Anyway, that's when he asked her to get the narcotics for him. I don't have to tell you what she told him."

"I dig. How'd she get unfixed?"

Seth shifted in his seat so that he was looking directly at Pharoah.

"Ella Hurst helped her."

Pharoah took the cigarette from his mouth and flicked the ash out the window. "For a recluse, she manages to keep in touch."

"Ben had told her about it. Ella called Ada on her own."

"Did she know Sister cat?"

"Not personally."

"Then why the Girl Scout act?"

"Ella took a perverse pleasure in crossing Ben. And Ben got a perverse pleasure out of watching her do it. That strange old lady was his match, and he never tried to top her. They had a funny relationship."

"I got to meet that Ella cat real soon."

Pharoah swerved around a corner and Seth reached over to steady the carton. He heard glasses tinkling. "What've you got in here?"

"Glasses."

"Been shopping?"

"Borrowed." They were crossing the bridge. "Got to ask you something, cat. What's the purpose in this book?"

"I have to write it."

"You name names and you'll be spending the rest of your life in court."

"I have to piece together his life."

"Cat, I hope someday somebody feels that way about me."

"It's for myself, Pharoah Love. I never said I'd try to get it published. It's only for myself right now. I have to know what it was about him and what it was about me that brought us together and led to murder."

"Kismet."

"I'm not a fatalist. When I find out all there is to know about Ben, maybe I'll find out all there is to know about myself. Sounds crazy, doesn't it?"

"Far from it, cat. There's a few things I'm trying to find out about me too, only I can't write."

Seth took the plunge. "What is there about you, Pharoah? Are you married? Or do you have a girl friend?"

"No and no." Seth decided the expression around his mouth was a smile. "I'm a lonesome cat. But I'm in the market. I don't believe in getting hooked up just to keep myself busy a couple of nights a week. Wasn't till recently I made up my mind what I wanted."

They were heading up the West Side Highway and Seth could see his apartment house towering in the distance. "Where are we going?"

"Feel like a drink?"

Seth flipped his cigarette out the window. "You mean my place?"

Pharoah chuckled. "No, I was thinking of Ida's Place."

"What did you think of my place?" asked Seth.

"Cat, you were wildly funny last night."

"I don't remember very much after Jameson's fit."

"You were wildly funny."

"Then it was you that got me home."

"Who else was there?" He patted Seth's thigh. "It's okay. You didn't give me much trouble." Pharoah veered off at Seventy-ninth Street and headed crosstown toward Columbus Avenue.

"What time does the Ida cat open for business?"

Seth looked at his wrist watch. "It's after five. She'll be open."

"I'm sure she'll be delighted to get her glassware back."

"You got those glasses from Ida?"

"You know of an easier way to get fingerprints?"

My glass, Seth was figuring. And Veronica's. Jameson's. And Adam's. He cleared his throat. "They match any you found in Ben's apartment?"

"Everybody's been to the deceased's apartment, cat." He turned into Columbus Avenue.

Ida stared at the pizza and the pizza stared back at her. They found each other tasteless. Ward helped himself to a slice, keeping an eye on the two couples at the bar in case they needed refills. He swallowed a bit and grimaced.

"Ice cold."

"Who asked you?" grunted Ida. She was watching Seth and Pharoah getting out of the Jaguar parked at the curb. Like everything else in her life, her window needed cleaning.

"Here comes Seth and the spook." Pharoah was carrying the carton with one hand. Ward stared out the window and dropped the remainder of the slice back onto the tray, wiping his hand on his apron.

"Remember," said Ida in a whisper, "I don't know a frigging thing about the shit you were peddling for Ben."

"Okay! Okay!" Someone called for a refill and he walked away from Ida as Seth and Pharoah entered. Pharoah put the carton on a bar stool while Seth kissed Ida.

"How's your head?" she said, laughing.

"Behaving," said Seth.

"Thanks for the use of the glassware," said Pharoah, as Ida snapped her finger and Ward walked back, reached over for the carton, and placed it under the bar.

"When the waiter saw you taking them glasses," said Ida, "he spent the rest of the night with a cold towel on his head." Pharoah chuckled and asked Ward for a beer.

"The same," said Seth. Then he said to Ida, "Was out in Brooklyn paying my respects to Ben's mother. That's where I caught up with—" he jerked his thumb at Pharoah—"this one."

"Hey, bartender cat." Ward held the steins steady in his hand as he drew the beer. "Met your mama today." Ward looked up as the beer foamed over. "So you and Ben Bentley were kids together." Ward flipped the tap back in position and dried the steins with his apron.

"He was my best friend."

Ida cut in jovially. "That's how come he's working here. I took him on as a favor to Ben."

Pharoah lifted his stein. "So you're a good-Samaritan cat."

"I ain't sorry," said Ida. "He does a good job, and the customers like him."

"I got no complaints," said Pharoah, and he sipped his beer. Ward couldn't stop wiping his hands with his apron. Ida shifted her attention to Seth.

"Veronica called a few minutes ago. She's looking for you."

"Thanks."

"Bartender cat . . ." Ward leaned against the cash register with one foot propped up on the sink. "When'd you last see your buddy?"

"The night before he died. He was in here having a few drinks."

"I still can't get over it," cried Ida. "One night a guy's sitting at your bar boozing it up, the next day—" she clapped her hands together—"in memoriam!"

"Sad," agreed Pharoah. "Very sad." He sized up Ward and knew nothing would alleviate the bartender's very bad case of nerves. "Ever do any business with him?"

Ward's foot dropped to the floor. "What do you mean 'business'?"

"Sell things for him."

"What do you mean?" Ward hoped this was what Madame Grabatkin meant by underplaying.

"I mean, did he ever give you little packages to pass on to other people in return for some cash in some small envelopes?"

"Say, what's this all about?" flared Ida. Had she been a student, Madame Grabatkin would have approved.

"Well, Ida cat, since I like you, I'm going to tell you." Ida folded her arms and leaned on the bar. "Little Benny was a very industrious little cat. He knew how to get his hands on peyoti. You heard of the stuff."

"In this place you hear of everything."

"He used to peddle it. Except not always direct. So he needed a go-between, and you do heavy traffic here."

"Oh, Jesus God!" cried Ward. "You mean *that's* what the stuff was?" He waited for applause from Ida, but her fists were too clenched.

Pharoah's mouth formed a half-smile. "You didn't know?"

Seth looked at Ida, watching the perspiration blossoming on her brow.

"I didn't know. Honest. I owed him the favor. I couldn't say no when he asked me to hold the stuff for whoever would pick it up."

"No cut for you?" asked Pharoah.

"What are you talking about?"

"Don't jazz me, cat."

Ida saw an opening and took a dip. "Why didn't you tell me about this, Ward?"

"I didn't think it was important," he pleaded. "People are always leaving things here for other people to pick up."

"That's true," said Ida to Pharoah.

Pharoah placed an elbow on the bar and propped up his chin with his hand. "You ever see the *Mikado?*" he asked Ward.

"No."

"There was a Jap cat in that show who had a little list. So did your friend Ben. There's a Moishe Gabriel on his little list. And your mother calls her son, the bartender, 'Moishe.' "

"Okay, okay," said Ward, paling. "But Ida didn't know."

Ida's eyes pleaded with Pharoah. Seth put his hand on Pharoah's arm. "This sort of thing isn't Ida's style."

"I know," said Pharoah.

"Give the boys another round," cried Ida. "On the house, boys."

"I'm not ready yet," said Pharoah.

"When the boys are ready," Ida said to Ward. She reached under the bar for a paper napkin and mopped her brow.

"Moishe," said Pharoah, "I want you at the station tomorrow morning at ten." He dropped a card on the bar and Ward put it in his pocket. "That too early for you?"

"No, no, it's fine. Listen," he pleaded, "I didn't know what it was all about. Honest!"

"Tomorrow, cat. I'm too tired now. Ida, how's business?"

Ida wadded the napkin and flung it under the bar. "Can't

complain. Listen, Ward's a good kid. You know what I mean?"

"I ain't asking for references," said Pharoah, tapping his fingers against his half-empty stein.

"This is for free," said Ida evenly, and Seth admired her for not backing down. "He's a cool cat behind the bar and he minds his own business." She dug into her pocket and pulled out a red velvet bow which she pinned in her hair, "So he made a mistake. Okay. He didn't know it was a mistake when he was making it. You got no inkstains on your own ledger?"

Pharoah's eyes were riveted on the red velvet bow. "Ida cat, I wish my late daddy was alive to see you. He'd swallow you in one gulp."

"Even with my legs kicking?" she riposted. Seth burst out laughing and Pharoah signaled for the second round. I've met some spooky spooks in my time, thought Ida, but this one's the kinkiest. What bothered her even more, he was stirring up her stagnating juices, and she couldn't even spell integration. "What a life," Ida continued. "Somebody fries a kid in his bathtub and the shit hits the fan for half the population of New York. You just never know." The wall phone rang and Ida lifted the receiver. "Good evening. Ida's." She listened a moment and motioned to Seth. Her lips mouthed "Veronica." Seth sighed and took the phone.

"I was going to call you in a few minutes."

"What's this line of crap Ruthelma's feeding me?" Veronica snapped, staring out the window of her office at a couple in a warm embrace in a hotel room across the street.

Seth motioned for his stein which Ida handed to him. "Which line of crap are you referring to?"

91

"I want first crack at the book!" Veronica raged. "You owe it to me. Get me that outline."

"Veronica," Seth said, in the tone of voice that usually irritated his wife, "you're giving orders again. You know what happens to me when you start giving orders. I don't obey. I retreat. Nobody, but nobody, gets a look at this thing until I'm good and ready. *Capisce?*"

"Now listen, Seth." Her voice trembled. "You need some advice on this thing. You're not only sticking your own neck into a noose, you're sticking mine and a lot of other people's! You write one word about what happened between Ben and me and so help me God, I'll kill you!"

Seth licked some foam from his lips. "Did you ever say that to Ben?"

"Drop dead!" She slammed the phone down. She swung around in her swivel chair with a violent jerk, hitting her knee against the desk and letting out a yowl of pain. The couple in the hotel room were sinking slowly beneath the horizon of their window sill and Veronica's eyes smarted with tears, out of both pain and envy. She got to her feet and began pacing the room. What's that idiot trying to do, crucify us all? It's that goddamn psychoanalysis! Seth was as pliable as silly putty until he began to hit the couch. Soft and malleable. That wasn't the way he sounded on the phone. His voice was firmer and sharper and stronger, and Veronica loathed other people's strength. All her life she had feared domination, and that's why she had set her cap for Seth. She didn't want a man who could handle her. She wanted a man she could handle.

"You don't want a husband," Seth said the day he left her. "You want a kid brother."

She sank into the chair and fumbled in her purse for a cigarette. She picked up the desk lighter and it suddenly seemed heavier. The window shade was drawn in the hotel room, and she wished them luck. She puffed at the cigarette. Seth has to be beaten.

The cocktail crowd was beginning to file into Ida's. Seth and Pharoah had moved to a table and the jukebox was straining its lungs. They had switched from beer to martinis, and Seth was feeling very pleased with himself. Pharoah dug into a bowl of pretzels and munched away contentedly.

"Tell you a theory I got," he said, munching both words and pretzel. "Ben cat's murder wasn't planned."

"Possible," said Seth.

"Probable." Pharoah stamped the word officially. "Otherwise his desk would have been cleaned out before we got to it. O at least there would have been a mess in the place. And it wouldn't have been the radio. It'd have been a knife, or a gun, or they'd have held his head under water."

"That would eliminate a woman."

"Not a woman the size of Ida cat."

"Aw, come on!" Seth snorted. "She had nothing to do with Ben."

Pharoah pushed the bowl of pretzels over to Seth who helped himself to one. "I'm not saying she did, and who's to say she didn't?" More bait, thought Seth. Was Ida on Ben's little list too? "I was just giving you a for instance." Pharoah took a moment to admire a girl who passed the table and then turned back to Seth. "Look at it logically. Did whoever did it know he'd be taking a bath at the time? Of course not. You left the door to the apartment unlatched because Ben cat told you he was expecting the maid. But the maid had a key of her own. And she doesn't arrive until at least an hour after he was killed. And the maid says that's the time she always comes to clean the place. So according to the coroner, Ben cat is dead about an hour—killed sometime between when you left and the maid arrived. Which means he was either expecting another visitor or somebody arrived at the apartment hoping to find him in. Now whoever that somebody was, I figure they was blazing mad. You didn't happen to run into anyone you know on your way out?"

"Not a soul," said Seth, and sipped his martini.

"He died approximately around ten A.M." Pharoah was making a pattern on the table with the pretzels. "You say you left a half hour earlier. Now whoever killed him had to know he was leaving for Mexico and had to get to him before he went. That can narrow down the little list. Because not too many people would know Ben cat's plans. Whoever did it might have been hanging around waiting for you to leave. But you have to scratch that if Ben cat said to leave the door unlatched."

" 'Tis a puzzlement," said Seth, wondering if he dare indulge in another martini.

"Let's have another drink," said Pharoah, snapping his fingers for the waiter, and solving Seth's problem for him. "Now then—" Pharoah exhaled—"who beside you might have known Ben cat was taking off? Probably Hurst and his squaw. Probably your snotty wife—" and Seth couldn't ignore the emphasis he put on "snotty"—"and maybe Moishe, the bartender, since Ben cat was boozing here the night before. That could therefore include Ida. And probably the fat recluse cat, Ella Hurst, who ain't listed in the phone book. How do we get to her?"

"Well . . ." Seth sighed, as he hungrily eyed the fresh drinks the waiter was setting on the table. "It's an involved and very slow process."

"So's solving a murder."

"Ada and Mrs. Bergheim might have known."

"About what?"

"Ben's trip to Mexico."

"Get back to Ella Hurst."

Seth sipped the fresh martini. "Well, Pharoah Love, first one sends her a telegram. You state your business. Then you rendezvous a phone call with her. She calls you, so you have to hang around the phone till she's good and ready to dial—*if* she's going to dial at all."

"Why don't we just phone her direct?" The "we" gave Seth a cozy sense of security. "I got her number in Ben's little black book."

"She doesn't answer her phone. She doesn't answer her door. It all has to be prearranged. Nobody takes Ella by surprise."

"Send her a telegram now. She'll get it in an hour. Ask her to see us tomorrow afternoon."

"Wouldn't you rather see her by yourself?"

"I got no secrets from you, cat." The voice was warm and friendly and the words patted Seth on the head.

"Okay," said Seth, rising, "I'll get some change and send the telegram."

7

Oh, my sainted mother! Oh, my blessed sainted mother!" Hurst's hands were clasped in supplication while his eyes rolled to the ceiling as though there might have been a mural of his mother there. "The man's gone mad! Utterly, completely mad!" He decided the ceiling needed repainting. "Is there no stopping him?" He looked from Adam to Veronica. Adam was stretched out on the floor doing deep-breathing exercises, and Veronica was watching his chest rise and fall, wondering what he'd be like in bed.

"Veronica!" snapped Hurst, demanding attention.

She reluctantly steered her eyes at him, then settled back in the couch with a sigh and kicked her shoes off. Adam sat up, inhaled, did a back flip onto his feet, and Veronica applauded.

"Drink time," said Adam, and went to the bar.

"Pour me one of the subtler brandies," commanded Hurst.

"Scotch and water," said Veronica.

Adam filled the orders swiftly, grateful for the silence that had settled in the room. Could Seth's book really hurt them?

He wasn't worried about himself. He could hold on to Jameson as a meal ticket for as long as he wanted. But what about Ella? She could be the bombshell, and he knew that was uppermost in Jameson's mind.

"Perhaps there's a legal way to stop him." Hurst tightened the obi on his Japanese kimono and stared out the window at the garden and the greenhouse, knowing full well there'd be no Lieutenant Pinkerton there. The greenhouse reminded him of something and he groaned, "Oh God."

"What now?" asked Adam, distributing the drinks.

"The bloody greenhouse!" cried Hurst. "The peyoti cacti I've got growing there!"

Veronica sat up as though she'd been prodded with a knife. "Destroy them, for God's sake!"

"But it's the last of it!" cried Hurst. "Ben was going to Mexico to bring back more."

"You can live without it," said Adam flatly. "It's not habit-forming."

"Don't you tell me what I can or can't do without! I like what it does for me." His face was enraptured. "Ten glorious hours of uninhibited technicolor spectacle. Say," he near-shouted to Adam, "what about that family of yours in New Mexico? Couldn't you get them to send us a CARE package?"

"Forget it!" Adam's words cut into Hurst's like a tomahawk.

"What about *Seth?*" demanded Veronica.

"Oh, how I loathe reality." Hurst sighed. "Seth." He stared at the Persian rug thoughtfully. "Of course it'll be ages before he gets to finish the damn thing."

"Don't kid yourself." She placed her drink on the coffee

table. "Once he gets going, he writes at a dead heat. And good, bad, or indifferent, every publisher in town will snap at it."

"You don't suppose it's the sort of thing they'd serialize in the *Ladies' Home Journal?*"

"Jameson!" He was amused by the agony in her voice.

"Well, what do you want me to do, Veronica, try to buy him off?" She contemplated the idea. "Do you think he might be for sale?" Hurst continued. "But then, if this entire case bursts across the front pages like a fireworks display, what difference will it make?"

"You have influence! You could get to the police and quash the more sordid details."

"Yes, yes, yes, everything is possible." He ran his fingers through his flaxen hair. "It's the blackamoor that has me worried. Pharoah Love, indeed. I'd love to kill the archaeological expedition that excavated him. Well—" he sighed— "we have one last hope."

"What's that?" Veronica asked eagerly.

"Ella." Adam had been waiting for this.

"What could Ella do?"

"My dear Veronica, there are times when Ella can work miracles. You know that, darling."

Adam's voice was so modulated that it came as almost a shock to them when he spoke. "I thought you wanted to keep her out of this."

"Too late," said Hurst. "The detective saw her at the funeral. He's bound to want to see her, and Ella can't resist the challenge. After all, in many ways she was closer to Ben then I was. She played games with him, and Ben doted on games. He was one of the few to really appreciate Ella and understand her. Ella can handle the detective person, and I think she just might be able to handle Seth. I shall see her at once!"

"Do you have to send her a telegram too," Veronica asked, wrinkling her nose piquantly, "or do you share a secret knock?"

"I call softly through her keyhole. That's what we did when we were children—when Father would lock us up in separate rooms—" His voice hardened—"always trying to separate Ella from me. But we were inseparable. In her heart Ella loathes me, but she will never sever the tie that binds us. Because it is inseparable."

Seth and Pharoah had finished dinner at Ida's and now sat over stingers. It was after ten, and several couples were dancing the frug.

"In this," murmured Seth, "the winter of our discothèque . . ."

Pharoah looked at his wrist watch. "What time do you go on tonight?" His eyes twinkled. Seth laughed.

"I don't think I'll be doing any singing tonight. I want a clear head when I go through Ben's papers tomorrow. What time, by the way?"

"Oh noonish. I don't think I'll need much time with Moishe." He jerked his head toward the bartender.

"Are you sure nothing was taken from Ben's apartment before you got to it?"

"Pretty sure. Everything was very neat and very orderly. A frantic cat would have left the place looking like India after a monsoon. No, cat, the murderer left in a very big rush."

"I wonder why."

"Tell you about it sometime." He yawned. "You suppose

that Ella cat is circling the phone about now, wondering whether or not to dial?"

"Look, if you're tired, you go and I'll wait for the call."

"Want to be on your own for a while, cat?"

"If I did, I would come right out and say so."

"That's how I'd like it to be with us, cat." He tapped the table lightly. "Everything spread on the table."

"I might even end up dedicating the book to you."

"I could use a little dedication." One of the dancers fell against him. She was a tiny pretty blonde of about twenty.

"Gee," she said, as he helped her up, "I'm so sorry."

"Be my guest."

"Yeah?" she gurgled. "Where's your hotel?" Her partner grabbed her hand and pulled her back into the fray before Pharoah could answer.

"Cute little chick," commented Pharoah. "You dig the type?"

"Too blonde, too small, too young."

Pharoah's next words seemed to descend from mid-air, as though they had been hovering in space for hours, waiting for a signal to land. "That Veronica cat got much of a temper?"

"She can spit, scratch, and bite like most cats." He didn't add "why." He just waited.

"She ever throw things?"

"Like radios?"

Pharoah was about to speak when the wall phone rang.

Ella read and reread Seth's telegram during the better part of an hour. She sat in one corner of the cramped apartment, in a wing chair that had once been her father's. When she was a baby, he would sit in this chair and bounce her on his knee or cuddle her until the nurse came to claim her. Now the chair was worn and badly in need of recovering, as was Ella.

The telegram was propped up against a lamp on the table next to her. Ella giggled to herself. The black veils swathed around her face softly diffused the already dimly lit room. This was how Ella liked it. This was Ella's world, and Ella's world called for subdued lighting, veiled face, grotesquely obese body, black-gloved hands, huge strands of purple beads, and the near-sickening odor of incense. It burned in the cup at the feet of the ivory Buddha.

She sipped her brandy and stared at the phone.

Let them wait a bit longer. Let them grow impatient. Let their appetites be whetted until they groaned under the weight of their anxiety to hear from her.

That fool Jameson. It's no wonder Daddy loathed him. What a mincing, simpering brat he had been! Had he at least attempted to behave like a little man, instead of capering in front of Daddy in odious imitations of Mother, our childhood might have been more bearable. Poor Mother. Dear Mother. Dead at twenty-six. How beautiful she was. Or was she? Ella was barely five when Mummy fell from the window of their country estate, cracking her skull on the patio stones below. She was sitting in the window combing Ella's flaxen hair, singing "Today is Ella's day, today is Ella's day," when somehow she leaned backward and lost her balance. There was no guard rail on the large window in Mummy's room. She always loved to sit there on the narrow window seat and call down to Daddy. Was she calling down to Daddy that day? Was she leaning out? Ella couldn't recall. It was over so quickly.

101

"When I want a woman," Daddy had shouted furiously when Jameson came clopping into the study in Mummy's high heels and her big picture hat, "I'll buy myself another," and he had slapped Jameson in the face. Served the little stinker right. How long ago was it? Sixty years? Was it sixty years? I look a hundred years. Jameson looks forty years, and he has the scars to prove it.

Silly Jameson. A thing of beauty is a boy forever. Face lifts and hormone injections. Why must he grow old gracelessly. How we hate each other! How we need each other! Who passed this evil sentence upon us? Why have I never married?

She picked up the telegram and read it again. The grandfather's clock in the foyer struck eleven. She looked at the telephone. Time to struggle out of the chair. This flesh. This meat. This ugly padding. This wall I've built around myself, year after year, layer by layer. She lumbered slowly to the phone, clutching the telegram in her right hand. She adjusted her veil to read the number better and then dialed. The voice at the other end said, "Good evening. Ida's."

Seth and Pharoah watched Ida as she answered the phone. They saw her mouth "Yes" and then she turned and waved at Seth.

"Bingo, I hope," said Pharoah as Seth went to the phone. "Hello?"

Ella's voice was pitched like a whistle.

"Tomorrow at four," she said, and hung up. Seth replaced the receiver and returned to the table.

"Okay, Pharoah Love." He sat down and picked up his drink. "We see Ella cat tomorrow at four."

"Should we wear anything special?"

"A poker face will do."

The little blonde was wiggling her fanny a few inches from Pharoah's face and he thought of pinching it, until he reminded himself of the more important pinch he was after.

"I better brief you a bit on what to expect." Pharoah moved his chair closer to Seth. "Don't blanch when you enter her apartment. It was decorated by the Collier brothers. It stinks of incense and obesity, and she sits in the far corner of the room in a very old wing chair. She never lifts the veils from her face and all she serves is brandy. It's laid out for us before we get there. She never budges from the chair because it's too much of an effort. Her voice is piping shrill—pitched so high I sometimes think only birds and dogs can hear her.

"At four sharp the door will be unlatched for us. We sit on the couch in the center of the room. The drapes are drawn tight across the window and the room is dimly lit."

"Can she see through the veils?"

"Sometimes I think she can see through walls. She has a sharp mind and a sharper tongue. And if she doesn't like you, you'll know it soon enough."

"Yet she went to Ben cat's funeral."

"Don't ask me to explain Ella. I only met her a few times, and that was because of Ben. She adored him. Don't ask me to explain that either. Ben evaded most of my questions about her. All I know is that she's a spinster and she exiled herself about fifteen years ago after an accident to her face somewhere abroad, which brought her back to this country with Jameson."

Pharoah looked puzzled. "How long did they live abroad?"

"About twenty years, I think."

"Even during the war?"

Seth lowered his stinger. "They lived in the south of Spain for a while, then Switzerland, then Portugal. And she loathes her brother. She'll let you know that soon enough. Anything else?"

"No. I'll catch the rest of the plot myself after the curtain rises." He stifled a yawn. "Cat, I'm tired. I think I'll cut. You want a lift to your pad or you staying?"

"I'm staying awhile." Pharoah signaled to the waiter and mouthed "Check."

Seth shook his head. "Forget it. Tonight's on me."

"No, thanks, cat. I pay my own fare."

"I said it's on me." The note of insistence and irritation in Seth's voice jarred the detective. "I'm flush. I collected a couple of residual checks today."

"Okay, cat. If you insist." It seemed to Seth that he was giving in too easily. He knew the man was surrounded by a wall of stubborn pride, and he even seemed embarrassed by Seth's gesture. Let him get used to it, Seth decided. Practice what you preach, Pharoah Love. Give and take. Share and share alike. You're your own man, now I'm my own man. And you better get to know that.

"See you tomorrow." Pharoah winked and left the table. He said "Good night" as he passed Ida, flashed a knowing look at Ward, and then winked at the tiny blonde. She rewarded him with a smile while her escort glared.

Ida joined Seth. Her face looked like a piece of wrapping paper that had been scribbled on with a heavy crayon. "I got a feeling I'm coming down with diarrhea."

"Don't let him frighten you," said Seth, lifting his empty glass so the waiter could see it.

"This place is all I got, Seth." He patted her hand. "You know what happens if they pull your license just once in this town. The ABC Board cracks down on you and it's hell trying to get another. I don't have that much fight left in me."

"Nothing's going to happen, Ida. Once you get to know him, he's kind of a nice guy."

"Fuzz don't know from nice when they're on a job. I wasn't kidding him. He knows I knew what Ward was up to. I read him easy."

"I wish I did."

Ida stared at his handsome, tired face. Something had chipped away at his chiseled good looks. The slight flab in his cheeks was gone. They were hollow now, and the muscles of his jaw were tightly drawn.

"He seems to like you well enough."

The waiter brought the fresh drink, and Seth leaned back in the chair and then smiled at Ida. "The last time somebody said that to me, they were speaking of Ben. As of now, I'd like to see well enough let alone."

"Ah, come on! I see how you handle him. He's got respect for you. That's why—if you could put in a word with him— you know, friendly like . . ."

"He won't touch this place, Ida. That's a guarantee."

She pinched his cheek affectionately. "By me, you're all the nice people in the world. Any time you want to make it with me, baby, just leave a trail of rice and I'll follow it."

In the space of five hours Ward broke seven glasses, cut his finger on one, unwittingly short-changed three customers, and forgot to charge two. He knew he'd be up all night rehearsing his meeting with Pharoah. The trouble was, he might know his lines by ten o'clock in the morning, but what cues would Pharoah throw him? Maybe he was being punished for not having gone to Ben's funeral. But it was either that or laying that kid from Bennington. And he had paid his respects to Ben often enough in the past twenty years. He'd pay his respects to the Bergheims on Sunday, if he was a free man. He broke another glass.

Ida glared at the bar, muttering out of the side of her mouth to Seth, "This frigging mess is beginning to cost me more than it's worth. Why don't you grab me by the hair and take me away from all this? Uh-oh."

Seth looked up. Veronica was entering with Adam Little-storm. She spotted Seth immediately and nudged Adam. Adam smiled and waved. Seth winked and folded his arms on the table as Veronica, followed by Adam, pushed her way past the dancers to his table.

"I can steer them to the back," offered Ida.

"No." Seth smiled. "I can handle this."

"Well," piped Veronica, "and where's the Corsican brother?"

"I thought you weren't talking to me," Seth rejoindered.

She smiled coyly. "You know I can't stay mad at you long." She slid in next to him and Adam sat next to Ida.

"How's Mr. Hurst?" Ida asked.

"He's okay," Adam replied. A waiter came for their order. "The same?" Adam asked Veronica. She was repainting her lips and grunted "Uh-huh." "Two scotch and water. Seth?"

"Not at the moment, thanks. Where's Jameson?"

"Off in a world of his own."

"He's with Ella," snapped Veronica, "and *very* upset about the book."

"What book?" asked Ida.

"Hasn't he told you?" She plopped the lipstick into her purse. "He's writing a book about Ben Bentley."

Ida thought a moment. "Why not?"

"I love you, Ida." Seth was livening up. "Why not indeed? What's all the fuss about? Everyone's been reading things into what I haven't even written yet."

"You have no control as a writer." Veronica clipped each word like a coupon. "You need an editor, someone to help you shape your material the way I always have. Cut away the fancy dross."

"You didn't cut, sweetheart, you eviscerated. You'll never lay your hands on anything of mine again."

"You ungrateful son of a bitch!"

"You should never raise your voice, Veronica. It lowers your guard." Seth's words hit her like cold sleet. The downpour didn't abate. "You take a perverse delight in cutting people down to what you decide should be their size. 'I did this for you.' 'I did that for you.' " He mimicked her savagely. "You don't do anything for anybody unless it nets you a profit."

"Seth!" she gasped. The waiter brought the drinks and departed hastily.

"I'm telling you right here and now, and in front of witnesses, you keep trying to scuttle this project of mine and so help me, you'll sink along with it. This book is going to be written because it's the first honest thing I've done in my life."

"Ha-haaaah," shrieked Ida.

"That's the sort of line that needs editing," huffed Veronica, not easily beaten.

"Everybody needs editing, baby, everybody. But since my ambition seems to give you such pain, let me salve it a bit by telling you it's simply going to be a study of a kid who went wrong. I'm just going to show why. It's going to be a short book because it wasn't a very long life. But I'm going to feel better for having written it. And, sweetheart, I haven't felt good in a long, long time. About ten years, I think it's been. From the day I said, 'Yes, dear, I'll marry you.' "

She flung her drink in his face, snatched her purse, kicked her chair back, and stormed out.

Seth was extremely pleased with himself. He didn't feel embarrassed.

After Pharoah left Ida's, he settled behind the wheel of his car and suddenly felt too tired to switch on the ignition. Where's this case taking me, he wondered. This yellow-brick road I'm following won't land me in Oz, though I've met the cowardly lion, the tin woodman, a scarecrow, and a witch. What happens when I find what I think I'm going to find at the end of the road? I was a good cop and I think I'm a good detective. I got there on my own steam. Nobody helped. Nobody pushed. Nobody tried to hold me back, either. I got a Jaguar. I'm the first cat on my block ever to own a Jaguar. And in another couple of years it'll be all paid up. Time to trade it in.

Time to trade a lot of things in. Protection traded for information. Pride traded for affection. Loneliness traded for love. Inferiority traded for dominance. Will everybody be willing to swap? I mustn't like the Seth cat too much, but he reaches me. What am I to him so far? He's a suspect in my murder case. He needs my help to get his book written. Damned fool. It could be the last book he'll ever write.

I could use a little dedication.

I like that cat too much. I haven't liked anybody in too long. I need to care about somebody. I'm forty and I need to care. I'd care for some chick except I saw what my folks did to each other. Folks!

A cab pulled up at the corner and he saw Veronica and Adam emerge. Why didn't Seth tell him that they were joining him? Was that why he was so anxious to see me cut? Shit. Maybe he doesn't even know they're on their way to Ida's. Hadn't she hung up on him when he spoke to her? That was five hours ago. The only other time he used the phone was to take Ella's call. Why do I give a damn what he does or who he sees?

Veronica's mouth never stopped moving as she and Adam walked past the Jaguar without seeing Pharoah.

Snotty cat. My boy can sure pick them. He switched on the ignition and the motor purred. He shifted into gear and drove off slowly.

Order had been restored at Seth's table. His face was washed, his hair combed, and he had a new glass of stinger to fondle. Ida was back at the bar, and Adam was proving to be pleasant company.

"I was a very promising athlete in high school back in New Mexico," Adam was telling him. He was on his third Scotch. "I even dreamed I'd make the Olympics. But hell, it didn't work that way at all. So I left home and started working my way east."

The tiny blonde was being wildly uninhibited on the dance floor, and Ida was wondering whether to step in and censor her. The less attention Adam paid to her, the more frantic her gyrations. But Adam had Seth's undivided attention, and undivided attention was something Adam rarely got.

"I used to work in summer resorts and winter resorts. Then I met this broad who asked me to drive her to New

York. It was an exhausting trip in more ways than one, but she gave me a hundred bucks when we landed here and told me to forget her name." He chuckled. "God, was she a bimbo! Am I boring you?"

"Not at all," said Seth.

"Then I began waiting table in the Village. The Hungry Poodle. You know the place?"

Seth knew it well. A haven for advertising-agency executives, directors, producers, actors, bankers looking to let their hair down and drop their inhibitions.

"You ever hear of Rod Monks?"

"I did a TV script for him once."

"Well, he's the first one who convinced me I could be a—" he snorted derisively—"masseur. So I pummeled him for a while, then somebody else, and so on ad infinitum. The money was good and the living was easy and I didn't give a shit any more. And when Jamie saw Ben the bastard easing out of his life, he began easing me in. What the hell! It's no sweat. And I've grown to like the old bugger an awful lot. Boy, if they ever got wind of this back on the reservation. When that little prick threatened me about it once . . ."

"Ben?"

"Who else? Boy, did I belt him one."

So that's what had happened, thought Seth.

"Get off my back, will you?" Ben lay on the couch with a piece of raw steak pressed to his eye. "Ain't it bad enough it's costing me that modeling job tomorrow?"

"I thought you never got into fights," Seth persisted, as he waited for the red light to glow on the electric percolator.

"Oh, for crying out loud! There was no fight. I tripped and

fell against a doorknob at Ella's, that's all. Isn't that frigging coffee ready yet?"

The tiny blonde made a lot of noise as Ida pushed her and her escort out the front door. "Beat it," she shouted through the door, "or I'll call a cop!" Ward broke another glass.

"So it was you who socked Ben in the eye that time."

"There would have been more times, but—" he chuckled—"Ella told me to lay off. There was no shaking loose of that little bug. Well, I guess he's shook loose for good now. Boy, I wanted to send you a medal when I heard him tell Jameson you two had split. You're a nice guy, Seth. A real nice guy. How do you get yourself mixed up with lice like this?"

"How do you?"

"Why'd I know you were going to say that?"

"When'd you last see Ben?"

"If it was important, I'd remember. But it's not important. Poor Jamie. He's gonna miss him something awful. His stockpile of peyoti is running awful low."

"Did you introduce it to him?"

"Shit, no. He found it himself in Mexico when he was there with Ben back in sixty-two. I'm just a coincidence. I hate the stuff. My old man used to use it when I was a kid. But at least that was a part of a religious ritual. He belonged to a sect in which chewing buttons was part of the religious ceremony. But then my mother decided to become a Protestant because she liked the organ music in church. So he became a Protestant too, and me, and my brothers and my sisters." He grinned. "There's eight of us. I have a very tired mother." He sipped his drink. "I've been trying to get Jamie off it ever since I went to live with him. But that little bugger

111

Ben out-talked me. Well, he's going to be off it soon." Then he sighed. "He'll probably find something else, though. Want another drink?"

"No, thanks."

"Me either. You got something going for you, you know? Like I mean, you can write. I got nothing to fall back on. I walk out on Jamie, I got no place to walk to. I ought to go to night school or something. I used to think once maybe I could be an artist. I used to draw real good when I was a kid. Did all right at the government school. Shit. Do you think it's too late?"

"Adam baby, it's never too late when you make up your mind to do something."

"Like the way everybody's hemorrhaging over this book of yours. Boy, I'd like to stir up a little action like that. I'm too . . ." He snapped his fingers. "What's the word?"

"Passive."

"Passive!" He brushed some cigarette ash from his shirt. "It'd be nice, just once, to do something you don't have to be ashamed of. You know what I mean? Everybody could say it stinks, but I wouldn't give a damn because it's something I did, something I'm proud of. Ahhh . . ." He waved his arm as though he were warding off evil spirits. "I used to listen to them razzing you—Jamie, Ben, Veronica . . ." Seth felt the blood draining from his face. "But they razzed everybody who did things they couldn't do."

Razzing . . . Ben . . .

"But you're spitting in their eye and that's what I like about you. You're gonna write this book no matter who tells you not to." He winked knowingly. "It's gonna be a good book. I feel it in here." He thumped his chest. "You're bigger then any of them." He chuckled. "You need a good masseur? On the house."

Seth mustered a grin. "I've taken enough beatings lately."

"Okay." Adam chuckled. "Rain check. But remember, I'm on your side."

And I need all the help I can get, thought Seth, and I wish you weren't so tight so I could ask you again when was the last time you saw Ben Bentley.

Adam shook his head violently and sat erect. "I better get back. Heap too much firewater!" He flung his head back and laughed uproariously.

Ida said to Ward, "No more drinks for Tonto, or I'll have to eighty-six him. And don't drop that glass, fer Chris'sakes!"

The waiter brought Seth the check and he dropped some bills on the table. "Come on, Adam. I'll get you a cab."

"Let's go back to your pad for a drink."

"Not tonight." Seth helped him to his feet. "I got a heavy day ahead of me tomorrow and I'm going beddy-by." Adam rose somewhat unsteadily and held on to the back of the chair.

"Wow," he whispered. "Happens every time he goes to see Ella. I guess I just can't cope with Ella. Poor Ella." Seth helped him to the door, waving good night to Ida and Ward en route.

It was a clear night and the cool air refreshed them both somewhat. Seth hailed a cab and Adam got in. Seth gave the driver the address on Gramercy Park and then poked his head through the back window. "Good night, Adam. I'll see you soon." Adam patted his cheek and Seth moved back as the cab pulled away. He crossed back onto the sidewalk and

113

wondered if he had the strength to walk the ten blocks to his apartment house.

"I used to listen to them razzing you. . . ."

He began walking.

"It'd be nice, just once, to do something you don't have to be ashamed of."

Seth felt stiff all over. He could use a massage.

8

Jameson stood at the window, his hand holding the curtain aside, and tapped his foot impatiently. Under a peacock-blue satin dressing gown embroidered with gold and red forget-me-nots, tied around the waist with an orange brocaded sash, he wore purple silk pajamas. His slippers were oriental in style, green and fuschia, with a tiny bell sewed on the tip of each. All he lacked was a pot of gold at his feet.

He puffed impatiently as he watched Adam pay the cab driver, fumble for his keys, get the gate open, slam the gate shut, and then weave his way to the front door. Jameson tinkled his way to the door and pulled it open. Adam stumbled forward, poking his key into Hurst's stomach.

"Oof! You oaf!" Adam straightened up with a friendly, if somewhat hazy, smile, as Hurst slammed the door shut and swept back into the living room. Adam followed, removed his jacket and flung it on the floor. Jameson spun around on his heel, hands firmly planted on his hips, and demanded in an ugly tone, "Where have you been?"

"Out."

"What did you do?"

"Nobody." He slumped onto the couch. His eyes focused on Hurst's irate figure, and for a moment he thought someone had left on the colored television set.

"You've been to bed with Veronica!"

Adam groaned and his head fell back.

"Answer me!"

With an effort Adam pulled himself erect. "You give me a pain in the ass." Jameson gasped, lifted a porcelain ash tray, and hurled it at the fireplace. Adam leaned forward, his face in his hands. Very slowly he parted his fingers and his right eye dollied in on Hurst. "Peek-a-boo."

"I've been home for hours! You didn't even check in to see if I was all right." Adam began drumming on the coffee table. "Listen, you. In this country we use telephones." Adam folded his hands.

"How was Ella?"

"Ella was a perfect wretch tonight! I left her dissolved in tears. I'd have preferred leaving her dissolved in acid!" He stormed to a chair and sank into it. "She's seeing Seth and that detective tomorrow afternoon."

Adam was suddenly sober. "Is Ella out of her mind?"

"Ella can take care of herself. She's been doing a very good job of it for a good many years."

"Ella's looking for trouble, baby."

"Ella thrives on trouble." He lit a cigarette.

"I wish you'd see the last of Ella."

An evil smile formed on Jameson's face. "You don't like Ella because she loved Ben. Ella doesn't like you."

"You know what I might do?" said Adam menacingly. "I

116

just might tell Seth all about Ella. You wouldn't like *that*, would you?"

Jameson exhaled through his nose. Here sits the dragon challenged by Saint George. "You wouldn't dare."

"How do you know?"

"You're upsetting me, Adam."

Adam got up and began unbuttoning his shirt. "You can go to hell." He crossed to the hall and went up the stairs. Jameson lunged out of his chair and jingled in pursuit.

"Adam!" He jingled up the stairs, retrieving the shirt where it had been dropped. "Adam!" He crossed the hall into Adam's bedroom where the Indian stood in his shorts, lighting a cigarette. "You do—you just do—and I'll kill you! Do you hear me? I'll kill you!"

"How?" asked Adam, exhaling. "I don't play the radio when I take a bath."

Jameson began to convulse. Adam cried "Shit!" and rushed to him.

Veronica sat up in bed and reached for her robe. She flung it around her shoulders and got out of bed, crossing to the dresser for her purse. She found her handkerchief and dabbed at her eyes.

"Don't you worry. He'll come crawling back to me. I'll get my hands on that book if it's the last thing I do."

A sigh emanated from the vicinity of the bed.

"He knows I mean business, and when I mean business—*I mean business!*"

The bed creaked and then sighed with relief as it was unburdened of the second weight.

"He's just going through a phase of hostility. Everyone in

117

analysis goes through that stage. I've been reading up on it. You can't say I don't enter the battle unprepared."

He took her in his arms and kissed her. "Get back into bed and get some sleep. A good warrior needs all the rest she can get. Oh God, that drive back to Darien."

Veronica watched him as he began dressing. She wondered if there was any chance of separating Daniel Saber from his family.

Ada awoke with a start and switched on the night light. She listened. Nothing. Pray God Mama's sound asleep. She fumbled for a cigarette, found one, and lit it. Then in a sitting position, she drew her knees up and hugged them with her arms. A book about Ben. What crap. How ironic if the damned thing turned out to be any good. Well, why not? There were a lot of biographies of Oscar Wilde. Why not one for our Benjamin? I suppose Seth will be calling again to ask questions about his childhood. No doubt he'll do his research thoroughly. I hope he's decent enough to use some discretion. Oh God. Supposing he's honest. Supposing he paints the little bastard for what he really was. Will he write about the abortion?

Oh Jesus! He wouldn't dare! I'll kill him!

Pharoah Love slept with his head under the pillow and the blanket scrunched up around his shoulders. One leg hung over the edge of the bed and he breathed heavily. He whimpered once, then he laughed. He whimpered again, and then he growled. He murmured, "Got you, cat!" and began laughing wildly. He woke himself up. He stared into the darkness.

"Who's there?"

He leaped out of bed, grabbed his service revolver from its holster, and turned on a lamp.

He was alone in the room. He flung the revolver on the bed and sat down. His aloneness enveloped him, grabbed at him, stifled him. He began to shiver and crossed back to the bed. He picked up the revolver and placed it on the night table. He got under the covers, then stared at the lamp he had forgotten to extinguish.

"Go to sleep, baby. Mama's gonna leave the lamp on. The hobgoblins won't come when the lamp's on. They's afraid of the light."

Pharoah got out of bed, crossed to the lamp, and pulled the switch. He stumbled back to the bed, kicked his foot against the chair, yelled "Damn!" but not because he had kicked his foot.

Ruthelma slept with her head propped up against two huge pillows with her chubby arms folded across her stomach. Eighteen curlers were snugly set for the night in her hair. She wheezed and snored. The wheezes emanated gently. The snores were italicized.

Ward sat at the edge of the bed and stared at the clock. Five more hours. Five more hours till the countdown. Why hadn't he done that scene from *Detective Story* at Madame Grabatkin's? How should he play it with Pharoah Love?

Like Marlon Brando. "Uh—wha'—uh . . ." Scratch, scratch. "Uh—wha' yuh after—uh—cop?" Wrong.

Maybe tell him a few jokes. Jack Lemmon style. "Gee, Officer, if I had a dollar I'd pass the buck." Forget it.

Jean Paul Belmondo! *"Je ne sais pas rien,* flic."

Ida nudged him with her elbow. "Get going, will ya? It's late."

Seth sat in his kitchen sipping a cup of instant coffee. On the table in front of him were several sheets of paper. One sheet was headed "Motives." The second sheet was headed "Who." The third sheet was headed "Titles." Other than for "Motives," "Who," and "Titles," the sheets were blank.

Then Pharoah's face loomed large on the "Motives" sheet. Seth scribbled over it.

The night doorman at Ella Hurst's apartment house had often sworn she was an occasional nocturnal prowler. He had sworn he once saw her return at five in the morning, arms laden with junk she had probably collected from garbage cans and refuse piles. Hurst never denied this was possible.

Tonight her bed was empty.

9

THE WEST-SIDE dogs were in full voice Saturday morning. Seth could hear the cacophony of yaps, yips, and barks as he finished dressing and, without looking out the window, could describe in detail to himself the small army of dog lovers and their four-legged children. There would be Napoleon (red leash) with his slim redheaded mistress who nightly seemed to entertain agents, producers, and other assorted "Johns" in her studio apartment, occasionally raising her voice in song, but never in protest. There would be the middle-aged architect from the fourteenth floor with his great Dane, Victor (chain leash), assuring mothers he was as gentle as a lamb, the great Dane, not the architect.

The two boys from the Venezuelan Legation would be airing their Airedales (brown leash and green leash), arguing in Spanish while the dogs exchanged bored looks. Seth was convinced the Airedales were bilingual. There'd be an impatient shout of "I said *heel,* Evangeline" (boxer, red leash, Bloomingdale's) from the window trimmer (bantam weight, pink ascot, Bloomingdale's).

They didn't annoy Seth this morning as they annoyed him most mornings. He was enjoying the best frame of mind he had enjoyed in months. He had worked on the sheets marked "Motives," "Who," and "Titles" until five in the morning, and he took a perverse delight in the results. The suspects were pinpointed (unless a dark horse loomed on the horizon, and that seemed unlikely); their motives were clearly drawn (though Ben's papers might add or subtract from his deductions), and he would call the book *Ben: A Wasted Life,* unless he could find something better in Shakespeare than "This Too, Too Solid Flesh."

There was an hour to spare before his noon appointment with Pharoah (invisible leash), and he decided to treat himself to a good breakfast at Stark's. He even permitted himself to hum while waiting for the elevator and commended himself for greeting the day in high spirits. It might even last a few hours. At the sixteenth floor the elevator stopped to pick up another passenger.

The slovenly lady who wore no brassière shuffled aboard, clutching the mangy old poodle under her beefy old arm.

"We're going to settle this once and for all when we get back upstairs." The dog defied her by staring at Seth. "Do you hear me? Phyllis! Pay attention when I'm talking to you! You're not going to have it your way any longer!" Phyllis yawned and the slovenly lady grabbed the dog's head and twisted it until they were staring into each other's eyes. "I've had enough of your insults, you rotten thing!" The elevator doors opened and she flung Phyllis onto the lobby floor. Phyllis raised her tail in an obscene gesture and headed for the revolving door. "I don't want to go that way today," the slovenly woman shrieked. "We're going out the service entrance." Phyllis sat down and stared at her mistress in confu-

sion. If looks could kill, thought Seth, as he pushed the revolving door.

The Venezuelans were arguing vociferously, oblivious to
Napoleon's mistress caroling "I Could Have Danced All
Night." The architect was assuring a mother of three (children) that the great Dane was as gentle as a lamb, and the
window dresser favored Seth with his fixed, half-dressed
smile which Seth ignored. He didn't realize that like the
faulty taps, the stubborn ovens, and the rotten reception on
Channel Nine, he was a mystery and challenge to his neighbors.

Seth strode briskly to Broadway, pausing only to buy the
morning newspapers before entering Stark's. He found a
table near the window and a waitress near the table, gave his
order, and concentrated on the newspapers. Still nothing
about Ben Bentley's murder. Monday, he thought, Monday
it's bound to hit the fan, if his letter makes tomorrow's New
York *Times Book Review*.

He dug into his breakfast with relish.

The bird chirruped from the branch directly over Jameson's head, and he stared at the intruder ominously. Adam
was stretched on the grass with his eyes closed, sun-bathing.
He had refused coffee; he had refused toast; he had refused
jam. Jameson hoped his head would explode as he spooned
more kumquat jelly, imported at great expense from Hong
Kong, onto a thin sliver of rye toast. He popped the lot into
his mouth, crossed his legs, and then folded his hands over
his bony kneecap. The jelly tasted like slime; the toast tasted
like straw, and Jameson prayed he would swallow it without
gagging.

After last night's fit he had lain in bed chain smoking, staring at the ceiling, where an invisible operator had projected a motion picture entitled *The Life of Jameson Hurst*. Had he been a professional critic, he would have given it a brutal panning. Watching it had filled him with remorse, disgust, sorrow, pity, and occasional exhilaration. He didn't think the story was too bad, but the continuity was flawed by several outrageous contrivances. There was no rewriting, recasting, or reshooting. This was the finished product and it was doomed to be a commercial failure. The ending couldn't be changed because it was inevitable. He would die soon. More than one doctor had warned him. He was an old man and his body could no longer cope with the increasing number of convulsions.

He managed to get the toast and jelly down and, with trembling hand, lifted the cup of coffee to his lips. The bird twittered and Adam opened one eye and asked, "What's that?"

"A yellow-bellied Mother Fucker," snapped Jameson, and sipped his coffee. Adam rolled over, facing away from Hurst, and played with the grass. Last night's convulsion had frightened him. He should have called the doctor after Hurst came out of the convulsion and went into hysterics. He had thought of calling Seth Piro and still didn't understand why. He had thought of Seth most of the sleepless night and by daybreak had begun to hunger for his company.

"You ought to eat something," he heard Jameson say in a very strained voice. Adam sat up and stretched. He turned to Jameson, and it was as though he had seen him for the first time in his life. Was this what the picture of Dorian Gray looked like after time had ravaged it? Jameson unfolded his hands, uncrossed his legs, and lit a cigarette.

"Last night was rather ghastly, wasn't it?" Adam got to his feet, sat down at the table, and poured himself a cup of coffee. He would miss this garden. Jameson held on to the table lighter as he stared at Adam.

"When do you plan to go?"

"I'm not thinking of going, unless you want me to." Both were relieved by the lie.

"It's Ben's murder that's doing this to us," growled Hurst, slamming the lighter down on the table. "Once this mess is over with, would you like to go to Mexico?"

Adam fixed him with accusing eyes. "You said last night you were finished with peyoti."

Hurst's eyes widened innocently. "Peyoti isn't *all* Mexico has to offer, my dear. We could go to Greece if you prefer." He mustered a pathetic smile. "Or are you bored with old ruins?"

"Jamie," said Adam, "I'm lonely."

Hurst transferred the cigarette from his left hand to his right hand as he spoke. "You have me. You have my friends."

"But I don't have *my* friends." The bird chirruped, but no bird chirruped in reply.

Hurst sighed as he readjusted the fold of his dressing gown. "I suppose you should be off on your own more often. Meet more people your own age." Aimlessly Hurst began to hum, not realizing the song was "This Is the Beginning of the End."

"I don't care how old they are," said Adam, "as long as it's someone I can relate to." There wasn't a breeze in the garden, but Hurst felt a chill.

"Did you meet someone last night?"

Adam stirred his coffee.

"Well, did you?"

"I can't explain it. For the first time since I've known him, I spent an hour talking to Seth last night, and when I got home, I began to miss him. That's all there is to it. I haven't missed anyone since I came East. Suddenly I know I'm lonely." Adam's voice hardened. "And don't start thinking all sorts of nasty thoughts."

"I'm not." The lie dropped into his lap and expired of exhaustion. "If you want to see more of Seth, then by all means do so. Of course, it takes two to tango."

"Seth as *Seth* means nothing to me."

"Methinks the lady doth protest too much."

"Look at it this way, Jamie. No matter who comes and goes in your life, you'll always have Ella."

"There's *no* need for you to be sarcastic."

"Ah, the hell with it. What's the plan for today?"

"Well . . ." began Hurst, and got no further. A green stain appeared on his chest as the bird chirruped, fluttered its wings, and took off. Adam would have laughed had there been any laughter in him.

Ward left the police station and headed for the nearest phone booth. Ida answered on the first ring.

"There was nothing to it," he said elatedly. "Absolutely nothing to it."

"You're jazzing me."

"I'm not! He wanted to know everything I knew about Ben and then everything I knew about Seth Piro." There was a pause. "Ida? Ida, are you there?"

"I'm here."

126

"Then he asked me some questions about you. . . ."

"Yeah?" she said anxiously.

"And I told him you run a clean place."

"What about the peyoti?"

"Just warned me to lay off passing things for the customers. I think we ought to put up some kind of sign, Ida."

"He didn't ask nothing personal about me?"

"Like what, for crying out loud?"

"I don't know. Just personal. The hell with it. I'll see you at the place." She hung up.

Ward felt around in the coin return, but there was no jackpot. He found another dime in his pocket, inserted it in the slot, and dialed.

"Hello?" said a tiny blonde voice at the other end.

"Hi, kid. Ward Gabriel."

"Oh, hi. Sayyy, that fat slob had a hell of a nerve eighty-sixing me last night."

Ward snuggled up to the mouthpiece. "Would you like to try for another number?"

"Come on in, cat. Sit down."

"How are you this morning?" asked Seth, settling into the only other chair in the small office.

"Wide-eyed and bushy-tailed," said Pharoah, swiveling around in his chair and transferring a legal folder from his work table to the desk. "Want some coffee?"

"No, thanks. Just had breakfast."

"Uh-huh." He kept his hand on the legal folder as he smiled at Seth. "Much action at Ida's last night after I left?"

Seth returned the smile as he reached in his pocket for a cigarette. "Veronica arrived with Adam Littlestorm. She and

I had a brief altercation. She showered me with a drink and left me with Adam. We had a long talk. Then he went home and I went home." He struck a match and lit the cigarette. He wasn't too startled by the strange expression on the detective's face.

"I didn't know Hurst let him out of sight long enough to have long talks."

"Hurst was with Ella."

"Uh-huh. That Indian—he a nice cat?"

"Very nice cat."

"Talk much about the deceased?"

"Never mentioned him more than two or three times."

"Such as?"

"Such as Ben once threatened to let his folks back on the reservation know the kind of life he was leading, and Adam took a poke at him." He marveled at how easily he told this to Pharoah. He had a good feeling it was going to be a very easy day.

"Guess that's as good a reason as any to put the whammy on Ben cat. People have killed people for less."

"Adam's not very high on my list."

"What list, cat?"

Seth leaned over and flicked his ash into a tray. "I made a list of suspects and motives last night "

"Yeah?" Pharoah looked very pleased. Seth cat was on the beam and he liked that. "Come to any conclusions?"

"That you're right about whoever did it, did it in the heat of anger. No plan. No premeditation. That's manslaughter, isn't it?"

"That's right, cat."

"What's the rap for manslaughter?"

"Up to twenty."

Seth indicated the legal folder. "That the stuff?"

"That's the stuff." Pharoah upended the folder and the contents spilled onto his desk. "Cat, we are doing you a favor because we have official permission and we like you." His voice softened on the last three words. "I don't want you spilling any of this to your near and dear. You're going to have to watch yourself in case you happen to get angry."

Seth ached to plunge in, like a starving man confronted with a T-bone steak.

"You'll have plenty of time," said Pharoah, "till we meet Ella cat at four. I'm going to leave you alone with it for a while. I'm going to get me some lunch." He pushed the lot toward Seth and got up. "Want me to bring back some coffee?"

"Black. No sugar."

"I know all that, cat." He patted Seth on the back affectionately as he passed him and shut the door when he went out.

I know all that, cat. Seth moved around to Pharoah's swivel chair. He stared at the heap in front of him and wondered where to begin. The little red address book. Seth opened to the first page. "Ben Bentley" was neatly printed in block letters. His address and phone number were underneath. Ben had always been meticulous about his own possessions. His name, address, and phone number were printed on the flyleaf of every book he owned, under "Stolen from . . ."

Seth began with the *A*'s. Two names, both male. They meant nothing to him. The *B*'s began with Ada Bergheim and then Mrs. Molly Bergheim. There were five other names, three male and two female. Seth recognized one of the female's as the wife of a radio columnist they had met at Jameson's. Seth wondered if they ever got together.

The C's brought him up sharp. The first page was headed by a familiar epithet and there were approximately seventy-three names listed, some with phone numbers, some just with addresses, and about four with **** next to their names. Seth couldn't recall that many good restaurants listed in Michelin. Twelve had red check marks next to their name, and from the three names he recognized, two actors and a professional jockey, Seth figured there must have been a pay-off—or a fee. The C's carried over into the D's, and the E's were blank. F was headed by another familiar word and Seth totaled fifty-three names. Some were duplicates of the C's, and at least thirty names had red check marks next to them. The ten names Seth recognized with red check marks were wealthy and elderly. He had introduced three of them to Seth at dinner parties.

He wasn't sure if he was feeling faint or nauseous. But he didn't feel good, that was for sure. He was no longer elated and knew the rest of the day would not be an easy one. He forced himself into the G's and saw Ward Gabriel, and he was grateful to meet an old friend. If the page could listen, he would have told it his troubles. He plowed his way through to Z, where he found Zen Temple, and wondered when Ben had found the time. He shut the book and stared at it. Did Pharoah Love plan to interview all these people? How many of them had he already interrogated? Which of these now suffered sleepless nights or contemplated suicide?

His mouth was dry and he wished Pharoah would hurry back with the coffee. He turned his attention next to a composition book, the sort used by children in grade school. On the first page were Ben's name, address, and phone number in block letters. On the next page was a name. It was a well-known choreographer who had won himself four stars under both *C* and *F*. Seth wondered why Ben had never thought of holding a dinner and giving an award, like an Oscar or an Emmy, at the end of each year. Under the man's name there was a precise listing of dates and sums of money received. The last entry was dated two years ago. Seth remembered he had gone to London to choreograph a movie and had very wisely settled for expatriation.

One hundred pages were covered with names, dates, and amounts received. Jameson Hurst had the honor of being allotted three pages. The monies paid by him to Ben totaled well over one hundred thousand dollars. Seth's head was spinning. He rummaged around on the desk and found an envelope with a rubber band around it. Seth removed the rubber band and pulled out five bankbooks. Their balances totaled over sixty thousand dollars. What a windfall for the Bergheims.

The next item was a square envelope that contained some sixty typewritten pages. On the first page was neatly typed:

AVAILABLE
My Story
by
Ben Bentley

Underneath was printed his address and phone number. Pharoah was gone over an hour. When will he get back with that coffee? Or is he deliberately giving me time to get through this stuff by myself?

131

It took him less than an hour to read the typewritten pages. There was no continuity and there were large gaps of eliminated years. Seth recognized all of it. Ben had told him most of these stories, but it was the last six pages, written in ink, in Ben's tiny script, that brought him up short. He found out why Veronica had been blackmailed and he found out what Ben had really thought of him. He had cried at Ben's funeral, and he was crying when Pharoah returned with a container of coffee, black, no sugar.

"Want me to go out, count ten, and come back in again, cat?"

Seth shook his head no and wiped his eyes on the sleeve of his jacket. He took the container gratefully, tore off the lid, and took a deep swig. He sat back in the chair and looked at Pharoah who sat on the edge of the desk lighting a cigarette.

"Didn't you puke at least once when you read this stuff?"

Pharoah inhaled and dropped the burned match in the tray. "I made believe I was reading some of that crap they peddle in those Forty-second Street book stores." He moved from the desk to the chair, stuck his thumbs in his belt, and crossed his legs. "What I tried to figure out is, how much of it is true?"

"You can't argue with names, addresses, or bankbooks," said Seth, "but this—" his hand slammed down on the typewritten pages—"this can't all be true!"

"You'd of thought he felt a little bit self-conscious when he wrote it."

Seth guffawed. "About as self-conscious as a nymphomaniac at a gang bang. He must have colored a lot of it. I knew him as well as anyone could get to know him. The stories always varied. He used to forget from one day till the next what he told me."

"So help me, Seth, I laid her right there on the beach."
Ben was watching Seth baste the Thanksgiving turkey.
"What beach?"

"Acapulco!"

"Last week you said it was in the church in Taxco."

"Huh? Oh, that was the second time."

The carton sprung a leak and Seth quickly transferred it to
the wastepaper basket while Pharoah mopped up the stain
with some paper. "You still want to write that book, cat?"
Seth watched him while he replaced Ben's things in the legal
folder and made a firm knot in the ribbon.

When Seth finally spoke, his voice was hoarse and harsh.
"More than ever."

"You and the deceased really carry on the way he put it
down?"

"More or less."

"Cat, that analyst of yours must look forward to those
sessions with eager impatience."

Seth took Pharoah's cigarette, dragged on it, then stubbed
it out in the ash tray.

"And snotty cat—did you know that side of her?"

"No, so help me . . . No. I guess it's what the peyoti
used to do to her."

"One thing stumps me, cat."

"What's that?"

"No pictures."

"Wasn't what you read graphic enough?"

"What I read is one sick cat's word against a lot of others.
Somewhere, someplace, there were pictures. There was an
expensive German camera in his desk, but nowhere—not
nowhere—a snapshot, a negative—nothing. Cat, I think
whoever did our boy in has those pictures."

"You said nothing was disturbed in the apartment."

"That's right. Nothing was. Because the cat I'm looking for knew exactly where to find the stuff. The deceased probably kept it all neatly filed in a little box, and all the culprit cat had to do was just take the little box and go."

"And leave all this behind?" said Seth, indicating the legal folder.

"Like I said, sick cat's word against everybody mentioned there. Any good lawyer can have that stuff killed. That's why we've kept the newspapers out of this. When did he move into the apartment?"

"His?" Pharoah nodded. "The day he walked out on me. That was about four months ago."

"Then that narrows down the amount of people who would know the layout considerably. Considerably. Hot damn, cat, it's beginning to shape up. When are you going to start the book?"

"Couple of days, I think. I have to see if I'm going to throw up any of what I've swallowed. I have to figure out how to use the material without hurting anyone. Then I have to decide for myself which was fact, which was fantasy. And then what I have left has to go with the theme."

"What's the theme, cat? That interests me a lot."

Seth leaned back in the swivel chair and stared at the floor as though the theme were neatly printed there in block letters. When he spoke, he spoke slowly and deliberately, and Pharoah recognized that none of it was coming from the top of his head.

"Life," Seth began, "is a series of experiences—good ones, bad ones, delightful ones, rotten ones—some outweigh the others. Yet what prepares us to face life but experience? And we draw our experience from circumstances." He got up and the chair creaked. He crossed to a wall and leaned against it. "Some of us accept what we're given—good, bad, or indifferent—but some of us have the guts to reshape it all to meet our own demands. The cowards and the weaklings fall by the wayside, swallowed up by the quagmires of their own design. The ones who make life what they want it to be are the ones who face the challenges. The others get struck down. Life is a hit-and-run driver. And believe it or not—" he turned to Pharoah—"Ben crashed into life headfirst. He pummeled it, reshaped it, made a tool of it. What struck him down was circumstances. God knows the rotten little bastard was no hero, but in another environment he damn well could have been one."

Pharoah's chair was tipped against a filing cabinet.

Seth concluded, "I'm going to show what made him what he was, because, Pharoah cat, I've never had the guts until now to reshape life to meet my demands. I'm going to parallel my life with Ben's. And when I'm finished—" he sighed—"I might take a match and apply it to the whole frigging manuscript."

"Not before I read it, cat."

Seth moved back to the swivel chair.

"You see, cat, I think when you've finished piecing this book together, you're going to hand me a murderer." He looked at his wrist watch. "Quarter to four. Let's get going to Ella cat's." He got up, adjusted his hat, and opened the door. Seth rose slowly and took one last look at the legal folder.

I may hand you more than you bargained for, Pharoah cat.

10

ELLA SAT in the wing chair and adjusted the veils around her face. She smoothed the black lace gloves on her hands and then lifted the veils and sipped her brandy. The draperies were tightly drawn across the windows, and one lamp was lit on the table next to the sofa with a twenty-five-watt bulb. The incense burned and filled the room with memories of the Far East. On the coffee table in front of the sofa at the far end of the room two snifters of brandy sat on black lace coasters.

In a few minutes there would be a gentle knock on the door and her shrill, reedy little voice would pipe her visitors aboard. Earlier she had spent a disturbing hour with Jameson.

"Adam is drifting away from me." He kept lacing and unlacing his fingers and she thought his eyes were beginning to decay.

"They always do. You've always been prepared for it."

"Not this time. I thought Adam would see me through to the end."

"Perhaps that's how it is with Indians, dear." "Dear" grated on his ears like a fingernail drawn across a window-pane. "They enter silently and then just as silently steal away."

"He is beginning to find himself, much the way Ben did. I think it's Seth again."

"Seth?" She threw back her head and piped her shrill, reedy laugh. "How can a ship without a compass lead the convoy to port?"

"Dear God, Ella, haven't you absorbed any of what I've been telling you?" She's teasing me. Just when I need her most, she's teasing me. "Somehow Ben's murder has given Seth new strength. He defies Veronica. He mocks me openly. He's become a confidant of that dreadful detective. And now Adam admires him!"

"It's not admiration at all, you silly goose. Adam is simply attempting to transfer to another father figure. You are old and epileptic and far too demanding, and your face is begin-ning to drop again. It's been lifted so often your ears are horizontal."

"Oh God!" He began to weep bitter tears. Why does Ella force me to face my conscience?

"Oh, stop that childish sniveling!" she piped. Tears always embarrassed her, especially her own. She had never gotten over the surprise of them at Ben's funeral. Would she ever admit it was really Seth who had moved her?

"Who will look after me when Adam goes?" He hoped the despair in his voice would envelop her and give Ella a good shaking.

"My dear." She sighed. "You have a choice between a trained nurse or God."

137

"You bitch!" he shrieked. "You coldhearted, hardheaded, selfish, insulated bitch!"

"Go away, Jamie. You are tiresome. It isn't Adam's imminent departure that distresses you; it's your own. My dear, with your impeccable sense of camp, I should think you'd be dwelling on a *bon voyage* party for yourself."

He began to brighten.

"You're always planning grand entrances, darling." He didn't mind that "darling" was meant to strike him in the face. "Why not plan a grand exit? My dear, that's one party *I* might even attend."

"You wouldn't!"

"I just might."

"You're not afraid?"

"I went to Ben's funeral, didn't I?"

"That was stupid of you."

"At this stage of my life I can afford to indulge in stupidities." Her cackle rose and beat against the walls with ineffectual fists. "We could make such a memorable night of it, Jamie."

He was infected with her enthusiasm as his eyes shone, momentarily obscuring the decay. "We shall, my darling, we shall. We'll show them. And Adam . . . Oh God, poor Adam!" He collapsed with laughter. "How he shall suffer! Oh, Mother! Mother! How Adam shall suffer!"

"Don't mention Mother!" she screeched. "How often have I told you not to mention Mother! Get out of here. Get out, you mildewed pederast!"

Now she was alone and calm and prepared to cope with her guests.

There was a gentle knock at the door. She aimed her

mouth at it, piercing the wood with a shrill "Enter!"

The door opened and Seth came in, followed by Pharoah Love. "Hello, Ella," said Seth warmly.

"Shut the door. Sit on the couch, both of you. Your brandies are room temperature." They shut the door and sat on the couch, their eyes adjusting to the dimness, their noses making peace with the incense.

Seth cleared his throat. "Ella, this is Pharoah Love. Pharoah, Miss Hurst."

"How do you *do,* Mr. Love."

"Ma'am." He placed his hat on the coffee table.

"Who murdered Benjamin?"

"We're nowheres near a solution, ma'am," said Pharoah.

"I loved the boy," she cackled, "but he did need murdering." She lifted the brandy glass under her veils and sipped.

"When did you last see him?" asked Pharoah.

"At his funeral."

"I mean alive."

She thought a moment. "Oh yes." Pharoah's ears were adjusting to her voice. He thought it belonged on a peanut vending machine. "It was the night before he died. He came to bid me adieu." She sighed. "He certainly went."

"Ella," said Seth, and she cocked her head, "Mr. Love would like to know why you helped Veronica out of her predicament with Ben."

"And Ada Bergheim," added Pharoah.

"Dear, dear, dear." She brushed some lint from her dress. "I simply thought Benjamin was going too far. You know, there was really much finer stuff in the boy than anyone realized. Didn't you ever feel that, Seth?"

"Yes, at times I did."

139

"Also, Veronica's lawyer unearthed a great deal of Benjamin's sordid past. Had that been made public, we might have all felt the repercussions. So I simply paid Benjamin the money he requested from Veronica, and *that* was *that*. It made no difference to me. As for his sister, that was pure sentiment. You see, *I* am a sister too. And that loathsome brother of mine has frequently treated me contemptibly. I couldn't tolerate Benjamin's cruelty to Ada. I might add, Benjamin did show remorse at that incident. Though you know, she was never very nice to him when he was a child. She suffered severely from sibling rivalry. The father died when Benjamin was just a baby, and the mother had to go out and peddle her papers, leaving Benjamin in Ada's care. She mistreated him miserably. With such a sordid childhood, is it no wonder the boy went astray? That's why we understood each other. My childhood was no better. But Benjamin did need murdering. Yes, he certainly needed murdering. You haven't touched your brandies."

They both dutifully lifted their snifters and sipped.

"Can you tell me your whereabouts Tuesday morning between nine and eleven?"

Ella stared at Pharoah and then placed her brandy glass on the table. "I was sitting in this chair meditating."

"Were you alone?"

"Do you mean do I have an alibi? I do not. I was here and quite alone. I did not murder Benjamin."

"Wasn't he blackmailing you?"

"I paid him for his company."

Pharoah was almost amused at the agility with which the hulking woman side-stepped his questions. "Your payments aren't listed in his ledger," he said.

"His ledger?"

"Yes." Pharoah smiled. "He kept a very careful account of monies received. Strangely enough, you're not listed."

Seth wondered why he hadn't noticed that. That's why Pharoah's a detective and I'm not.

"I suppose," said Ella, "it was out of respect. He respected my desire for anonymity. I shall light a candle for him for that."

"Your brother's entries," said Pharoah, "cover several pages. It's possible the deceased bunched you with your brother."

"Bunched?" She repeated the word with distaste and then sighed. "Perhaps he did. Benjamin, as we all know, had rather strange habits. Now tell me," she interjected cozily, "who do you *really* think did it?" Pharoah subdued an urge to cross the room and pinch her cheek.

"I'm not sure."

"Seth, who do you think did it? Everyone's in an uproar about the book you plan to write about Benjamin. I think someone suspects you know the murderer's identity and that's what the book's really going to be all about."

"Maybe I'll know when I assemble the facts."

"Now don't play with me, Seth, although I do adore games. That's how I treat life, Mr. Love."

"How's that?"

"I treat life as a charade. It would be unbearable otherwise. Seth finds life unbearable, don't you, Seth?" She didn't wait for him to speak. "Seth looks for life in other people to sustain his. He's doing the same with this book, aren't you, Seth? Seth looks for life in others when he should be looking for life in himself." She was playing with her purple beads and tapping one foot lightly. The effect was somewhat sinister, and yet Seth had detected neither challenge nor accusation in her words. He was too busy admiring her astute observation.

"But perhaps now," she continued, her voice squeaking as though a brake had been applied, "for some oblique reason due to the late unpleasantness, the man Seth within the boy Seth is beginning to emerge. I think I suspect what writing the book is all about. In seeing Benjamin in a dispassionate perspective, perhaps Seth will begin to see himself."

Seth knew she was smiling wickedly, though he could not see through her curtain of veils. He thought it wise to compliment her observations. "You're very astute, Ella. I've always admired that in you."

"I knew I was right!" she piped triumphantly. "Now then, Mr. Love, do you still think I murdered Benjamin?"

Cat, he thought, you are flying jets while we're still traveling in covered wagons. He leaned back and crossed his legs, one arm placed over the back of the sofa. "You could have done it."

"Of course I could!" she snorted. "Don't you dare exclude me from your list of suspects. Where am I on your list? At the top? A few names lower? At the bottom?"

"My list isn't numbered." Pharoah smiled.

"I could recite that list for you." She drenched the room with her egotism. "There's Seth, and certainly Veronica. My ridiculous brother with his ridiculous fits. Possibly Benjamin's sister, but somehow I find that thought disagreeable." She paused for effect. Then she said, "What about my brother's Indian? Have you given him much thought?"

You're being evil, thought Seth. You're being very evil.

"He broods a great deal, and brooding breeds."

"I've given him some thought," said Pharoah.

"He'll like that," whispered Ella. "He doesn't feel he's given enough attention. You like Adam, don't you, Seth? Your face has been disapproving me." Pharoah stared at Seth. He looked more annoyed than disapproving.

"Yes, I like Adam," said Seth. "Does Jameson object?"

"You stole Ben away from him. Jamie would loathe lightning to strike twice."

"I know what you're insinuating, Ella, but you couldn't be more wrong. I intend traveling alone for a long, long time."

"Hitchhikers can prove irresistible when one is lonely."

"Miss Hurst," interrupted Pharoah, "what makes you think Adam Littlestorm might have killed Ben Bentley?"

"Ben once threatened to let Adam's family know about his relationship with Jamie. And Adam resented Ben's continuing influence over my brother. There were constant arguments about the sums of money my brother gave Benjamin —and the trips to Mexico for peyoti."

Chalk up one for me, thought Pharoah. "I suspected he was Ben cat's angel."

"Ben cat," Ella repeated. "Yes, how like a cat he was! Stalking the night . . . selfish . . . licking his chops at the sight of a likely prey . . . occasionally deigning to lie back and let his stomach be stroked. . . . Ben cat—how absolutely marvelous, Mr. Love." Then she became stern. "When Benjamin left Seth, Adam feared he might try to regain his position in Jamie's ménage. Yes," her voice trilled, "I think Adam is a very good suspect. You know, my brother has told me he doesn't account for his whereabouts the morning Benjamin was murdered."

"Is that so?" said Pharoah.

"Yes," she said flatly. "And now Adam is very sullen and very moody. He seems anxious to leave the country. I believe he and my brother have discussed the possibility of a trip to either Mexico or Greece." She stared at the two of them for a moment. "You did come here to find out things, didn't you? Well, don't damn me for cooperating."

"I'm very grateful indeed," said Pharoah softly. "Very grateful." He looked at Seth and Seth caught the signal to leave.

"Thank you, Ella," said Seth, rising. "We won't trouble you any longer."

"I am no longer troubled," piped Ella confidently. "Please see yourselves out. Goodbye."

"Goodbye," said Pharoah, and he preceded Seth out the door.

"Goodbye, Ella," said Seth, and shut the door. Pharoah collapsed against a wall and exhaled.

"That," he said, "is a most peculiar lady cat."

Seth held a finger to his lips and then beckoned Pharoah to follow him to the elevator.

"Why the need to hush up, cat?" whispered Pharoah.

"She listens at the door."

Like a rejected bale of hay, Ella leaned against the door with her ear pressed to it. She heard only retreating footsteps and then the elevator door opening and closing. Slowly she crossed to a Venetian mirror that hung over a sideboard, unwinding the veils around her face as she walked. She studied the reflection in the mirror with the practiced eye of a connoisseur.

"Mirror, mirror on the wall," she cackled, "who's the fairest one of all?"

The mirror held a diplomatic silence.

"Very well, you bitch," snapped Ella. "Then who's the smartest?"

"I feel the need for a powwow with Adam cat."

Pharoah was trying to pass a Third Avenue bus as he nosed the Jaguar uptown.

"Ella certainly pushed hard enough for him as a suspect," said Seth. "Who knows? Maybe I ought to move him up a few notches on my list."

"That's the trouble with lists, cat. They take a lot of revising." Pharoah inhaled deeply. "Man, I don't think I'll ever clear that incense out of my lungs. Did Ben cat ever catch a look at her face?"

"He never said if he did."

"Ever mention how she smashed it up?"

"I think it was a car crash in Spain."

"With all that Hurst money, I'd have thought she'd buy herself the best plastic job in the world."

"Those operations don't always take."

Pharoah uh-huh'd and finally made it past the bus. "I did a lot of research on the Hurst cats yesterday. They must have been born abroad. I couldn't find a thing on them at the Hall of Records. Went back almost seventy years, but couldn't find a birth registration. You know if they were born in Europe?"

Seth's mind was on Adam Littlestorm, and Pharoah's questions were an annoying intrusion. "They might have been. I think the mother was French. I know old man Hurst had a lot of investments in Europe and spent a lot of time there. Come to think of it—" he sighed—"I know very little about Ella and Jameson's origins."

"Maybe they jes' growed." Pharoah chuckled. "Like Topsy cat."

"Maybe." They weren't born on a government reservation in New Mexico, that's for sure. They weren't one of eight children or watched their parents chew peyoti during a religious ritual. They didn't travel across the country doing odd jobs and living off the bounty of an occasional woman. They weren't indoctrinated into a life of homosexual prostitution by older men who knew a likely initiate when they saw one.

"Where are you, cat?"

"What?" said Seth, startled, as Pharoah's question shook him out of his reverie. "Sorry. I was thinking about the Hursts."

"Uh-huh. I'm heading back to the station. You can pick up Ben cat's stuff. I'll make you a nice neat little package."

"How long can I hold on to it?"

"Long as you like. You're getting Photostats."

Life, Seth decided, was one long, lonely procession of reasonable facsimiles.

"You think there was ever anything between Ben cat and the Indian?"

"I doubt it." He hoped it sounded authoritative.

"But it's possible."

"With Ben," said Seth, "everything was possible." And everyone was a challenge.

"I hate that word 'no.' " Seth had been sitting at Ida's bar gulping martinis, hoping they'd drench the flames of anger singeing his insides. The argument with Veronica an hour earlier had been one of their violent ones, and he wondered if the annoyingly persistent young man perched on the adjoining stool realized his life was in danger. " 'No' means 'the end,' " the persistent young man persisted, "and I don't like anything that's final, unless I call the shot."

Seth mustered his unfriendliest look as he turned to the handsome young man. "My mother told me never to talk to strangers."

"So did mine." He grinned amiably. "But if I didn't, I wouldn't have ended up with any friends. Come on. You look so sad. Let me buy you a drink. Ida knows me. My name's Ben Bentley. You live around here?"

"Hey, cat! Come alive!" Pharoah nudged Seth with his elbow. "I'm beginning to feel like I'm driving a hearse."

"Sorry," muttered Seth. "My mind's on the book."

"You didn't hear a word I said." He was smiling, but it didn't mask the injury in his voice. "I was telling you how Mama Cat Hurst went to her reward."

Seth sat up. "Go ahead. Tell me again."

"Maybe I'll sing it for you this time. That'll keep you awake for sure." Seth turned to Pharoah and favored him with a smile. "I know, cat, I know. We all got a lot on our minds these days. Anyway, Mama Cat Hurst was sitting in her window and apparently leaned out to call to her papa cat sitting out in the patio. She lost her balance and fell out, cracking her head. She was holding a comb in her hand, or so said the newspaper clipping I dug up. Local paper in Oyster Bay. But whoever the reporter cat was who wrote the story, he found out from the undertaker she'd been wearing a hair net. So whose hair was she combing? Ella cat's? Jameson cat's?"

147

"Does it matter?"

"It could matter if Mama cat was pushed."

Seth's mind had no intention of wandering again. "But they were just kids when she died."

"Cat," said Pharoah, "there ain't nothing more dangerous than an angry kid. And some angry kids grow old and reach their sixties, but that don't mean they grew up. You dig me, cat?"

"I dig." He had often commented to Ben that Jameson was the biggest baby he ever knew. How big a baby was Ella? Was there a skeleton in the closet that Ben had rattled once too often?

"Mind you," said Pharoah, "Mama Cat Hurst might have been preparing to remove the hair net and comb her own flaxen locks. But when you live in a big mansion with a lot of servants, I kind of think there might have been a maid to do it for her. Anyway, Papa cat sure bundled those kids off to Europe in a hurry. Know how he died?"

"Yes. He went down on the *Titanic*."

"Did you know that when they yelled 'Women and Children First,' he tried to make it with them by dressing up like a lady?"

"No," said Seth, his mouth dry and parched. "You certainly do your research when you research."

"Cat, that's the trick with these kind of cases. If you don't find what you're looking for on the surface, start digging."

Yes, thought Seth, you are not a psychiatrist, Pharoah cat, but you could qualify.

11

I HATE making *luncheon* dates on *Saturday*. *Especially* a luncheon date with this *witch*.

"Perhaps Madam would prefer a plum tart?" the waiter suggested.

Veronica stirred her demitasse overenergetically as Ruthelma studied the pastry tray. A diamond merchant would have appreciated the care with which she examined each jewel for a hidden flaw.

"I don't like plums," said Ruthelma in her mind-your-own-business tone of voice. Veronica wished she'd hurry and make up her mind so they could go on with their conversation. Please, God, she began her usual silent prayer when dining with Ruthelma, don't let her select anything that drips.

"I'll take *that!*" decided Ruthelma, pointing at a blueberry and apple torte dripping in chocolate syrup and topped with a pyramid of whipped cream. "Whipped cream isn't as *fattening* as most people *think,*" she said to Veronica. "It's almost *all* egg white."

The waiter kept a straight face and a steady hand as he

delivered up the sacrifice to Ruthelma, then retreated discreetly.

"I know this isn't *de rigueur,* but I'm going to eat it with a *spoon."*

"Ruthelma, we've been friends for a very long time . . ."

"Mmmmmm . . ."

". . . And I've given you a great deal of business . . ."

"Mmmmmm . . ."

". . . And I think you ought to consider seriously what we've been discussing."

Two streams of syrup were descending, one from each corner of Ruthelma's mouth. She caught one with her napkin and Veronica wondered about helping stem the other, but Ruthelma's tongue darted out and retrieved it before Veronica could come to a decision.

"Well, dear," said Ruthelma, "I find it *very* bad business to try to dissuade *my* authors from undertaking projects of which *I* or *others* might happen to disap*prove."* She lingered over the last spoonful of dessert, like an ill-starred lover departing at a railroad station. "I've been giving *this* a *great* deal of thought. Seth has had a *serious* writer's block for almost two *years* now. If *this* is going to help him *break* it, then I think *neither* of us should *brook* any interference."

"Don't you realize how much damage it could do to him if it's ever published?"

Ruthelma pushed the plate away, wiped her mouth with the napkin, examined her bosom for stains, on which miraculously there were none, and then began ladling sugar into her cup of espresso. "Veronica *dear,"* she began pointedly, "his *last* book, which I *begged* Saber House *not* to publish, is what did the damage. Seth's a *very* good writer, and I'll never *stop* believing in him, but he has to *find* himself again. I think if *anyone* interferes *now,* it might be *fatal.*" She was now studying Veronica shrewdly. *"What* made you change your *mind?"*

"What do you mean?"

"Yesterday you were *demanding* a first refusal. *Today* you want the project *abandoned."*

"I began to realize that a lot of people besides Seth could be hurt by this book."

"Truth is *always* painful. I didn't *like* Ben Bentley at *all,* but then I don't like De Gaulle *either,* but *that* wouldn't make me dis*courage* an *author* who wanted to do a book on *him."* Ruthelma hoped she had thoroughly derailed this train of conversation, but she was underestimating an engineer like Veronica.

"Then you've got to give Saber House first crack at it."

"You mean, give *you* first crack at it." She was tired of pulling punches. She wanted to get home and air her mother in Central Park and then tackle the brief case full of manuscripts she had taken home for the weekend. "Haven't you done Seth enough *damage?"*

Veronica was bristling with indignation. "What the hell do you mean by *that?"*

"You *know* what I mean," purred Ruthelma in singsong. "You *cas*trated his books the way you tried to *cas*trate the man." Veronica opened her mouth, but Ruthelma overrode her. "Let me finish, dear, and I'll pay for the lunch. I've *known* you a *long* time, dear. I'm familiar with your *dichotomy."* She sounded like a general practitioner discussing a vital organ. "You *suffer* from a love-hate *syndrome.* You *married* Seth because he had *promise,* but you *never*

151

stopped putting him *down* in public. Now I *know* it's something you do unconsciously with a *lot* of people. I *remember* you didn't even like Edith *Piaf* . . ."

"Oh, for crying out loud . . . !"

"But that's what I *see,* dear. Now you're doing it *again* to Seth. Why don't you just leave him *alone?*"

"God damn it," hissed Veronica, "I could kill you and I could kill him!"

"Veronica *dear*—" Ruthelma smiled—"are you *capable* of *murder?*"

In the small park at the foot of East Fifty-seventh Street Adam Littlestorm sat on a bench facing the East River. He stared through the iron railing at a passing garbage scow and wished the past could be hauled away as easily. He had eaten no breakfast or any lunch. The gnawing in his stomach was a hunger for escape. Decisions did not come easily to him, but once made, they were never reversed. Living with Jameson Hurst was like living in the hall of mirrors at an amusement park. And Adam was fed up with distortion.

A rubber ball rolled to his feet. He picked it up and turned around. A small boy with large brown eyes and a tiny mouth stared at the ball with a proprietary air. Adam smiled and tossed it to him. The boy caught the ball and scampered back to his nursemaid who sat on a bench reading a paperback love story.

Adam turned back to the river and studied the people on a sight-seeing boat that was passing. Take a look, he wanted to shout. Take a really good look. Here's a man who's come to a decision and really means to stick to it. Goodbye, Jameson. Goodbye, Ella. I may be losing a meal ticket, but I'm gaining my self-respect. Will there be severance pay?

His thoughts wandered back to Seth Piro as he looked at his wrist watch. Maybe he's home by now. Ella wouldn't give them too much of her time. Ella never gave too much of anything to anyone. Just enough to amuse herself. He rose, fished in his pocket for a coin, and began looking for a phone booth.

"It's all yours, cat."

The Photostats were tied in a fresh legal folder. Seth studied the package as he dialed his answering service. "How many people in Ben's address book have you contacted?"

"A dozen or so. Some of those cats no longer exist. Most of those I got to didn't remember Ben cat. Or so they said."

Seth listened as the service gave him his messages.

"What time did Mr. Littlestorm call?"

Pharoah lit a cigarette.

"Okay. Hold on to the other messages. I'll call you when I get home. In about half an hour." Seth hung up.

"So Adam cat is sending you smoke signals."

"He calls occasionally."

"Would you be surprised if he turns out to be our pigeon?"

Our. What am I supposed to be? Watson to his Sherlock? Boswell to his Johnson? Mouse to his cat? Seth sat down and lit a cigarette.

"Whoever *our* pigeon is, it will come as a surprise to me."

"I don't think so, cat."

Seth looked at him quizzically.

"Cat, I think you got some definite idea of who did in Ben cat." He smiled. "I'm not asking you, mind. I'm just telling you that I know you are doing a lot of private deducing, and two heads are better then one. All I know is, pigeon cat is probably wise to it, or else why would you do the book? And

153

pigeon cat might try to walk in and steal your typewriter."

"It's insured."

"You going to be up at Ida's tonight?"

"No," he said, indicating the legal folder, "I'm going to start working on this."

"Ah, come on," the detective cajoled. "Drop in around ten for a little nightcap."

"Not tonight, Pharoah. There's too much to do."

"Working against a deadline?"

"I've given myself one."

"Was that the kind of deadline you were working on the morning Ben cat phoned and pulled you away from it?"

Seth drew on his cigarette and studied Pharoah. He exhaled and Pharoah continued talking.

"I phoned your agent. She said you hadn't had an assignment in a long, long time." He drew out the word *time* perfectly, imitating Ruthelma.

"Pharoah cat," began Seth, "it's like I once told you. Like most people in this worst of all possible worlds, I lie." He smiled beguilingly, almost with a trace of mockery. "But it was just a tiny lie. I eventually told you why I went, didn't I? I put it right on the table where you said you always want to see it. Maybe there was no deadline, but I was working on something. An article on peyoti. If you don't believe me, I'll show you the four sentences I accomplished that morning."

"You know, cat," said Pharoah, "when you do the kind of work I do, it's hard to divorce yourself from it, even with people you sincerely like. And if you don't know it by now, I like you very much."

"Even though I'm a suspect in this case."

"That's before the fact. Now come on, drop into Ida's later. Saturday night is the loneliest night of the week."

"There's always television."

"I saw all the pictures they got listed."

"I can't promise. Don't be sore if I don't show up."

"Well, if you don't show up, I can always go home and take a nice hot bath and play my radio. That's one thing the deceased had in common with me. Hot damn. I like to loll in that tub with the radio going." Then he chuckled. "But I keep it on a very high shelf."

Seth rose and picked up the folder.

"Maybe I'll give you a call later, cat."

"I'll be home." Seth left the office quickly. He was out on the street in a minute and breathing deeply. His body was damp with perspiration, his hands clammy, gripping the folder tightly.

Cat, I think you got some definite idea of who did in Ben cat.

Yes, Pharoah cat, I've got a likely prospect in mind. But would it really come as a surprise to you if I told you who?

Jameson adjusted the chin strap, then turned away from the mirror to face Adam.

"I suppose no amount of reasoning will change your mind."

"None."

Jameson crossed to the chaise longue and draped himself across it like a comforter. He reached for a cigarette and lit it. Adam flicked some ash from his into the fireplace and prayed there'd be no convulsion.

"Can you bring yourself to stay through Tuesday night?"

"What's so special about Tuesday?"

"I'm planning a farewell party." He guffawed. "Not for you, dear. I couldn't indulge myself in *that* kind of irony. It

155

was originally for *us*—" "us" emerged as a prolonged hiss—
"and I suppose in a sense it still is. You're leaving me and
I'm—" he gave an airy wave of his hand—"just leaving."

"Mexico?"

"No, my dear, I think farther away than that."

"Supposing they won't let you leave town?"

" 'They?' You mean the police? That detective person?
Don't be ridiculous. When Jameson Hurst decides to go, darling, he goes. Will you stay through the party?"

"If you want me to, I will."

"It should be a terribly delicious soiree. I've phoned two
dozen people the past hour and all accepted with alacrity."
Adam stood as though he were nailed to the fireplace. "Have
you made any plans?"

"I found a rented room on the west side and then I'm
going to look for a job."

"Doing what?"

"Anything I can get."

"You can always go back to massaging."

"I'd sooner cut off my hands."

"I see," said Jameson quietly. "Then it's to be a new life
altogether."

"That's right."

"I rather thought you might be moving in with someone
else."

"Such as?"

The phone rang and Adam looked at it with gratitude.
Jameson lifted it to his ear and purred, "Hello?" He listened,
and then the corners of his mouth curled as he held the
phone out to Adam. "It's for you. It's Seth." Adam crossed
and took the phone from him.

"Hi."

"Sorry I took so long getting back to you," said Seth, "but it's been a bitch of a day." He sat in front of his air conditioner in his shorts, but the perspiration wouldn't dry. "You said you wanted to see me about something. Can you get away for a drink?"

"Yes," said Adam. Jameson was trying to look nonchalant as he attacked his nails with a buffer.

"How's about an hour from now?"

"Fine," said Adam, and hung up.

And this was to be an easy day, thought Seth.

Adam sat across from Jameson. "I'm going up to have a drink with Seth."

"So *that's* it!" spit Jameson.

"That's *not* it at all!"

"Oh well." Jameson sighed. "Who's to fight it when youth calls to youth?" Jameson's mind was a vast filing cabinet of old silent screen titles.

"You couldn't be more wrong."

"It doesn't matter. Out of sight, out of mind. I'm too old and too ill for any more of this nonsense. Will you join me later for dinner, or do you plan to spend the night with him?"

Adam fought to restrain his temper. "I'm going to his place for a drink. If you'd like me to have dinner with you, I can meet you later."

"Why don't I phone you at Seth's?"

"Why don't you stop being a bitch?"

"At this stage of my life, darling? It would be easier to move the Eiffel Tower to Disneyland." He flung the buffer aside. "Oh, all right. Come home when you're finished. We'll eat in. You can help me with the party."

"Fair enough." Adam rose and left the room. Jameson leaped to his feet and began pacing the room. There was no holding back the tears as they began to sting his cheeks. He crossed to the terrace windows and flung them open. He went out and leaned against the railing, staring into space. The tears were a nuisance as he groped in his pocket for a handkerchief. Then he felt himself losing his balance and, with a yip of fright, grabbed the railing with his left hand and steadied himself.

My God, he thought with relief, I almost toppled over the damn thing. I could have fallen onto the patio and cracked my skull.

It was then that he threw up.

Seth carried the bucket of ice from the kitchen to the living room. The air conditioner was turned off and two windows were flung open. The legal folder was on the top shelf of his closet in case it piqued Adam's curiosity. He toyed with the idea of mixing himself a martini, then decided to wait for Adam. He settled into an easy chair with feet outstretched and lit a cigarette. Strange, no message from Veronica all day. Stay angry for all I care.

The newscaster on Channel Two was telling Veronica the water shortage was growing critical. She stared at him defiantly and squelched an urge to open every tap in her apartment. Earlier he had told her the air-pollution index had risen and her lungs were filling with deadly toxins. At the start of the program he had decimated what was left of her indestructibility with the ominous warning that cigarette tar was causing her lungs to shrivel and decay. The rye bread commercial provided her with an oasis of relief, and she wondered if you didn't have to be Jewish to murder Ben Bentley.

She lay on the couch in her flimsy slip under an open window, breathing the deadly air, staring at her deadly cigarette, listening to the deadly drip-drip of the leaking faucet in the kitchen. The commentator was back with the news that Russia was believed to have detonated its deadliest bomb to date in Siberia.

"You're a bundle of joy," she muttered as she got up and turned off the set. The phone rang, and for a moment she was afraid to answer it. The mouthpiece would be covered with millions of deadly germs.

"Hello?"

"Veronica, my sweet!" Jameson's voice leaped at her ear, each word wearing a tutu and precisely on *pointe*. "I'm giving a gala on Tuesday night and your shimmering loveliness is requested as decoration!"

"What's the occasion?"

"It's a farewell party."

"Who's leaving?"

"I am, darling. I'm planning to fly to parts unknown. Did you know I've been abandoned? Adam is defecting. I believe he's at this very moment seeking asylum in Seth's apartment. Isn't it too amusing?"

Veronica believed that if she convinced Jameson, she would convince herself. "Seth and Adam? I think that's highly unlikely."

"Well, my dear, if Adam could spell it, he'd push for a liaison. But perhaps I'm being overemotional about it all. Ella thinks what's happened is for the best. I have to ring off, dear. My tub is almost full and it's time to sprinkle it with lavender. Tuesday night, from nine." There was a click.

The dead air pierced her ear like a laser ray, but Veronica was too dumfounded and disturbed to replace the phone in its cradle. How would the commentator on Channel Two handle this piece of news? She slammed the phone down and burst into tears.

"Now, Veronica," she could hear her mother's brittle, matter-of-fact voice, "you can't have your way all the time. Daddy says you're terribly spoiled. Don't we want to prove to him he's wrong? Go into the parlor right now and tell him you've changed your mind. You don't want a new pair of roller skates. Then next week," she said, with her conspiratorial wink of the eye, "when he's forgotten all about it, I'll buy you a pair."

It's wrong, damn it, it's wrong. I still love Seth. I'm still his wife. And by God, I'll get him back. I'll have him back where he belongs. Right under my thumb.

Adam wandered from the walk-in closet to the bedroom and back to the living room. "You have a great layout here, Seth." He sat down and the ice in his drink tinkled.

"It's not bad for the price. And the view's great."

"Terrific."

"But of course there are the dogs, and the kids and their bicycles, but I suppose you get that in every apartment house."

"You were lucky to get such a great buy. I just took a rented room up on West Eightieth. It's not much, but by the time I move—" he managed a smile—"I should be speaking Spanish fluently."

"You're leaving Jameson?"

"Yup!" Seth envied the triumph and relief in Adam's voice.

"What will you do?"

"Live." He placed his glass on the coffee table and lit a cigarette.

"Is that what you came to tell me?" No complications, please. Please, no complications. Not now.

"I want your advice. It's about something I did. It involves Ben."

If you're going to say what I think you're going to say, don't say it. I don't want to hear it.

"I was in his apartment the morning of the murder."

12

"I DIDN'T KILL him," said Adam. "He was dead when I got there."

"Why'd you go there?"

"To give him some money."

"Had Jameson sent you?"

"No. He doesn't know I was there. For two hundred dollars Ben promised me the negative of a photo of myself."

"You too," said Seth flatly.

Adam shrugged. "It was a picture of me in the greenhouse. Me and somebody. It doesn't matter who. They're not important. It was during one of Jamie's peyoti parties. I'd gone to the greenhouse to cut some more buttons. Somebody followed me. Made a pass, and Ben snapped a very embarrassing scene. Nothing actually happened, but the picture tells a different story. I had to get it back."

"Did you get it back?"

"What do you mean?" Adam's innocence almost shimmered.

"Pharoah Love's theory is that the murderer stole a box of negatives from Ben's apartment."

162

"Oh God! Then whoever's got them—"

"Doesn't dare make a move," interrupted Seth quietly. "To admit to owning those negatives is to admit to having murdered Ben. Did you see anybody when you went to Ben's?"

"No one. I almost ran into the maid. I heard her coming up the steps and ran into the incinerator room until I heard her go into the apartment."

"Was Veronica at that peyoti party?"

"No. Jamie told me she'd been to one but something happened that frightened her off from any others."

"Did he tell you what it was?"

"No. But I could take a guess."

Seth rose and crossed to the bar, asking as he went, "How's your drink?"

"It's okay."

Ella was on Seth's mind as he mixed a martini. She had fingered Adam as a more important suspect than either he or Pharoah had figured. Had she taken a shot in the dark and found her target, or did she know more than she had been willing to admit? Ella had loved Ben, yet she spelled out her animosity toward Adam in capital letters. Was it because of Jameson? Had Jameson gone weeping to her that Adam was walking out? In some devious way had Ella found out Adam was in Ben's apartment that morning? How? From whom?

"Adam," said Seth, "Pharoah Love and I saw Ella earlier today."

"I know."

He turned and faced Adam. "I hate to tell you this, but she made a point of trying to convince Pharoah Love you might have murdered Ben."

Adam held his glass so tightly that Seth feared for a moment he might shatter it.

The phone rang.

"If that's Jamie," said Adam in a strange voice, "tell him to go fuck himself."

Seth picked up the phone. "Yes?"

"Working hard, cat?"

Seth hoped he was stirring the right dose of lightness into his voice. "Hi, Pharoah. Just about to get into it."

The phone booth was stifling, and Pharoah opened the door an inch.

"Why don't you let it go till tomorrow, cat? I'm feeling mighty lonely and a little depressed. Come on out and cheer me up."

"Look, I might make it up to Ida's later." Seth slid onto the couch, one foot hanging over the arm. "But that'll depend on how far I get with the stuff."

Pharoah sighed. "Don't let me pressure you, cat. I think this case is beginning to get me down a little."

"I think it's got a lot of people down," said Seth. The next question stung his ear.

"You alone, cat?"

"Sure I am!"

"Okay, cat. Maybe later then." Pharoah hung up, left the phone booth, and crossed to his car which was parked across the street from the entrance to Seth's apartment house. His temples throbbed, his face was burning as he slid behind the wheel. Never jazz me, Seth cat. I saw the Indian going into the house. I know he's in your pad right now. He drove off and Veronica stepped out of the shadows of a doorway and crossed swiftly to the apartment-house lobby.

"Would you like something to eat?" Seth asked Adam.

"No." Adam ran the edge of his hand across his neck. "I've got it up to here."

"You ought to tell Pharoah Love about being in Ben's apartment."

Adam ran his fingers through his hair and emitted a noise that sounded like a muffled war whoop. *"How* can I prove I didn't kill him? Supposing he locks me up on suspicion?"

"Even if he does," said Seth, "he can't hold you very long. Any good lawyer could spring you. They can't hold you on insufficient evidence."

"Oh Christ." Adam sighed. "I suppose it would look better if I got to him right away."

"I think he's heading up to Ida's."

"Christ, I promised Jamie I'd be home for dinner. If I call him now and tell him I might not make it, he'll think . . . Oh Christ."

"Tell him the truth. What difference does it make? You've handed in your resignation."

Adam shook his head in frustration. "It's not that easy. He's got it in for me. He's already made a crack about not knowing my whereabouts the morning Ben was murdered. Don't you know what he's like when he thinks he's being crossed? He's already used Ella to make it look bad for me." He jumped to his feet and agitatedly began pacing the room. "He doesn't give a damn about anything any more. He doesn't even give a damn about himself. He's dying. The convulsions are getting worse. His doctor warned him. He took three fits in the past five days. Any one of them could have been fatal. That's why he doesn't care *what* happens."

"Well," began Seth, "maybe if you stuck with him a while longer . . ."

"I can't!" cried Adam. "I can't. I can't take it any longer."

Chimes filled the room and it took a startled Adam a few seconds to realize it was the door. He looked at Seth questioningly, but Seth was staring at the door. If that's Pharoah, Seth was thinking, how will I explain Adam's presence to him? If that's Pharoah, he has a hell of a nerve coming to the apartment when I told him I planned to be busy. If that's Pharoah, I'll . . .

He pulled the door open and Veronica stood there, clutching her purse. "I had to take the chance you'd be home," she said briskly as she crossed the threshold. "I would have called first, but . . ." She stared at Adam.

"Hullo," he said dully.

"Oh."

Seth shut the door, took Veronica's arm, and guided her to the sofa. "We were having a drink. Won't you join us?" The mockery in his voice stood out like a bas-relief. Veronica pulled her arm away and sank onto the sofa.

"Did Pharoah Love just call you?"

"Are you psychic?" asked Seth.

"Do you know where from?"

"How the hell do I know where from? His office probably. Why?"

"He was phoning from the booth across the street. And when he left that booth he looked damned mad." Her eyes shifted back and forth from Seth to Adam as she spoke.

"He must be tailing you," said Adam, his voice a pale imitation of itself.

"Must be," said Seth with an air of nonchalance. "What the hell! Why not? I'm a suspect in a murder case. Don't they always put tails on suspects? Who knows? Maybe we've all been attached to invisible shadows." Adam headed for the door. "Where are you going?"

"Up to Ida's."

Veronica's eyes widened innocently. "You don't have to go on my account, darling."

"I'm going on my account," snapped Adam, and left. Veronica winced as the door slammed behind him. She stared up at Seth.

"I didn't know I'd be interrupting anything."

"I'd ask you to swear that on a stack of Bibles except you don't believe in God and I don't have a stack of Bibles. Jamie send you here to break it up, whatever that sick bastard fancied needed breaking up, or is this a ploy of your own?"

Tears never came easily to Veronica, and Seth was equally surprised and chagrined to see her put her face in her hands as her body shook. He went to the bar and poured her a stiff scotch and water, then sat beside her, holding the glass out stiffly.

"You need a drink. Here."

"P-ut it d-down." She fumbled in her purse, found a handkerchief, and in sixty seconds order was restored. She picked up the drink and took a stiff swig, then fixed Seth with her most earnest look.

"I've never felt so frightened—so all alone—in all my life. Don't look at me like that!" Seth wiped the smirk from his face. "This isn't any helpless-female act. It . . . it . . ." She gestured helplessly. "It's as though the whole world was coming to an end. Seth, have you ever stopped to think? What happens to us when this case blows wide open? Do you realize how many reputations are at stake? How many lives can be ruined?"

"You're thinking of your own skin."

"Yes," she said weakly, "mostly. Seth, how much does

167

Pharoah Love know? How much has he told you? What did he find in Ben's apartment?" Seth restrained an urge to look at the closet door behind which the Photostats reposed.

"What are you afraid he's found?"

"Well—things—about everybody!"

"You mean things about you."

She put her glass down and took out her cigarette case. "Okay, Seth." Nobody could have feigned such weariness in their voice. Veronica was a woman of amazing strength and rarely admitted to being beaten. But she now looked her thirty-five years, with perhaps another five thrown in for bad measure. She lit a cigarette, exhaled, and then said in a voice that seemed to come from an echo chamber, it rang so hollow with resignment, "Did Pharoah Love say anything about finding some rather nasty negatives?"

"What kind of negatives?"

"Some pictures of me taken at one of Jamie's peyoti orgies. The reason why Ben was blackmailing me."

"What kind of pictures?"

"Incriminating," she suddenly roared. "Why the hell else do you think I'm pea green with fear? Pictures of me and some goddamn dyke rolling in the hay." His expression remained placid and Veronica was perplexed. "Aren't you shocked? God knows I was! It was the first, and let me tell you, the last time! I disgust myself every time I think about it, which lately is every hour on the hour." She was on the verge of tears again and choked them back with difficulty. "They wouldn't release that sort of thing to the papers, would they?"

"Not even if they knew where to find them."

"What?"

Seth borrowed her cigarette and took a drag on it. "The one thing they didn't find in Ben's apartment were snapshots or negatives of any kind. Pharoah suspects they must have existed and were stolen by the murderer."

"Oh God!" Her hand flew to her forehead. "Then there's another county to be heard from. Oh God!" She fell back against the back of the couch, legs splayed outward and cigarette ash showering over Seth. "Who?" she yelped. "Who could it be?"

As though it was offering her an answer, the phone rang. The intrusion irritated Seth. "God damn it!" He crossed to the phone and spoke sharply. "What?"

"Seth?" piped a familiar voice at the other end. It startled him.

"Ella?" Veronica sat up sharply, head cocked, mouth gaping.

"A bit of an emergency, dear. Is Adam with you? He was to have dinner with Jamie, and Jamie couldn't bring himself to call you."

"No, Ella, he's not. He left a short while ago. He might be up at Ida's Place. That's the number on the telegram I sent you yesterday."

"I shall refer your information to Jameson. Seth?"

"Yes, Ella?"

"You haven't been poaching on Jamie's territory again, have you?"

"Of course not, Ella."

"I'm glad." She sounded sincere. "I have a spot of fondness for you, Seth. You touched me very deeply at Ben's funeral. People so rarely weep for each other. I wept too. Not for Ben. For you." Veronica was now circling Seth impatiently, clouding the room with cigarette smoke. Seth pressed the phone to his ear to catch Ella's piping words. "The few times Ben brought you to visit me, I sensed more substance in you than in any of the others. You know what I mean?"

"Thank you, Ella."

The phone clicked. Slowly he placed the receiver in the cradle.

"Ella!" said Veronica, as though Seth had just been knighted. "Was that *really* Ella? But she never phones *any-body*!" It was almost a perfect imitation of Ruthelma.

"She was running an errand for Jameson," said Seth, "and I'm sure I don't have to tell you what it's all about." Veronica nodded and went to the bar.

"You hungry?" asked Seth.

"No. You?"

"No."

She turned and leaned against the bar. "Were you shocked?"

"Ella?"

"I don't mean Ella. I mean me and what's on those negatives."

"It's not important."

"I love you, Seth. Please believe me, I love you."

There was one hunger Seth could no longer resist as he crossed to Veronica and pressed his mouth against hers. Their tongues renewed an old friendship, and Veronica's hands eagerly caressed his head. Her thumb tingled victoriously.

"Why'd you wait till now, cat?"

"I was afraid."

"What made you finally own up?"

"Seth." Their eyes finally met. Pharoah and Adam sat in the farthest corner of Ida's restaurant, the one her regulars referred to as the isolation ward. There was no escaping the blaring jukebox or the raucous Saturday-night crowd that packed the place, but here they would be comparatively undisturbed.

"Were you with Seth cat when I phoned him earlier?"

"Yes."

Pharoah's finger traced an invisible pattern on the tablecloth. "That why you went to see him, to tell him you'd been at Ben cat's that morning?"

"Yes."

"Why Seth cat?"

"I don't have any friends." Pharoah lifted an eyebrow effortlessly. "I had to get some advice. He told me to come here and look for you. Listen, I swear to God I didn't kill Ben."

"I know you didn't." He said it so quickly that Adam reared back in his seat in astonishment. He didn't realize Pharoah was as equally astonished. Pharoah said very slowly and pointedly, "Not because I'm positive, but because I don't think your kind kills. And I don't say you didn't go there with murder in your heart, but thinking and doing are two different things." He signaled a waiter and ordered refills. "So it shouldn't be a total loss, cat, what goes with the brother-and-sister act?"

"The Hursts?" He wished he had a tranquilizer. "What do you mean by 'act'?"

"If they claim to hate each other so much, how come they're so thick?"

Adam hesitated briefly, then cleared his throat. "They've only got each other. There are no other relatives."

"How long you been shacked up with Hurst cat?"

"Couple of years."

"Then you should be an authority on the subject. He ever discuss his parents?"

"Not much."

"Ever tell you how his mother died?"

"Yes. She fell out of a window when he was five years old." Careful, Adam told himself, go slow. This man listens between the lines. You owe Jamie something. Not much, but enough.

"Did he ever say if he or Ella cat was with Mama cat at the time?"

Adam thought a moment. "No. Not that I can remember."

"Uh-huh." Pharoah was watching Ida lead a party to a table and had a sudden urge to see her on a skateboard. "Adam cat, which of that curious twosome do you think murdered Ben cat?"

"I . . . I don't know," Adam fumbled. "I . . . Oh Christ." He moved his broad shoulders expressively. "I can't see either one of them killing anybody. Anyway, when I left the house that morning, Jamie was still at home."

"And Ella cat says she was at home 'meditating.' You hungry?" If it was an invitation to join the detective for dinner, Adam was startled. He wanted to get away. Even Jameson would be an improvement on this.

"I—uh—promised to have dinner with Jamie."

"Uh-huh." Pharoah laid the menu down and sipped his drink. It was watery and he looked around for the waiter with the refills. "Seth cat mention if he was staying in tonight?"

"I don't know. Veronica was with him when I left."

Pharoah's face looked suddenly grim. "Old snotty cat doesn't give up, does she?"

The waiter finally appeared with the fresh drinks. "It's a madhouse tonight. A madhouse." He whisked the empties from the table and darted toward another group which was crying impatiently for service. Adam wondered if he dared excuse himself. The detective had accepted his confession too easily. Was this all there was to it? No being hauled to the station? No intensive questioning hour after endless hour? Had all those Humphrey Bogart pictures been a fraud?

"Is this all there is to it?"

For a reason he would never explain to himself, Pharoah was saddened by the Indian's naïveté. "For the time being. I don't carry a rubber hose with me." He didn't look at Adam for a reaction. Sitting ducks were no challenge. Instead he asked, "You think there's any chance of Seth cat and snotty cat getting together again?"

"I don't know. It doesn't make any difference to me one way or another. Does it matter?"

"Yeah, cat. He's too good for her." Pharoah leaned back. "If you're itching to cut, cat, then cut."

"Well . . . I did promise Jamie, and . . ."

"Good night." He looked at him. "Keep within reaching distance."

Adam nodded, got up and burrowed his way through the crush, ignoring Ida and Ward as he passed them, eager for the freedom of the street, eager to savor the freedom that was his, eager for Wednesday morning and the start of his new life.

"Ella! Ella!" Jameson exalted. "It shall be the most memorable party of the season." He glowed at his beatific expression in the mirror and entertained an urge to lean forward and kiss it. "The garden will be festooned with Japanese lanterns. I've hired a five-piece combo and the rugs will be removed for dancing. And at midnight . . ."

"I shall appear," piped Ella gleefully.

Jameson's eyes suddenly filled with tears as he sank to one knee and clasped his hands together. "Ella . . . Ella darling," he whispered hoarsely.

"Darling!" she cried, mimicking him cruelly.

"Yes, darling. Don't be cruel to me, Ella. Not now. Not this close to the end. What I'm trying to say isn't coming too easily, but it must be said."

"Then get on with it! You turn stomachs faster than you turn phrases."

"Ella!"

"Sorry."

"I have loved you all my life, Ella."

"Idiot."

"I have. I *have!* It's the burden of the dreadful secret we've shared these sixty years that has caused us to be mean and petty to each other. In your own way haven't you loved me?"

"I suppose."

"Don't begrudge me the truth," he pleaded. "We have protected each other all our lives. Doesn't that speak for love?"

"So you finally realize that," she said quietly. "Why else would I have stayed at your side all these years? Didn't you realize, you damned pederast, I sacrificed myself to your happiness? Isn't sacrifice *love,* you simpering, adorable, lovable fool? Now get out of here before we drown in this sea of sentimentality. Adam's probably at home waiting for you.

Find out what he's told that monstrous Hawkshaw! And, Jamie . . ."

"Yes, darling . . ."

"Don't forget to invite him to the party."

"How could I?"

"Jamie." He was struck by the sudden fear in her voice. "You don't suppose Adam told him? You don't suppose we've been betrayed?"

"Don't! Don't even think it. Adam wouldn't dare." He stood bravely erect, a knight in invisible armor. "It would mean incriminating himself. He's gone far enough, hasn't he, in daring to leave me? Ben was far shrewder than Adam, yet in the end he was defeated. No, my darling, I can safely say that Adam has not betrayed us. The pitiful fool. Oh, how I hate what we must do to him! But then," he exclaimed gaily, "so many of us are expendable! Ta ta, my sweet."

"Ta ta."

"Hey! Cheer up, will yah? You're giving the place a bad name. Detectives aren't suppposed to look depressed, or are you in disguise?" Ida wedged herself into the chair opposite Pharoah. At two in the morning everything thinned out in her restaurant except Ida. Pharoah gazed at her unsteadily for a moment, then blinked his eyes and refocused them. They couldn't sustain the weight of two Idas.

"I like you, Ida cat," he mumbled thickly.

That's all I need, she thought grimly. A drunken spook isn't bad enough, but a drunken-spook detective—that's white on white. She reined in the laugh that tried to gallop out of her mouth.

"Hows about a cup of coffee?"

175

"Uh-uh," he said, rubbing the back of his neck with both hands. "That ain't what I need, Ida cat."

"Then how about something to eat? You must be starved."

"I am starved, Ida cat. I am starved for many things. I am starved, for instance, for a murderer."

"You won't find one on my menu."

"I know, Ida cat. I have already looked."

"Listen," she said, folding her arms and weighing down on the table, "what happens if you can't pin this on anybody?"

"Ohhhhh," he chortled, "I will pin it on somebody, Ida cat, or I will be replaced. And I do *not* intend to be replaced. Oh no, Ida cat. I will have me a murderer—and very soon. I can feel it in my bones. But things got to get moving a little faster because it's beginning to close in on me. And when I want something bad enough, Ida cat . . ." His voice trailed off. He heard the rumble of thunder and looked toward the window in time to see a brilliant flash of lightning.

"There it is, Ida cat. There it is. A sign!" Then his hand dropped listlessly to his side, and his head fell on his chest.

"Hey." No answer. "Cat! Hey!" He looked up with an effort. "You sick?"

"No, Ida cat." He sighed. "I ain't sick. I'm just in love."

"I feel *mar*velous!" Veronica danced across the bedroom floor in her bare feet, zipping up the back of her dress.

"Sure you don't want some coffee?" Seth shouted from the kitchen, wondering if the rumble of thunder and the flash of lightning would make her decide to spend the night. He hoped not.

"No no no no *no!*" she sang gaily. "It will keep me awake, and I plan nine full hours of sleep tonight." She slipped into her pumps and walked briskly into the living room, searching for her purse.

"I'll call down for a cab." He entered the room, balancing the cup of coffee in one hand and a ham-and-cheese sandwich in the other.

"Don't bother! I want to walk a few blocks."

"At this hour? Are you nuts?" He had reached his desk safely with the cup of coffee and the sandwich. "The streets around here are barely safe in broad daylight. And it sounds like rain."

"Who cares? Who cares? Who cares?" She rushed to him and kissed the tip of his nose.

Oh shit. She really thinks the past couple of hours were all that important.

"What's the matter?" she asked.

"What do you mean?"

"You've got the strangest look on your face."

He turned and stared at himself in the mirror. "I don't look any different to me."

"Don't kid *me*." He knew that tone of voice well. It was as familiar as a Con Edison jackhammer breaking up the streets. "You're sorry we banged." He was about to bite into the sandwich. Now he wished it was her jugular vein. He dropped the sandwich back onto the plate and sat back.

"Okay. It's change-of-mood time. What's up?"

"I don't reach you anywhere any more, do I?"

"For Christ's sake, Veronica, can't you ever do anything without spending the next two hours dissecting why?"

"You went to bed with me because you needed to go to bed with somebody. That's all it was, wasn't it?"

"What the hell do you expect? Applause?" She considered

hurling her purse at him, but she wasn't sufficiently rehearsed for the recriminations.

"Oh well!" she said airily, not surprising him one bit, "we're still married and I suppose it's the least a wife can do for her husband."

He bit into the sandwich.

She took a deep breath. "*Is* there something between you and Adam?"

Seth groaned. "Veronica, the only thing Adam and I have in common is that we have nothing in common. Now go home, will you? I didn't mean to use you tonight, and I didn't plan it because I didn't know you were coming. But on the other hand, you came here tonight thinking there was something to break up between Adam and me, and when you found there wasn't, you decided to go for broke. I took advantage of it, okay? Oneupmanship."

She sat down abruptly and crossed her legs with a positive gesture. "I think we should get the divorce."

"So do I," he said, chewing on another bite, "but I can't afford it."

"I'll pay for it," she snapped, "and from here on in, sweetie, no holds barred!"

He threw the sandwich down. "Okay! Okay!" he shouted. "Pull out the stiletto and start hacking at my balls. No holds barred! What are you going to do? Ruin me? Destroy me? Tell the world you married a switch hitter? You think I give a shit *what* you do? Go on! File in New York! Name the late Ben Bentley as corespondent!" He leaned forward and smiled. "And I'll countersuit and name Daniel Saber."

A chameleon would have envied the swiftness with which she shed the nasty look on her face. "Aw, Seth sweetie, we care too much for each other for these silly threats and counterthreats." She got to her feet and smoothed her dress. "Let's both sleep on it."

"Don't dismiss it that easily!" he shouted, jumping to his feet. "I've got it over you, baby. I know where I stand with myself now. I'm in the driver's seat this trip. From here on in, keep out of my life."

"Seth!"

"Stop trying to mess me up." She backed away from him, frightened, as he advanced at her in a rage. "Stop your stinking interfering. And if you do anything else to keep me from writing the book, so help me . . . !"

She was out the door and rushing down the hall. The door slammed and Seth stared at his hands outstretched in front of him. He thought his fingers were frozen, frozen around an invisible neck. Veronica's neck.

He rushed into the kitchen, and with his elbow he jolted the cold-water tap. He held his hands under the icy downpour, wheezing rasping, staccato sobs, until the muscles in his fingers relaxed. Then he leaned against the sink, exhausted, staring at the water emptying into the drain and wondering who the hell could be phoning at this hour. He turned off the tap, dried his hands on the dish towel, and picked up the kitchen extension.

"Hi, cat," said the drowsy voice at the other end. "You are my favorite cat, cat. My most favorite cat." And then, after a slight fumbling, the receiver was replaced on the other end.

Seth hung up, went back to the living room, sat on the couch, and lit a cigarette. Oh, Dr. Shlacher, he thought elatedly, it is no longer important how he "handlez" me. Seth

179

baby is in the driver's seat, dear Dr. Shlacher, and Seth baby has no intentions of losing control of the wheel.

Adam was in the kitchen finishing some scrambled eggs when Jameson returned. He swallowed the last mouthful as Hurst sauntered into the kitchen carrying the morning papers.

"So there you are," sniffed Hurst. "I thought we were going to have dinner together."

"So did I," said Adam, crossing to the sink with the plate and fork. "I've been back over an hour."

"Oh." Hurst put the papers on the table. "Well, I waited and waited and then decided I'd been completely abandoned. So I sought solace with Ella."

"Want some coffee?"

"Just a trickle."

Adam got the cups and saucers from the cupboard and crossed back to the table where the electric percolator gurgled seductively.

"Ella phoned you at Seth's, but you weren't there. Or so he said."

"I suppose," said Adam with a trace of a smile, "I should be flattered Ella broke with tradition just to check up on me."

"We *weren't* checking!" said Hurst petulantly. "You said you'd be back for dinner and I was too proud to phone Seth myself." He watched Adam pour the coffee and then sat down opposite him.

"Did you eat?" asked Adam.

"I wasn't hungry."

"Do you want me to fix something for you?"

"No. Where were you?"

"I went up to Ida's."

Hurst's eyes narrowed. "What did you tell that detective?"

Adam's head shot up. "How'd you know I was with him?"

Hurst clapped his hand over his mouth.

"You've been following me," said Adam. Hurst lowered his hand and assumed his naughty-little-boy look. "Well, I did follow you to Ida's, but when I looked through the window and saw you with the blackamoor—well, I just went off in a high dudgeon and went back to Ella's. Ella was a bit worried, Adam. She's afraid you may have been a bit indiscreet about us." Then he added sharply, "Were you?"

"No, God damn it," snapped Adam, "I wasn't. But I fucking well should have been. What's the idea of Ella trying to plant in Love's mind I killed Ben?"

"Oh dear, dear, dear." His hands fluttered nervously. "Did she do that? I shall chide her for it." Then he said placatingly, "She was just being wicked. You know how Ella gets."

"I've got news for you and Ella. I was at Ben's place the morning he was murdered."

"Oh! Oh!" His hands covered his eyes as he agonized.

"But he was dead when I got there, and I told that to Pharoah Love. And put this in your pipe. He doesn't believe for one minute that I killed Ben."

Hurst lowered his hands and pursed his lips.

"And chew on this while you're at it. He's been doing some checking into your mother's death. . . ." Hurst emitted a squeal of horror. "And don't take a fit, because I'll leave you laying there!"

Hurst, quite calmly, stirred his coffee to cool it. "I'm inviting Mr. Love to the party Tuesday night."

"Any more surprises?" asked Adam, playing with a bread knife.

"Yes." Hurst smiled. "But I'm saving those for Tuesday night." He lifted the cup to his lips and sipped. Then, lowering the cup, he smiled beguilingly. "Do you know something, Adam? You seem to have aged in the past few hours. I find it terribly becoming."

Adam stared down at his hand. It was clenching the knife hilt.

"Careful, my dear. You might cut yourself."

With a sudden, uncontrollable rage Adam plunged the blade into the table top and then rushed from the room. Hurst giggled and tapped the hilt with his finger. The knife trembled slightly but remained imbedded. Hurst stared at the knife in fascination.

"My dear," he whispered in astonishment, "the bloody thing could be fatal!"

13

To the Editor: I would appreciate information, photographs, etc., for a biography of Ben Bentley (Bergheim), who died on Tuesday, June 11th.

Seth Piro
203 West End Ave.
New York City

SETH COULDN'T estimate how many people read the book section of the Sunday *Times,* but he figured if he received a dozen replies, he would be ahead. The squib served its most important purpose. It proved he meant business. He was grateful to see it in print. It was the first time in almost two years he hadn't received a rejection slip.

He sat at his desk in pajamas and robe, hair tousled, eyes still heavy from lack of sleep, mind still troubled by the gothic horror of a nightmare, heart still heavy from those last despicable moments with Veronica, fingers still aching from typing copious pages of notes until six in the morning.

183

The phone was still off the hook as he reread the telegram that had been slipped under his door. COME AS YOU ARE CHEZ MOI. TUESDAY. FROM NINE. GALA FESTIVITIES. HURST. Then he riffled the twenty pages of typewritten notes, pausing every so often when a particularly telling line caught his eye and held his attention. Then he reabsorbed the final paragraph for at least the tenth time that morning.

Yes, he thought, a very likely, a very plausible murderer. He poured his third cup of coffee, lit his sixth cigarette, and then reached over to reunite phone and cradle. There just might be someone who had already read the Author's Query and was anxious to get through to him. He replaced the Photostats in the legal folder, tied it tightly, and crossed to the linen closet. He made a wedge behind the pile of laundered bed sheets and inserted the folder.

In the bathroom he opened the medicine cabinet and found the bottle of mouthwash. He swished a healthy swig around his mouth, silently whispering adieu to the millions of tiny germs the mouthwash was guaranteed to destroy, and then spat into the basin. He stared at himself in the cabinet mirror and winked conspiratorially. Seth tried to remember the last time he'd been so pleased with himself.

Back at his desk, he paper-clipped the notes, opened the bottom drawer, took out a folder marked "Income Tax" (big private joke), and carefully inserted the sheaf. Then he crossed to the sofa and stretched out, cigarette dangling from his lips, hand over his eyes, trying to re-create as many incidents of the nightmare as he could recall. He wanted to go over them carefully and have them thoroughly analyzed before his next session with Dr. Shlacher.

First he assembled the cast of characters in no particular

order of appearance. Once these were established, he knew
most of the incidents would fall into place. There was Veronica, then Adam, followed by Hurst and Ella and the never-to-
be-forgotten Pharoah Love, who needed no introduction.
There was Ada and Ida and Mrs. Bergheim, and in the bathroom a small boy with beautiful big eyes and a Buster Brown
haircut with Cupid's-bow lips, toweling himself briskly and
singing at the top of his lungs to the accompaniment of the
ever-present radio.

And there was, of course, the star of the nightmare, Seth
Piro, rushing from Veronica to Ida and to the strange, face-
less man who sat in the chair with his fly half unzipped, pol-
ishing his eyeglasses with the tip of his tie, seemingly deaf to
Seth's terrified, agonized cries, "Save me! *Au secours!
Ayudame!*" Seth chuckled. Southern Spanish girl. Ayuda
Mae. Help me. Save me. Rescue! "The big black cat!" he
cried. "Save me from the big black cat!" The feline monster
stalked him from room to room, six feet tall, razor-sharp
claws, menacing Seth with its penetrating yellow eyes and
baring its fangs. There was no escaping it. Then he was cor-
nered in the walk-in closet and the big black cat pounced,
pinned Seth against the wall, and licked his face, purring contentedly, and Seth awoke with an erection.

Hot ash sprinkled on his chest and he sat up swiftly and
spat the cigarette stub into the tray. He picked the cigarette
paper and tobacco residue from his lips and then sat back
with his hands clasped behind his head. He whistled a merry
little jig through his teeth, keeping time with his right foot,
enjoying himself, loving himself, proud of himself. Everything and everyone was falling into place and all because he,
Seth Piro, was now in complete control. All niches were oc-

cupied and carefully labeled. Veronica. Pharoah. Adam. Ella. Hurst. Even Dr. Shlacher. Seth Piro was no longer being manipulated. This was his show now, his own production. And as God is my witness, I will never let go of the strings. Chimes began to accompany his delicious sense of euphoria, and he grinned with delight until he realized someone was at the door.

Pharoah Love stood in the doorway, wearing a brightly colored shirt and sports jacket, holding a brown paper sack.

"Well!" said Seth, not too surprised. "Come on in."

"Greetings, cat." Pharoah ambled in and Seth shut the door. "I tried to phone first, but your signal was very busy, cat." He held up the paper sack. "Trade you some jelly doughnuts for a cup of very black, very strong coffee." He looked around as Seth went to the kitchen for cup, saucer, and plates. "Are we alone?"

"Who were you expecting to find?" asked Seth, as he rattled the plates to keep himself from getting rattled. "The Schola Cantorum?"

"Got any aspirin?"

"Medicine chest. Help yourself."

A few minutes later aspirin had been swallowed, coffee had been poured, and jelly doughnuts were laid out on a serving plate. Pharoah slouched in an easy chair and Seth sat at the desk.

"I am a very hung-over cat this morning." Pharoah sighed, lifting his cup. "Did I call you at what is usually referred to as an unearthly hour last night?"

"You did." Seth nodded, transferring jelly from his fingers to a napkin.

"And what was the extent of the conversation?"

"Well," said Seth, smacking his lips, absorbing powdered

sugar, "you told me I was your most favorite cat and hung up with, as I recall, some difficulty."

Pharoah managed a smile. "As long as I didn't lie. You have been on my mind all morning."

You were on my mind all of my very short night, Pharoah cat, but it wouldn't make sense to you out of context.

Pharoah reached for his jelly doughnut, examined it, then put it back on the plate. "I saw the *Times*. You do mean business after all, don't you, cat?"

"Did you ever doubt it?"

"For a while I did. Had a meeting with my chief an hour ago. This little squib of yours has stimulated some interest among the other newspapers. We won't be able to hold back the facts of Ben cat's murder much longer. When the bloodhounds get on the scent, Seth cat, they start howling, and we got to throw them a little something. How much work you get done last night?"

"A lot. Every chapter's outlined, subject to whatever alterations my little Author's Query forces."

"And if it brings nothing?"

Seth shrugged. "Then I go with what I've got."

"Tell me about the last chapter."

"Not yet."

"Why not?"

"It's not fair."

"To who?"

"Me."

"Why?"

"Because I could be wrong about whomever I've pinpointed as the murderer."

"Supposing we prove to be of one mind?"

"Why were you following me again last night?"

"Don't change the subject, cat."

"We'll get back to the subject. Why were you following me?"

"Protection."

"From what?"

"Like I said, there are cats that don't want this book written."

"I'm not afraid."

"Ohhhh." Pharoah sighed. "I know you are not afraid. That is why you are my favorite cat. You are treading where angels fear . . . and there is somewhere an angel who is thinking of playing quoits with his halo."

"His? No hers?"

Pharoah chuckled. "Well, cat, that gives me a clue."

"Cat—" Seth smiled—"I might have thrown you a red herring."

Pharoah lit a cigarette and took his time about it. Seth poured more coffee, whistling between his teeth again, savoring the fantasy of the glorious spotlight in which he would bask when *Ben: A Wasted Life* was published. Possibly a review spread across the front pages of the *Times'* and *Trib's* Sunday book reviews. The *Times* review by some eminent psychoanalyst or maybe John Rechy if somebody had a proper sense of camp. An interview on "Author Meets the Critic," and he might even be invited to banter quips with Johnny Carson. Certainly there'd be a plug on the "Today" show. By the sixth or seventh printing there'd be literary luncheons, autograph parties at Brentano's, Doubleday's, and possibly Korvette's, a lecture tour, and then a fat advance for his next book. With the current lowering of censor bars there might even be a movie sale. It could possibly be grist for William Wyler's mill, possibly Richard Brooks (*Lord Ben!*) with Warren Beatty, or more likely Fabian, playing the lead ("He's big with the teen-agers, Seth, and you've got ten per cent of the gross. And don't fight the new title, kid. It's been tested in Oklahoma and it's a winner! *Beach Blanket Ben!* They got Henry Mancini to do the score. *A Wa-a-a-asted Li-i-i-ife!* Gets you where you live, doesn't it, kid?").

"Where are you, cat?"

"What?"

"You are wearing a big cat's smile and not hearing a word I'm saying."

"I was thinking about Hurst's party Tuesday night."

"I've been invited."

"Typical!" roared Seth. "Absolutely typical! Hurst goes down in my book as the great original of our time. Shall we go together, arm in arm, sporting jaunty hats and bachelor buttons?"

"It's a date." Seth's ebullient spirits were disturbing him. "What about lollipop cat?"

"Hurst?" Pharoah nodded. "What about him?"

"Did he do it?"

"Adam said Hurst was at home when Adam went to see Ben."

"That's what he said. That doesn't mean we take his word for it."

"If Adam lied about that, he could have lied about finding Ben dead."

"That's right. I still don't think he's the killer type, but wars have proved that theory wrong before."

189

"Why don't you stop fishing and take me for a drive, unless you've got other plans?"

"Don't you want to stick by the phone in case some fish start jumping at the bait?"

"The answering service can handle it." He rose and headed for the bathroom. "I'll get cleaned up."

"Cat." Seth stopped in his tracks and faced Pharoah. "What's this party all about? Got any ideas?"

Seth leaned against the wall. "It could be about a lot of things. It could be he just feels like throwing a party. He gives them quite frequently. Or else he's being a bitch and giving Adam a proper send-off."

"And where does Adam cat think he's cutting to?"

"A rooming house on the west side. He is leaving Jameson's bed—bored."

"Well, well, well, well, well."

"Pour yourself another cup. I won't be long."

Pharoah was trying to remember if he noticed a radio in the bathroom.

Ada Bergheim folded the Sunday *Times Book Review* and stared out the window of her bedroom. One line about my abortion, Seth Piro, just one line, and I'll stick a knife into you. How much of me will there be in that book? For crying out loud. Me. In a book. A book about Ben. He'll have to have *something* about *me* in the book. Ada Bergheim! Is that book about *your* brother? Good heavens! Everybody! I want you all to meet Ada Bergheim. Then she would hear the whispers and the hushed asides: That's Ben Bentley's sister . . . can you imagine such a wonderful person having such a rotten brother? She's been bearing up under the scandal magnificently. So you're Ada Bergheim. Yes, Dr. Spock, I am. Why, I'd love to come to your home for dinner. What? Join your new research center? I'd be thrilled. No, I don't mind the fuss at all. To be perfectly honest, I just *love* all this attention.

There was a light tapping on the door. "Ada?" said Mrs. Gabriel. "My Moishe is here to pay his respects."

"I'll be right out." She stood up, and the sunlight pouring through the window cast her long shadow across the opposite wall. Her face was magnificently aglow with a long-sought-after happiness, and in that brief moment she made peace with her dead brother.

In the subway heading toward Brooklyn, Ward Gabriel read the Author's Query. By God, that little stinker's really getting a whole book all to himself. Okay. Okay. So he'll never read it. But with a book he's immortal. Shit. Some guys have all the luck. So what, Moishe? Forgive me, I mean Ward. Somewhere there's a pedestal with your name chipped into the base. You'll be up there with the big ones one of these days. A very hotsy twosome at LaRue's, Ward Gabriel and Tuesday Weld (Sheilah Graham). Ward Gabriel Schwabbed it with Carol Linley (Sidney Skolsky). Richard Burton's on the set of *The Ben Bentley Story* every day. Could it be those torrid love scenes between Liz and Ward Gabriel, Metro's hot new bet (Mike Connelly)? Add don't invitems, Richard Burton and Ward Gabriel (Walter Winchell). And the winner is—Ward Gabriel—*The Ben Bentley Story!* I won the Oscar! Ladies and gentlemen! This is—Mrs. Norman Maine! I mean Ward Gabriel!

The dozen passengers sitting across from the young man

with the big smile and tears streaming down his face were getting very nervous. Under that stack of newspapers could the nut be hiding a switch blade?

Ruthelma Kross wagged her finger playfully at the near-senile old lady sitting on the bathroom throne. "Now *remember!* Call me when you're *finished.*" She smiled and blew a kiss and went back to the living room where the Sunday *Times* was strewn all over the floor, chairs, and table. She sat at the table and buttered a cold croissant, spooned raspberry jam over the butter, and then popped it into her mouth, where the repast received no mercy. Author's Query. By *God,* he's *really* going to *write* it. *Goodness!* (She wiped jam from her chin.) This is my fourth *tingle* this morning. It's *here* positively! He may *really* have a *winner!* At the very *least,* it might get the Catholic Book Club (Ruthelma, Ben was Jewish. So what? We're integrating *everything,* aren't we?). It should get at *least* a fifty-thousand *advance* for paperbacks. I could put *Mother* in that *rest* home, take a *cruise* to the West *Indies,* and maybe meet a *widower.*

"I'm finished," trembled the voice from the bathroom.

"No, you're *not.* It's too *soon.*"

Now where *was* I? . . .

Ida read the book section of the Sunday *Times* to keep up with her customers. She had it spread across the kitchen floor. She reread the Author's Query, snorted, and then dumped the pail of garbage over the papers. With five swift movements she had a neat bundle with which she crossed to the window that overlooked the back yard, flung open the window with her left hand, stuck her head out to zero in on the garbage pail directly underneath, took aim, flung the bun-

dle, missed, shut the window, sat down on a chair, lit a cigarette, exhaled, and said "Shit."

"I just can't stop crying, Daniel, I just can't. Daniel, are
you there?"

"Miss Urquist," said the very businesslike voice at the
other end for his wife's benefit, "can't this wait till tomorrow?"

"I suppose so," wept Veronica, "I suppose so," and she
hung up. She sank to the floor with a sob, recalling the sight
of Seth advancing toward her with hands outstretched, fingers poised to clutch her throat and choke her. Well, maybe
just throttle her, but she was frightened. She had run down
twenty-five flights of steps, propelled by fear and hysteria,
past the startled night doorman, screaming at the taxi on the
corner waiting for the light to change. Bastard. Seth, not the
cab driver. Bastard. You're in the driver's seat, are you?
Well, cars have been run off the road before, sweetie. I'll
fight you and that stinking book tooth and nail. I've protected myself all my life and I don't mean to stop now. You
heard me! No holds barred!

She was holding on to herself tightly as she rocked back
and forth, waiting for the plot for revenge to take hold in her
mind, wondering if her lawyer was a specialist in libel laws.

"Now don't be grumpy this morning. I'm sorry I upset you
last night. Let's do all we can to make our last seventy-two
hours together pleasant and memorable ones. Smile?" He
was coaxing. "Smile?"

Oh, what the hell. Adam smiled. He would miss this
garden, but there would be other gardens. Seeing Seth's name
in print when Hurst had showed him the item had somewhat

pleased him. Jameson was poring over a list and making check marks as he spoke.

"Ella doesn't believe he'll ever write the book." His words poured forth like an army of tiny soldiers bearing shields and swords, making swipes at thin air, knowing full well there'd be no counterattack. "She thinks he might yet change his mind." Adam sipped his coffee. "Things *could* happen to make him change his mind."

"He could also be hit by a car," offered Adam.

"Don't be morbid, dear. I have had enough of death the past few days. Adam, what did the blackamoor want to know about Mother's death?"

Adam crossed his legs and reached for a cigarette. "Who was with her when the accident took place."

"I see. Did you by any chance think of providing me with an alibi for the morning of Ben's murder?"

"I told him you were here when I left."

"You *are* sweet. I shall miss you."

"Stop carrying on," said Adam. "I'll be just across town from here. There's no reason why we can't see each other from time to time when you get back."

"Are you so sure I'm coming back?"

Adam exhaled and said nothing. Jameson rubbed his chin with the pencil end, studying Adam and silently cursing the plastic surgeon who had removed the cleft during his most recent operation, erasing forever his faint resemblance to Cary Grant.

"Strange, Adam, but do you know Ella has become terribly fond of Seth?"

"He's a very nice guy."

"She thinks there's more to him than meets the eye. Of

course, the only reason he's writing this book is as a sort of catharsis. The final attempt to have Ben out of his system." He sighed. "Ben was never easily removable. Even now he is more alive and more threatening than he has ever been. Amazing. A boy who took everything and gave little in return, who actually had very little to give when you come right down to it, receiving an immortality he never dreamed of awaiting him, and all through the simple act of murder. And here is Seth, struggling for his own kind of immortality, more or less trying to ride in on Ben's coattails. Ella would like to see him succeed. She hopes he finds the strength to go on with the book regardless of what happens." His eyes twinkled. "Ella's going to do all she can to help him carry it off. She has a plan to free him from at least one fury she's positive is pursuing him. She's going to drop the future right into his lap."

"Supposing he won't take anything from Ella?"

"Ella's mind is made up. He has no choice. She'll tell him Tuesday night." Jameson yelped as Adam's fist swiftly slammed down on the table.

"You keep her out of here Tuesday!"

"But why, sweetums, why? Don't tell me you're *afraid* of Ella?"

"Ella is insane!" Trembling, Adam had spit each word.

"That's just your opinion, my dear," said Jameson quite calmly. "There are others who would admiringly describe her as—unique. Light me a cigarette, will you, dear? My hands seem to be shaking."

Dr. Shlacher sat in his office, his fly half unzipped, holding the speaker to the tape recorder a few inches from his mouth.

"Djune zigzteenth. Zeth Piro. Ze payshent haz gone to remarkable eggztremez to regain hiz ego. Zere iz now ze hope he vill zeaze to fear zis analyziz and zeaze to lie aboud himzelf and to himzelf. Zere iz effry reazon to hope he vill zeaze hiz constant zenz uff omizzion und combletely give himzelf over to ziz treatment."

He stared at the ceiling as if a teleprompter might be suspended there to cue his troubled thoughts.

"Ze payshent phoned to canzel his appointment tomorrow wiz ze eggscuse he muz correlate hiz notez for hiz bewk. Hiz tone uff voize wuz firm, azzured, und pozzitif. Zere was no childitch zign of ze fear of a reprimand. Und yet I zee in ziss a danger zignal. Why iz ziss?"

He clicked off the tape recorder and placed the speaker on his desk. He reached for a cigar, bit off a tip, spat it on the carpet, clicked the desk lighter with his thumb, plunged the cigar into the flame, and took five rapid drags until the cigar glowed like the beacon he was seeking. He put the cigarette lighter down with a thud and stared at the autographed photo of Sigmund Freud and shook his head dolefully.

"Ach, Zigmund. Vod foolz ve immortalz be."

14

THE GAS station attendant finished wiping the Jaguar's windshield; Pharoah handed him a tip, and Seth completed his phone call. He strode nonchalantly from the booth to the car and got in next to Pharoah.

"Sorry to take so long," said Seth in rare good humor, as Pharoah segued into the Long Island traffic heading back to New York. "Spoke to my answering service and my analyst."

"I wasn't wondering." Seth knew better. "Any bites?"

"Strangely enough," said Seth, "not one. Maybe there'll be some mail tomorrow."

"Maybe you didn't expect any bites."

"What makes you think so?"

"Let's face it, cat. How many people who knew Ben Cat Bentley Bergheim would admit to it? Maybe some kids he went to school with. Things like that. The rest are scratching their heads wondering whether he was poet, peasant, or overture. Half the times I read them Author's Queries I say to myself, now who's Sophie Satchmo, someone should want to

197

write a book about her? Come on, cat, you used that device to make it official to yourself. Anything else is gravy."

"You've really been doing a character study of me, haven't you?"

"That's right, cat."

"Is that why you've been tailing me?"

"I explained all that."

"I know, and listening to you, I tried to keep a straight face."

"What do you mean by that, cat?"

Seth's words were heavily coated with self-confidence. "You're very, very interested in me. Not just as a suspect, but just plain me. What do you have in mind, Pharoah?"

"Just like that, eh, cat?"

"Just like that."

"Well," began Pharoah, eyes staring straight ahead at the rear end of the car in front of him, "I been thinking of getting me a bigger pad with maybe somebody there to keep me company."

"And you are now doing me the honor—"

"Don't jump me, cat," Pharoah cut in. "I have been contemplating you as a possible candidate. But nobody's twisting your arm. Play around with it awhile. I'm lonely, that's all. I think we'd be good for each other. I need a friend and you need a lot of what I've got to offer."

"Remember, I'm still recovering from an undesirable roommate."

"Yeah, cat, but you had different kinds of hooks in each other. My blueprint calls for a better kind of layout. Anyway—think about it. It would certainly turn snotty cat piss green."

198

Everything's falling into place. Everything's working. Seth repressed the urge to pinch his own cheek. This is the way Ben would have maneuvered it. Subtly. Cleverly. Until every detail was checked and rechecked and in the end Ben would emerge the winner.

Ben had said that day at the Central Park Zoo, "I don't know, Seth. Do you really think it could work? I know we'd have a lot of fun and all that, but there are times when I have to be left to myself. You know what I mean? Ah, who knows? After Jamie you might be like a vacation."

And he had known all along that the offer would soon be forthcoming and that he'd keep Seth on a string for a while and then assent. Ben had examined all the angles for weeks. Seth had examined nothing but his own emotional needs. Seth was examining every angle now. Oh, Dr. Shlacher, are you in for some surprises!

"We heading for your pad or what?" asked Pharoah.

"Anything you like." Seth smiled. "I haven't a plan."

"No work?"

"Not today. I need to clear the cobwebs. Tomorrow, though, I start early and work right through."

Pharoah chortled. "Come on, cat. Stop stringing me. Who you got down for the murderer?"

"When I'm ready, Pharoah, when I'm ready."

When Seth arrived home shortly before midnight, his answering service told him a Miss Ada Bergheim had called. He decided it was not too late to return the call and dialed. Ada answered.

"Hello. It's Seth. How are you? How's your mother?"

"Mom's okay. I only called to tell you, Seth, Mom and I

have talked it over. We'll help you with the book. But you've got to promise me to leave out that other thing. You know what I'm talking about."

"I can't avoid an allusion to it."

Her breathing was heavier.

"But I promise you this, there'll be no identification that the matter concerned abortion. I just want to illustrate Ben's inability to perform a decent act for his own family. It has to be, Ada. Believe me, I plan to show you in a completely sympathetic light."

"I'll have to trust you." There was a pause. "My mother's going up to my aunt's place in the Catskills for a week or so Tuesday. That's when the mourning ends. Can you wait till she gets back?"

"Sure."

"Listen." The sudden lightness in her voice relieved him. "You want to hear something funny?"

"I can always use a laugh."

"I've been invited to a party at Jameson Hurst's Tuesday night. Do you think I ought to go?"

"Will you be in the mood for it?"

"You mean maybe I shouldn't go to a party so soon after Ben's death?" A deaf man couldn't have missed the disappointment in her voice.

"No, not at all. If you're up to it, go by all means. But I'm warning you, it'll be no party like any party you've ever been to."

"Listen." She sighed. "I could use a change."

"Then you be there. I'll be there and I'll look after you."

"You will?"

My God, Seth thought, has anyone in her entire life ever said, "I'll look after you?"

"I promise."

"Well, okay then. What time should I get there? I mean, don't people always make sure to come very late to parties like that?"

"Come after ten. I'll be there by then."

"Okay. And, Seth, thanks."

"Thank you, Ada."

She hung up and her Mother called from the bedroom, "Who was that so late?"

"Just a friend of mine, Mama." Somehow she couldn't say, "That was Seth." Yesterday's Seth was that man living with her brother. Today's Seth was the man who promised to look after her. She went to the mirror and immediately disapproved of the drab she saw reflected there. I'll get a facial and maybe—oh, what the hell, why not?—maybe a henna rinse. Wouldn't it be crazy if she and Seth . . . Why not . . . why not?

Maybe Ben would spin in his grave.

Seth had changed into pajamas, humming to himself. There was Pharoah's proposition to consider and how to handle it. Could he stall the decision until he finished the book? He needed a private session with Ella but decided it was wiser to wait until after the party. Until Adam had departed the Hurst premises. He was even willing to guarantee himself Ella's reaction when he hinted at the murderer's identity. He'd play a game with Ella, and Ella couldn't resist games. And if Ella loathed the person as much as he suspected she did, the cat was in the bag. The phone rang.

Cat?

Seth stretched out on the bed and reached for the extension. "Yes?"

"It's me." It could have been Judith Anderson in *Medea*. "Veronica."

"I should have called you. I'm sorry about last night. I guess it was just nerves."

"Seth." It was now the Little Match Girl. "So help me, if you weren't already in analysis, I'd tell you to see a doctor."

"I said I was sorry." He was annoyed.

"I've never seen that side of you before, Seth." Portia. "I never knew there was violence in you."

"Veronica," he said wearily, "it's very late and I'm very tired." I've had eleven hours of Pharoah Love. From breakfast to drive in the country to dreary Italian movie to drinks in the village to dinner at the Harlem Chicken Roost to drinks at Elaine's Restaurant to home at last.

"I had a drink with Lew Porsch."

"How's Lew?"

"He advised a Mexican divorce."

"I hear it's nice down there this time of the year."

"Very well then." Hedda Gabler. "Then that's that."

"Seth." He was beginning to hate the sound of his name. "For auld lang syne—" and here's one auld acquaintance, he mused, that will soon be forgot—"would you escort me to Jameson's party?"

"Sorry. But I'm going with Pharoah Love."

"Really!"

"And I'm meeting Ada Bergheim there. I promised to look after her."

"Ada *Berg*heim! What'll *she* be doing there?"

"Administering first aid. How the hell do I know?" Will you for crying out loud hang up? "She's been invited and she won't know anybody, so I'm taking her under my wing. If there's any room left, you can move in alongside her."

"What the hell's gotten *into* you?" she screeched. "Have you gone *mad* or something? What's that doctor *done* to you?"

"He grew me a new pair of balls!" He slammed the phone down.

Veronica rushed to the bathroom, ran the cold-water tap, held a towel under it, wrung it out, and pressed it to her head. He's having a nervous breakdown! That's what it is. A nervous breakdown! Wonderful! Then he'll never write the goddam book. A nervous breakdown! She stared into the mirror. Medea positively. A nervous breakdown. Those things can be helped along.

Seth rolled over and buried his head in the pillow. The phone was ringing again. No, no, no. Why doesn't the damn service pick up? He answered it.

"*Now* what?"

"*Se-e-e-e-e-eth!* It's Ruth*elma!* Your line was *busy* so I knew you weren't *asleep.*" She bit into the pizza. Frozen isn't as good as the real thing, but when you pile it with leftovers, roast beef, salami, Velveeta, it can be as equally satisfying.

Seth relaxed. "What are you eating?"

"A *diet* wafer. Seth, I saw the *Author's* Query and, so help me *God,* I haven't stopped *tingling.* I have to *admit* the book *really* had me *worried.* But now I feel *different.* So I had to call and *tell* you. Go to *work* and do a *brilliant* job. Do you *hear* me?"

"I hear you. God bless you, sweetheart."

"We'll talk *tomorrow.* Get a *good* night's *sleep.* Kiss *kiss!*"

Tomorrow was all to himself. Pharoah had mapped out a day of trying to track down some of the names in Ben's address book. Maybe tomorrow would bring some replies to the Author's Query. It would be interesting to see what turned up, if anything. Dr. Shlacher was canceled, and wisely, Seth was convinced. He didn't want to go into last night's nightmare. He knew well enough what it signified. Opening that fresh can of peas for the doctor to savor would have to wait. I've reached the most important crossroads of my life. Off with the old. On with the new.

He curled up and slept the most innocent sleep of his life.

Adam sat up in bed with a start. Someone was singing in the garden. He pushed back the covers and went to the window. Good Christ! The greenhouse was ablaze with light, and in the garden below, Jameson, a rose stuck behind each ear, was dancing on the grass, singing "The Merry Widow Waltz." He was stark naked.

Adam threw on his robe and raced down the back stairs into the garden. There were no lights on in the other buildings, and he prayed he could get Hurst back into the house before the spectacle attracted an audience. The stupid bastard must have cut himself a peyoti button.

Hurst passed a flowering bush, tore a bloom, and flung it at Adam.

"A peony for your thoughts!"

"Jamie! You damned fool!" He lunged at him, but with a triumphant giggle that rose and fell like an oncoming wave, Hurst deftly side-stepped and Adam tripped, falling into a bed of fuschia pansies.

Hurst did an arabesque around a lilac bush as Adam recovered and made a grab for Hurst's foot as he pirouetted past him.

"You missed!" cried Hurst triumphantly, bringing the sole of his foot down on Adam's face. Then Hurst darted gracefully in one door of the greenhouse, exiting through the other with a graceful *plier* that brought him into contact with a swift rabbit punch from Adam. Hurst fell to his knees and Adam deftly grabbed him under the armpits, pulled him roughly to his feet, and slung him over his shoulder.

He carried him into the house, up to Hurst's bedroom, and flung him on the bed. He knew Hurst would be out for the rest of the night. Adam rushed back down to the kitchen and pulled open drawers. He needed an implement with which to destroy the remaining cacti. The bread knife was nowhere to be found. He flung open a cabinet door and found a tool chest. He opened it and clenched the handle of a small hatchet. He crossed the kitchen to the garden, hatchet upraised, the image of an ancestor hunting scalps, and made for the greenhouse. Of the three peyoti cacti, only two were left. The remains of the third was scattered on the floor. Adam plunged the hatchet into one cactus and in a few seconds completely immolated it. He set to work on the second and, when he was finished, quelled a furious urge to smash every window in the greenhouse, destroy every plant, send flower-pots crashing to the floor.

Hatchet in hand, he returned to the kitchen. He stared up the back stairs, still trembling with rage, but reasoning that he must replace the weapon in the toolbox, or God knows what.

Five minutes later he was back in bed, still enraged, still trembling. He tried his deep-breathing exercises and they began to work. Soon a calmness overtook him and then, finally, sleep.

He dreamed the same dream he had been dreaming from time to time during the past two years.

He was strapped to a board at a side show, and the knife thrower was led in by a Seeing Eye dog.

15

PEOPLE WHO hate Mondays would have loathed
Seth Piro in the eager way he greeted the usually loathsome
day. He leaped out of bed at eight A.M., whistled merrily between his teeth as he prepared a pot of coffee and plugged it
into the wall, shaved in four minutes flat without a nick or a
welt, stepped under an icy, invigorating shower, yodeling at
the top of his lungs, then toweled himself with the dedication
of a flagellant. Five minutes later he was dressed in sports
shirt and slacks, puffing a cigarette and sipping the piping-hot
coffee. Ten minutes later the cup was drained, and clutching
a penknife, he entered the walk-in closet.

He attacked a large carton tied with rope, cutting the rope
in three swift strokes. From the box he selected a copy of
each of his two published novels and some gaily colored
wrapping paper which he remembered Ben had selected at
Jensen's at least two Christmases ago. He crossed back to the
desk with his treasure, opened the top drawer for an envelope
and a slip of personalized note paper, and wrote in a fairly
legible script, "Hey, cat! Thought these might interest you.

206

Gratefully, Seth!" with Seth underlined three times, the signature written with a Florentine flourish.

Seth wrapped the books, Scotch-taping the gift wrap after a fruitless search for some ribbon, and phoned Western Union for a messenger. If Western Union was astonished to hear the package was going to a police station, Seth detected not a note of it. He returned to the closet, retied the rope around the carton, then systematically went through piles of notes and manuscripts as he did at least once every six months, selecting items he decided were long overdue for the incinerator.

In an hour the neat pile of discards on the floor reached midway to the calf of his leg, and to these he added a wooden candy box on which was pasted a small card on which he had printed "Rejections." He opened the box and stared at the top rejection slip from the *Saturday Evening Post,* dated September 1946, and couldn't remember which short story it had been. He forced his fingers into the tightly packed box, felt around, was satisfied, then took the lot to the incinerator room down the hall and committed them to a fiery death.

On his way back to the apartment he intercepted the Western Union messenger stepping out of one of the elevators, introduced himself, guided him to the apartment, entrusted him with the package, and then raced back to the desk to answer the phone, a swift glance at his wrist watch telling him it was just past 9:30 A.M.

"Hello."

"Mr. Seth Piro?"

He didn't recognize the voice. My God! Maybe someone in response to the Author's Query.

"This is he speaking," he said anxiously.

"Mr. Piro, this is Mr. Zitzer."

"Yes, Mr. Zitzer?"

"Mr. Piro, I represent the Fred Astaire Dance Studios and—"

Seth cut in sharply. "This is an extremely cruel joke, Mr. Zitzer. I am confined to a wheel chair." He hung up and sat at the desk, lit a cigarette, and dialed Hurst's number.

By the fifth ring he was about to hang up when Adam's voice, sounding like he was being strangled by phlegm, said "Hello."

"Adam? Seth. Did I wake you up?"

Adam cleared his throat. "Oh no! I've been up for hours."

"I meant to call you yesterday, but I didn't get a chance. How'd it go with Pharoah Love?"

"Okay, I guess. He told me he didn't think I was the killer type." He thought better of adding, but he should have seen me last night when I held a small hatchet in my hand.

"Where's Jameson?"

"He's confined himself to quarters. He's planning to stay in his room all day and tomorrow until the party."

"Has he been giving you a hard time?"

There was a pause, then, "It'll be over soon. I can cope. I'm heading for the gym for a workout. Any chance you might get over there?"

Seth thought about it for a moment. "I'm not sure. I thought I'd stick by the phone in case I get any calls. Did you see that squib of mine in the *Times* yesterday?"

"Yeah!" The note of delight in his voice warmed Seth. "First time I've seen a friend's name in print. I got a big kick out of it!"

I wonder what kind of a kick it gave a lot of other people.

"Well, listen, kid, I just called to see if you were okay. If I don't see you at the gym, I'll see you at the party."

"Okay." The voice was dull again.

"I suppose it promises to be quite a wingding."

"Yeah. Big blowout. Seth . . . ?"

"Yes, Adam?"

"Would you be free for dinner one night this week?"

"Sure! You name it."

"How's for Wednesday? It'll be my first night away from . . . you know, on my own."

"Sure, Adam. Let's figure on Ida's around eight." By which time I hope to have seen Ella and the shit will have hit the fan.

"Thanks a lot, Seth. If I don't see you later, see you tomorrow night. G'bye."

Seth hung up and began whistling through his teeth again.

Adam held the phone for an extra fraction of a moment and, as he expected, heard the extension phone being gently replaced in its cradle. He hung up, lifted the tray holding Jameson's breakfast (stewed prunes, farina, chocolate-covered lady fingers from Denmark, and a pot of tea), and ascended the back stairs.

Jameson was propped up in bed holding an ice pack on his head. In response to the tap on the door he said weakly, "Come in, Adam," and Adam did as he was bid. Jameson looked at the tray and groaned.

"Oh, I couldn't. Oh, I just couldn't. Take it away."

"Don't you even want the tea?"

"Nothing . . . nothing." Wearily he lowered the ice bag. "I ache. I simply ache all over. You struck me last night, didn't you?"

209

"It was necessary. You kicked me in the face."

Jameson saw no point in masking his elation. "Did I really?" He peered closely at Adam. "I don't see any bruise."

"You were in your bare feet, right up to your neck."

"Dear, dear, dear. Did I disturb the neighbors?"

"I don't think so."

"Where are you off to now?"

"You know where I'm going."

"Now *how* would I know where you're going?"

"You were listening on the extension."

"Well, why not?" he snapped defiantly. "They're *my* phones! What do you bet Seth cancels that date Wednesday night?"

"Jamie," said Adam quietly, "don't make waves."

"You *are* naïve. You are so ri*dic*ulously naïve! Can't you guess what's going on between him and that odious detective? Integration, my dear, utter integration. How long have we been together? Hasn't *any* of my perception rubbed off on you? Even Veronica's figured that one out. I frankly don't understand it as far as Seth is concerned," he added maliciously, "what with that intensive crash psychiatric treatment he's been going through. But I'm sure," he continued, tapping his fingers delicately on his chest, "he has his reasons. Watch them when they're together tomorrow night. Two against the world. When will you be back?"

"Couple of hours. I thought I'd start getting my stuff together later."

"Of course. There's that. Well," he said with a sorrowful sigh, "don't get shriveled in the steam room waiting for Seth to show up." Adam left without a word, leaving the tray on the dressing table, knowing full well Hurst would plunge into it the minute he was alone.

Hurst stared at the door, then, hearing the front door shut, blinked his eyes rapidly as they began clouding with tears. Oh, Ben, Ben. Why did I let you go? Why didn't I fight? We were so right for each other. You would still be alive today, and there would be no need for tomorrow night. Tomorrow night. He wiped his eyes with a tissue and dialed the catering service.

"This is Jameson Hurst." He sounded as though he were pronouncing an edict. "Put me through to Mr. Rachel at once."

Seth pressed the phone tightly to his ear. The voice at the other end was so faint, it was as though the call might have been placed somewhere overseas.

"What time did you say, Mr. Montrose?"

Mumble.

"Could you speak up, please? I think we have a bad connection. I can't hear you."

The voice suddenly unscrambled. "Noon."

"How will I know you?"

"I know you." Mr. Montrose hung up.

It could be some crackpot, thought Seth. A lot of them probably answer things like Author's Queries, like those nuts who follow the obituaries and go to funerals either out of morbid curiosity or just to have a good cry. What the hell, he thought. Mr. Montrose just might come up with something usable, and he hadn't been to the Central Park Zoo since that day he had asked Ben to live with him.

Ben.

Strange.

He puffed the cigarette and stared out the window at the Hudson, watching some tugs pulling a liner out to the channel.

Ben. Four days ago I stood at your bier and wept. Four days ago I told Dr. Shlacher I was still hung up on you. It's not that at all any more. When did the ache go away? Friday? Saturday? Last night? Why, you son of a bitch, if you were alive today, you wouldn't mean that to me, and he snapped his fingers, stared down at them, and burst out laughing.

It is so lovely to be free.

The phone rang.

"Hello?"

"Hi, cat. I am very touched by this gift."

Seth smiled. "Let me tell you, Pharoah cat—" he knew this would please Pharoah—"there aren't many people I'd care to let read those books today. But I thought they might amuse *you*."

"I'm going to get at them tonight."

No date? Am I slipping?

"Thought I'd better rest up for tomorrow. Didn't sleep so good last night. How's for some lunch?"

I am not slipping.

"I'm meeting a Mr. Montrose at the Central Park Zoo at noon. We're going to watch them feed the seals."

"And who is Mr. Montrose?"

"He read yesterday's *Times*."

"Oh-ho."

"The only response I've gotten so far, so I'm going to make the most of it. Shall I call you when I'm finished?"

"Sure. If I'm not in, I'll leave word whether I can make it or not. I caught me one of those jokers in Ben cat's book and his only free time may be his lunch hour. Otherwise I'll try you later today. And thanks again for the books, cat."

"My pleasure. It's nice to know that somewhere I'm

being read again." The thought elated him.

"Call you later, cat."

Pharoah hung up and sat back in the swivel chair. You are being read, Seth cat. It's very deep and the print is kind of small, but you are double-spaced and I can pencil in little notes. And when you are properly edited, according to my own specifications, I shall publish you in a limited edition confined to a very select distribution of one.

Pharoah turned to the opening chapter of Seth's first book after snorting at the dedication, "for Veronica, without whom this book could not have been written." He read the first sentence, "Where did I go wrong?"

Where indeed, Seth cat?

Ruthelma read and reread the invitation to Hurst's party. I don't even *know* the man! Of course, I *did* have some contact with his *sister* when that *dreadful* Ben Bentley told me she was interested in writing her *memoirs*. What was that *strange* thing he said to me that day?

"Ella's a little way out, you know." He was sitting there with his legs outstretched and rubbing the insides of his thighs in that provocative way (*sex* maniac). "When she gets into one of her self-destructive moods, she decides to write her memoirs. You know, I've started to write my own. You might be interested—" he gave that sly *ferret's* smile of his which I suppose *intrigues* weaker-*minded* people—"in reading some of it."

I *wonder* if Ella Hurst ever *wrote* any of those memoirs. That *dreadful* Ben intimated she had *affairs* with some very *prominent* personalities. *He* said she once took *parachute* jumping lessons with Rudolf *Hess*. Rudolf *Hess*!

I *hope* I can find a *baby* sitter for *Mama* tomorrow night.

213

She bit into the fried-egg sandwich and became enraged. They forgot the ketchup again.

"What's wrong with you this morning?" asked Daniel Saber sharply.

"I don't know," said Veronica. "Maybe it's having come to the decision to get the divorce. I didn't sleep very well last night. Dan, I think he's on the verge of a nervous breakdown."

"Who?"

"Seth!"

Saber looked up from the editorial reports spread out on his desk, sighed, and shook his head.

"Veronica, Veronica. You'll never change, will you?"

"What do you mean?" she said, irritated.

"Whenever we lose an author it's usually, 'Oh, he's a lousy writer anyway,' or, 'Let's face it, Dan, his well's run dry.' You're losing Seth once and for all and it's, 'I think he's on the verge of a nervous breakdown.'"

"Well, he sounds like it," she snapped. "And I have a presentiment! And don't start laughing at me. I feel something horrible is going to happen. Oh God!" She held her handkerchief to her eyes to stem the flood. "I can't stop crying."

"Veronica," said Saber patiently, "why don't you take the morning off and see your doctor. You may be working yourself into a nervous breakdown."

Seth leaned against the railing of the seal pool tapping his foot impatiently. He glanced at his wrist watch for about the tenth time and cursed Mr. Montrose for keeping him waiting almost an hour. The seals had been fed and he hadn't, and he

214

found this sort of injustice intolerable. He found being kept waiting intolerable. Ben had always been late.

"I said I couldn't help it! What are you so sore about? If you're so sore, why'd you wait?"

Bastard. You too, Mr. Montrose. You have stolen an hour of my life and I'm tired of being robbed. Strangers have phoned me at home before at odd hours and I've been warned that's what sneak thieves do when they're casing an apartment. How many robberies has the apartment house had this past year? At least five that made the papers, and I know of at least three others that were unreported.

Seth paled. Was that phone call a fake? Was I deliberately lured away from the apartment?

"Hey, you dumb jerk!" the girl shouted as he went racing past her, hitting her elbow and causing her to drop her ice-cream cone.

Fifteen minutes later Seth flung open the door to his apartment, winded and gasping for breath, but fists clenched and face blazing with anger.

"Who's in here?" he shouted.

There was no response.

He looked in the kitchen, then the walk-in closet. He opened the bathroom door and pulled back the shower curtain. He rushed into the bedroom, slid back the closet door, and then looked under the bed. He opened dresser drawers, but nothing was disturbed. He hurried back to the living room and went to the desk. Nothing seemed to have been disturbed.

He pulled open the bottom drawer and found the folder marked "Income Tax" and spread it on the desk. He lifted the sheaf of notes and the paper clip fell off.

It had been hanging loosely.

215

Seth sat in the chair and with the sleeve of his jacket wiped the perspiration from his face. Then he riffled the notes.

For some reason he thought he might find a telltale paw print.

"Hello there, cat," said Pharoah. "Just got in and found your messages. What's up?"

"Mr. Montrose was a false alarm." He strained to keep his voice light, his conversation matter-of-fact.

"So was my pigeon."

"I think it was a trick to get me out of the apartment so it could be searched."

Pharoah's brows furrowed. "Anything missing?"

"No," said Seth, "I don't think so. But I'm pretty sure my desk was searched."

"Anybody else got a key to your apartment?"

"No."

"Do you remember if you double-locked it when you left?"

"It wasn't double-locked. I left in a hurry."

"Those single-lock jobs are a cinch for a professional. You want me to come over?"

"No," said Seth. "No—it's all right." Then he said, "Hold on a minute! I didn't check to see if the photostats are missing." He crossed to the linen closet and felt behind the stack of sheets. The legal folder had been untouched. He went back to the phone.

"False alarm. It's okay. It's just as I left them."

"Then relax, cat. As long as nothing's missing, you're still ahead."

Seth was staring at the typewritten notes spread across the

216

desk. He was about to say, "I think someone's read my notes. Somebody knows who I think killed Ben. In the wrong hands that information could be dangerous. I haven't tested my theory yet. If it doesn't work, an innocent person is in danger."

Instead he said, "You're right. I guess I'm still ahead. Talk to you later." He hung up and lit a cigarette, inhaled, and began choking on the smoke. He rushed to the kitchen for a glass of water and ended up with a painful case of the dry heaves.

Pharoah left his office, crossed the corridor, knocked on a door, and poked his head in. "Got a minute, boss?"

"Come on in."

It seemed an eternity before Western Union responded. Finally, "Western Union," said the voice that always sounded like a mechanical doll.

"A local telegram, operator," said Seth, dictating slowly. "Miss Ella Hurst . . ."

Jameson sat in bed staring at the television screen. He patted his head to make sure the curlers were secure and then resumed rubbing his face with hormone cream.

"John," said the actress to the blond young actor with the wisp of a mustache on his upper lip, "you've got to do something!"

The blond young actor looked slightly walleyed as he fumbled for his line, searching for the cue on the off-screen teleprompter.

"Joan," he said, and the actress knew he was in trouble.

"What about Joan?" she said swiftly. Her character name

217

was Arabella. Jameson giggled. He loved soap operas. Something was always going wrong, and more often with the performances than the plot.

"Uhhhhh," said the flustered actor, "maybe Joan can help us."

The actress was unfazed. "You've got to *do* something."

"Arabella," said the actor. The actress and Jameson relaxed. He reached for a tissue and wiped his greasy fingers, reached for the remote control, and switched the set off. Ben had indoctrinated him into the soap-opera cult.

"They're a camp! I love them!"

Tomorrow night, thought Jameson, you would have loved tomorrow night, Ben. It will be an unforgettable camp, darling, wherever you are.

Ada emerged from the beauty parlor and wondered if everybody on the street appreciated the difference. Well, she *felt* the difference, and that's what mattered. Mrs. Bergheim had been furious when Ada left to keep the beauty parlor appointment.

"We're still sitting *shiva!* What will the neighbors say? It's a shame for the neighbors."

The hell with what the neighbors say, thought Ada, striding briskly, face aglow, an invisible halo encircling her head. What will Seth say? Someone whistled, and though Ada felt like jumping for joy, she didn't look back.

She would have seen a mongrel running to its impatient master.

Though the apartment was in semidarkness, Seth didn't move to turn on the lamps. He sat staring at the phone as though he might hypnotize it into ringing. The ash tray was piled high with butts, and the darkening circles under his eyes seemed to blend with the darkening corners of the room. Ella must have received his telegram at least five hours ago. He had to see her before tomorrow night. What if she doesn't call?

Then I put Plan "B" into action.

The bacon sizzled in a pan as Pharoah broke three eggs into a bowl. He synchronized beating the eggs to the rock-and-roll rhythm blasting from the radio. Very soon, Pharoah cat, there'll be eight strips of bacon sizzling in the pan and I'll be beating six eggs, and I will sport my citation from the department for having brought in a murderer.

"This is a tough one, Pharoah," his chief had said last week. "It might be months before Bentley's killer trips himself."

"Himself, Chief?" Pharoah smiled. "Could be herself."

"Okay, Pharoah. It's all yours. But don't get yourself knocked off in the process."

Not me, Chiefie cat. I got it made. I am a seven-day-wonder. Tomorrow will be one week since Ben cat was so crudely dispatched.

I think I'll wear the new Brooks Brothers tomorrow night. It's for special occasions, and tomorrow night is a special occasion.

Seth entered Ella's apartment house and found the doorman sitting on a stool in the vestibule reading the evening paper. He stood up and took off his glasses.

"Can I help you?"

"Do you know if Miss Hurst is in?"

219

"I don't know. I just came on duty. I'll try her," he said, crossing to the switchboard. "But you know," he added, "she doesn't always answer." He plugged in the cord and jiggled the button. "She's not answering."

"This is very important. I'll have to go up and try her doorbell."

"Go ahead." The doorman shrugged. "But she never answers that door unless she's expecting you."

Seth crossed to a waiting elevator and reached Ella's floor a few seconds later. He reached her door and knew his quest was hopeless. A cardboard square had been hooked onto the knob. It was a notice from Western Union. There was a telegram for her at the main office.

Seth tried the doorbell. Then he knocked, calling, "Ella? Ella? Are you in there? It's Seth Piro. It's urgent. I've got to talk to you!"

Five minutes later he was back on the street, walking slowly, deep in thought. Several minutes later he came to a decision.

He went home and got very drunk on six dry vodka martinis.

16

"RELAX, CAT. You look a little green around the gills. Was it so tough fessing up about who you think killed Ben Cat?"

"No," said Seth, stubbing out his cigarette in the ash tray and wishing the Coca-Cola would arrive. "Once I'd made up my mind to it, it was no problem. I'm just a little hung over."

"Go out tooting last night?"

"No. It was a solo performance at home. Somebody read those notes in my desk yesterday, and like I said, before it got too dangerous I had to let you in on it. You can't make a move, can you? I mean, since it's all supposition. You still have to get actual proof."

"Murderer cat'll slip up," said Pharoah, beckoning the young rookie who stuck his neck in the door. He entered with the Cokes and just as quickly left. Seth took a large gulp of his and then sighed in relief. Pharoah rubbed his chin and stared out the window. "You're so sure Ella Hurst is on to some of this?"

"Positive. She gave herself dead away when we saw her on Saturday."

"Well," said Pharoah, "maybe you're right. Maybe the slip-up'll take place tonight at the party."

"It's got to. Jameson said it was a farewell party. If he leaves town . . ."

"He ain't going anyplace." He sprung about and faced Seth. "Cat, you are one hell of a detective. There ain't a flaw in your reasoning."

"Stop kidding me. You'd already come to the same conclusion."

"Just about, just about." He took a swig of his Coke. "You got to be careful tonight, Seth baby. That's going to be a mighty crowded house. Anything can happen which nobody might notice. Stick very close to me, cat."

"Aren't I already?" Seth smiled, and Pharoah could smell eight strips of sizzling bacon and six eggs sunny side up.

Adam examined the wallpaper of the furnished room for the third time that afternoon and wondered if there were any rules about repapering. A male and female voice in the next room were raised in a loud argument. Spanish fell about him with the grace and speed of a heel-kicking flamenco accompanied by castanets. I'll get used to that in time. He pushed the empty suitcases under the bed and then lowered the shade on the solitary window. I'll find a good job. I won't be trapped here forever. I'll find a place overlooking the Hudson with a southern exposure, a place as light and airy, as comfortable and cheerful as Seth's. Jameson will go away, and with him will go Ella, and Ben's murder will be forgotten in time. I'll get through tonight. God knows how, but I'll do it. But if there's Ella . . . Oh God, if there's Ella . . .

Mr. Rachel stamped his foot and three slaveys scurried for cover. "Why don't you hirelings pay attention? I said Kelly green lanterns at the end of the garden, not strung along the greenhouse! Green on green will wash out!"

Jameson appeared on his balcony, hair encased in a net, his flowing pink Sulka dressing gown billowing in the breeze as he emerged. "Rachel!" he called sharply, and Rachel looked up. Jesus. If she breaks into song, I'll faint.

"What is it, Jamie?"

"Must there be such a commotion?"

"You want this dump looking the way you want it to look, then there's got to be a bit of fuss!" "Fuss" hissed its way up to Hurst and nipped at his ear. He "tsked" and swept back into his room where the hairdresser waited patiently to remove the net from Hurst's head and tease the flaxen locks till they screamed for mercy.

Mr. Rachel had seen to it he'd be on hand for tonight's gala. "After all, Jamie! Supposing something goes wrong with the buffet? We can't have you sweeping it off the table in one of your pets!" Mr. Rachel sat in a wicker chair and lit his corncob pipe. The last time he had smoked it in public he heard somebody say, "Looka the faggot hillbilly." Dear Jamie. How long ago was it we were lovers? Bette Davis was an ingénue, and *that* could have been the year Haley discovered the comet. Look at Jamie and look at me. I could be his uncle. And there's still Ella. Did Jamie really mean it? Would Ella really be at the party tonight?

That maniac.

Veronica stayed home from the office and rested in bed most of the day. The doctor had given her a prescription he assured her would repair her frayed nerves by ten that evening. Rather cute, that doctor. Strange I never noticed it before. He was so sweet when he told me I must learn to control my violent temper. Kill Seth indeed. As though I could ever kill Seth. I could destroy him, but that doesn't mean I have to kill him. She sighed contentedly. We'll see who breaks down first. Didn't I end up getting that little Ben bastard where I wanted him (thanks to Ella, of course)? But then, Ella just might cooperate in helping me nip the book in the bud. I'm not as dumb as she thinks I am.

Seth lay on the bed letting the cool Hudson breezes dry his body. Stay sober tonight, baby. Whatever you do, stay sober. You're facing the toughest night of your life. And then after this mission is accomplished, there's Pharoah to contend with. Who knows? You may have to end up sharing his pad for a while anyway. But that doesn't have to go on forever. Nothing does. Ben found that out.

Ada held the peacock-blue cocktail dress up to her neck and admired herself in the full-length mirror. Thank God Mama's out of the way and off to the Catskills. The house is clean and there are flowers in the vases. The house smells good, thanks to the lavender spray. Seth is bound to come up for a drink when he brings me home tonight. So what if he isn't Jewish? Did that stop Sammy Davis Jr. from marrying May Britt?

She went back to the bedroom and hung the dress up on the door. She brushed the material of the skirt lightly with the palm of her hand and then stepped back to admire it. Peacock blue. I always look lovely in peacock blue.

224

"That's a rotten color for you! You look like a Flatbush tart!"

"Ma! Tell Benny to shut up! You shut up, Benny!"

I'll wear anything I damn well please, and you've been shut up, Benny. You've been shut up for good.

Ruthelma glanced at her wrist watch. Only *eight*-five. It must have been *eight* at least an *hour* ago. Well. I can't be the *first* to arrive. I could have another piece of *chocolate* layer cake and a cup of *skimmed* milk. I better *not*. I'll get *crumbs* all over me and ruin this Lucy Brombart *original*.

The baby sitter's eyes were glued to the television set, sitting on the couch next to Ruthelma's mother, holding her hand and patting it every so often. "How can you *watch* that *junk?*" Ruthelma asked the seventy-year-old woman.

"You go to your church. I'll go to mine."

Ruthelma marched into the kitchen, poured a cup of skimmed milk, cut a thick slice of chocolate layer cake, tied a dish towel around her neck as a bib, sat down, and went to her church.

"You naughty boy!" The middle-aged bleached blonde at the bar next to Ward Gabriel laughed. "I'd like to turn you over my knee and kiss you."

"Ward!"

"Excuse me. It's the boss," said Ward, and crossed to the end of the bar where Ida stood in spangled blouse and bouffant yellow skirt, a paisley stole draped across her shoulders and green teardrops dangling from each ear.

"Now you listen," she said to Ward. "If there's any trouble here, you phone me, you understand? I won't be long. I'm just gonna put in an appearance and then I'll be back."

"Stay as long as you like, for crying out loud! Tuesday's always a quiet night here. Why don't you learn to enjoy yourself?"

"Why don't you go take a shit for yourself? I been to one of Hurst's parties before. They're drags. I'm only going because it's business. And listen." Her eyes narrowed in warning as she wagged the beefy index finger under his nose. "You tamper with them receipts and . . ."

"Ah, Ida!"

"Don't Ah, Ida me, baby," she called, nailing every word into his ear with her tongue. "For a buck you wouldn't stop at murder. Where's that effing Carey Cadillac?" She waddled over to the window, and Ward looked at her with a mixture of distaste and mockery. On one of those days you bathe, you fat slob, I'd just like to be in that bathroom with the radio going full blast and then . . .

"There's the Cadillac. Now remember! If there's trouble, call me!"

I've got to get rid of him, she thought, as she crossed the sidewalk and nodded at the chauffeur holding the door open for her. The chauffeur wondered if he should heave her into the back seat with his shoulder as she bent over with difficulty to get in.

She made it.

He shut the door, crossed around the car, got in, and drove off as Ida lit a Gitane.

I knew it, sniffed the chauffeur, pot.

Yes, thought Ida, he's got to go. When they get to be trouble, they got to go.

226

The Cadillac turned east into Seventy-second Street, passing the red Jaguar heading toward West End Avenue.

Pharoah maneuvered the car gracefully, his mind on the evening ahead of him, repeating the silent prayer that everything would go off without a hitch and he'd have himself a murderer. Then he'd have himself a full life. He had Seth bagged and he knew it. Only did Seth know it?

Seth gave himself a final once-over in the dressing-table mirror (he'd have to give this damn dressing table back to Veronica, whether she has room in the apartment for it or not) and approved of what he saw. He had to stick close to Pharoah. He had to get his signal, walk over to that person and say, "You know, I'm drunk enough to tell you. I saw you going into Ben's apartment after I left." Would it work? It had to.

The downstairs buzzer resounded and he rushed to the intercom.

"Hello!"

"Cat? Your chariot awaits."

Adam stared at Jameson as he paraded back and forth in the bedroom like a model at a private Paris showing.

"Well, my dear? Where does this grab you?"

The flaxen locks were teased into a towering pompadour. The green velvet dinner jacket sported a spray of lilies of the valley. The trousers were purple, and down each side was a thin length of carmine dotted with yellow and blue paiettes. Around his neck was a silk plaid cravat with a large opal stickpin. On eight of his ten fingers was a variety of jewelry that might have caught Paulette Goddard short of breath. On

227

each of his red velvet pumps was a yellow pompon. His nails were lacquered to a high sheen.

"Jamie," said Adam, "you're a vision." He turned and went to open the door. He looked extremely handsome in the navy blue suit and red-and-blue-striped tie.

"Don't move!" whispered Hurst hoarsely.

"What's wrong?"

"Just stand there a moment. I want to remember you as you are." Then he swept past him, leaving in his wake a trail of lilac scent. Adam sneezed and followed him.

Over sixty people were milling about downstairs and in the garden, and Mr. Rachel stood next to the five-piece orchestra with eyes glued at the head of the stairs. Hurst entered his line of vision and Rachel signaled the orchestra leader. The orchestra leader nodded and tapped his baton, then gave the downbeat. The room reverberated with "Land of Hope and Glory" as slowly, head erect, shoulders back, one hand stretched ahead for balance, the other poised delicately on his hip, Jameson descended the staircase. All eyes were glued on the host, and Ida bit her lip to subdue the rising hysteria. Veronica's face was as straight as the seams of her stockings, and a chagrined Ruthelma was caught holding a plate in her left hand and a ladle in her right heaped with dripping lobster salad. Ada crouched deeper into the corner at the far end of the room and cursed the blood that rushed to her face in embarrassment. The doorbell rang, but the hired butler had his instructions. He could hardly wait to get home and tell his wife, or would her raucous laughter bring on another miscarriage? Pharoah and Seth cooled their heels outside. Seth recognized the music.

228

"We'll have to wait. Hurst is making his entrance."

Adam remained at the top of the landing, praying that Hurst's threat of an appearance by Ella was just a cruel joke.

Hurst reached the bottom of the landing as the orchestra stopped, his face wreathed in an enchanting smile. He cried, "Welcome, my darlings! Welcome!" Sixty pairs of hands applauded wildly as the butler opened the door and Seth and Pharoah entered. Hurst spun about to greet them with arms outflung.

"Abandon hope, all ye who enter here!" The orchestra resumed; laughter clashed with the hubbub of voices, and Hurst crossed to Seth and took his hand. "I hope this will be the most memorable evening of all our lives."

"I'm sure it very well could be," said Seth with a smile, then waved to Adam who was descending the stairs. Adam smiled and wondered what was eating the detective. Their eyes had met briefly, and Adam was positive he detected a flash of hostility. I must have misread him, he told himself. It's me. Everyone seems hostile tonight. When did Jameson find the time to tell them all we're splitting? The orchestra leader examined the list Hurst had drawn up of his favorite selections and guided his crew into a spirited arrangement of "Love, Your Magic Spell Is Everywhere."

Hurst took Pharoah by the arm and led him into the crush. "I'm so glad you came! I'll wager you haven't the vaguest idea who most of these people are. Well, my dear, there isn't one that hasn't been involved with Ben Bentley at one time or another. Did you hear me, Seth?"

"I'm spellbound," said Seth, watching Adam elbow his way to the bar.

"There's at least half the material you'll need for your

229

book under this roof at this very moment," Hurst continued gaily. "Make hay, my boy! The crop is ripe for reaping!" He patted Pharoah's arm with his free hand. "Wouldn't it be marvelous? Wouldn't it be *simply* marvelous if you caught Ben's murderer tonight? Right here! Wouldn't it be marvelous, Seth? What a fitting climax to cap the evening! What a way to say goodbye!"

"Where were you thinking of going?" asked Pharoah.

"Off!" cried Hurst with a sweep of his hand for emphasis, knocking a glass of champagne out of Mr. Rachel's hand. "Oh, I'm so sor—" He glared at Mr. Rachel. He was wearing a duplicate of Hurst's dinner jacket. "Rachel," growled Hurst, "you bitch." Rachel pursed his lips and sniffed as he motioned to a flunky to clean away the debris. "Rachel was one of my first lovers, way, way back, during the French and Indian War."

From her corner of the room Ada spotted Seth following Hurst and Pharoah through the crowd. "Seth!" she shouted, and fifteen pairs of eyes riveted on her. She shrank back into the corner and, after a decent interval, moved from it timidly and made her way with difficulty toward Seth.

How do I get rid of this bore, wondered Veronica. She was trapped by an effete young man with tiny eyes and tiny nose, probably, Veronica decided, bcause so much space was needed for his mouth. "What I really mean," the effete young man said, inhaling, "is that I'm so fed up with these plays about lack of communication. Now this one I saw last night off-Broadway—I mean way off like Delancey Street, I think it was—opens with two long-distance operators sitting on opposite sides of the stage, and right away they get disconnected and it's like three acts before they get plugged back into each other, if ever. Do you still get much of that sort of stuff, I mean book-wise?"

Veronica caught Adam's eye and he read her signals. He pushed his way to her side. "Excuse me," he said to the effete young man. Then smiling at Veronica, he said, "You promised me this dance."

"Oh, Adam, I'm so sorry! I got so caught up in this conversation with Mr. er—uh—ah . . ."

"Yumptov."

"Yumptov! Will you excuse me, Mr. Yumptov?"

Mr. Yumptov excused them and watched them go off and then set his sights for his next victim.

Hurst guided Pharoah and Seth from guest to guest with lavish introductions. "A detective, my dears! A real honest-to-God detective! He's on the track of Ben Bentley's murderer! Audrey, stop looking so guilty!" Audrey was a tall, late-fortyish woman with a masculine haircut. She wasn't looking guilty at all. Somebody's high heel had just accidentally dug into her right sneaker, and she was stifling a howl of pain and resisting an urge to belt the offender with a right uppercut.

"I'm so sorry!" cried Veronica, shifting about in Adam's embrace to get a better look at the person she had stepped on.

"Hullo, baby," said Audrey. "Long time no see." Seth folded his arms and beamed with delight at Audrey, wondering if she photographed as handsomely as she looked.

"Oh!" gasped Veronica. "Audrey!"

"Who'd you think?" said Audrey huskily. "Simone de Beauvoir?"

"Why, Seth darling," cried Veronica in a rush, "I didn't know you'd arrived."

"Hullo, baby." Seth smiled. "Long time no see." Veronica's eyes narrowed into slits, and at any moment Pharoah expected to see Seth struck down by a deadly ray. Veronica pulled away from Adam and crossed to Seth.

"I'm sure Adam won't mind if we finish this dance, darling." She snuggled against Seth, leaving him no choice, then turned to the others and said vivaciously, "Has he told you? I'm filing for the divorce."

Good God!" cried Hurst, clasping his hands together and flashing a look at the ceiling. "It's really the end of an era! Now I know how the Hapsburgs felt when Austria collapsed! Come, Audrey!" he said, grabbing Audrey's hand. "I shall teach you the minuet."

Alone with Pharoah, Adam stared at the detective awkwardly.

"How you doing, cat?" asked Pharoah.

"Okay," said Adam glumly.

"You don't look too happy. Cheer up. The worst is yet to come."

"That's what I've been afraid of."

Pharoah patted him on the back and then edged past him toward the bar.

"If you don't behave yourself," said Seth to Veronica, "I'll turn you over to Audrey."

"Go ahead, sweetie," retorted Veronica. "Keep driving the nails into your coffin."

"Then get your thigh out from between my crotch."

"What's there to injure?"

Seth left her in the middle of the floor and headed for the bar.

"Abandoned!" cried Hurst as he and Audrey swept past Veronica. "And in her prime!"

"Hullo, baby," said Audrey.

Veronica elbowed her way off the dance floor and collided with Ida.

"Oof," said Veronica.

"Hullo, baby," said Ida. "How do you get a frigging drink around here? The bar's jammed."

"Signal a waiter," snapped Veronica, and plowed onward.

"Up yours too," said Ida, and she signaled a waiter.

The skinny man towered over Pharoah by at least five inches. "Well, hello," he said warmly. "We haven't met."

"We haven't," said Pharoah, waiting for the bartender to fill his order.

"I'm Herbee Howard. H-e-r-b-*double* e. What's *your* name?"

"Pharoah Love."

"What a *mah*-velous name! Are you part Egyptian?"

"No," said Pharoah wryly, "I'm half Jewish."

"Really!" said H-e-r-b-double e. "You don't look Jewish. I'm a window trimmer. What do *you* do?"

"When?"

Herbee snickered. "When you work, silly?"

"I'm a detective."

"Oops. Excuse me. My mother's waving at me." He swivel-hipped past Pharoah. The bartender handed Pharoah a Scotch and water as Seth arrived.

"One of those," he said to the bartender. Then he said to Pharoah, "My wife is looking for trouble."

"Want me to belt her one?" asked Pharoah pleasantly.

"No, thanks. I can handle her."

"Your friend Adam seems a little unhappy."

"They say Indians have premonitions."

"Maybe he'll do a dance and ward off the evil spirits."

233

"Seth!" gasped Ada.

"Hi, Ada! You remember Pharoah."

"Yes." Gasp. "Of course." Gasp. "Hello." Gasp. "I had a terrible time getting through this crowd. Where's your wing? I need to get under it."

Seth put his arm around her shoulder. "There. All protected. How about a drink?"

"Oh, I'd love a pink lady." Pharoah winced inwardly.

"A pink lady!" Seth shouted to the bartender, who winced outwardly. "Who would you like to meet?" Seth asked Ada.

"No one," she said with a grimace. "I'm happy where I am." She managed a weak smile for Pharoah's benefit. "Is it all right if I stick with you two? I'm so *lost*. And I spent a *fortune* on this dress!"

Seth picked up his cue. "It's worth every nickel. It's beautiful. Did your mother get away all right?"

"God, yes. I've got the apartment *all* to myself. You *must* come up for a drink." Pharoah concentrated on a chubby lady gorging herself at the buffet.

"Mmmmmmmm," said Ruthelma as she popped a smoked oyster into her mouth.

"Delicious, aren't they?" said Mr. Rachel. Ruthelma smiled at the pleasant-looking elderly gentleman with the smoky gray eyes.

"Mmmmmm." She finished masticating and swallowed. "What a superb *buffet!*"

"Thank you. I arranged it all."

"You *didn't!*"

"I'm Mr. Rachel." He pronounced it "Rah-shell."

"But you're a *genius!* I can't *tear* myself *away* from it."

"Go right ahead and enjoy yourself, dear, before the others descend like a plague of locusts. May I?" He picked up a napkin and wiped a drop of lobster salad from Ruthelma's bosom. Ruthelma giggled. "There!" said Mr. Rachel. "Pretty girls like you don't want to go around getting themselves spotted up."

"*Girl!*" squeaked Ruthelma from her newly erected pinnacle. "Why, I'm *practically* a senior *citizen!*"

"Nonsense!" Mr. Rachel smiled, pinching her cheek playfully. "You're young in heart, and that's what counts, Miss . . ."

"Kross," squeaked Ruthelma, "*Ruthelma* Kross. I'm a *literary* agent. I *represent* one of the *guests.* Seth *Piro.*"

"Oh yes."

"I haven't the *vaguest* idea *how* I came to be *invited,* unless it was through Miss *Ella* Hurst."

"Ella?" said Mr. Rachel in a hushed tone. "You know Ella?"

"*Well,* I never *actually* met the *lady,* but through an *intermediary* there was a discussion of representing her *memoirs.*"

"Her *what?*" shrieked Mr. Rachel, and he carried himself away in a gale of laughter.

Seth watched Pharoah dancing with Ada, as Ida maneuvered her way to his side. "Ain't this a crock of shit?" she said for openers. Seth turned to her and threw his arms around her.

"Hiya, sweetheart! Who's watching the store?"

"Moishe the actor. And if he taps the till, I'll break his ten fingers like this." She picked up a swizzle stick and cracked it with thumb and forefinger.

"Then he won't be here?"

"Why? What do you need him for?"

"Nothing special. I just thought he'd be here. Part of the theme."

"What theme?"

"The party. Everyone invited was mixed up with Ben."

"Baby, if everybody invited was mixed up with Ben, we'd be drinking in Shea Stadium. I'm getting the heebie-jeebies."

"Why, for crying out loud?"

"I don't know. Something's up someplace. Look over there—Adam and Hurst. Something tells me they're building up to a real winger."

"Control yourself!" snapped Hurst to Adam. "You're making a scene."

"What's gotten into you?" Adam pleaded.

"If Ella wishes to attend this gala, then Ella shall attend! And don't you dare attempt to bar her way, do you hear me? Don't you dare! Oh, there's Veronica! I have to talk to her! Veronica!" Adam downed his fourth straight Scotch and then stared into the glass. He looked around the room and found Seth standing near the bar with Ida. He began pushing his way across the dance floor, past Pharoah and Ada.

"You're a *marv*elous dancer!" exclaimed Ada. "You people have such rhythm! I mean . . ."

Pharoah changed the conversation graciously. "Feel better tonight, now that you're out enjoying yourself?"

"I sure am! Can you imagine," she said, her eyes sweeping the room with wonder, "Ben was once a part of all this! Oh well."

"You didn't much like him, did you?"

"No, and I can't lie about it either."

"I guess you don't give a damn one way or another if I ever catch his murderer."

Ada looked into his eyes. "It's like I said, whoever it is deserves a medal."

"You ever win any medals, Ada?"

Hurst grabbed Veronica's arm as she was heading into the garden. "Come here, vixen. I want words with you."

"Oh, Jamie, *now* what?"

"Don't you use that tone of voice with me! Are you planning a bit of a to-do with Seth tonight?"

"We just *might* come to blows, yes."

"Don't be a fool, dear. His black mother hen will scatter you to the four winds. Watch your step. Those two are up to something. They keep going into huddles and giving each other cryptic winks across the room. They don't fool me for one minute. I caught their reactions when I gaily suggested it might be delightful if Love caught his murderer tonight. Well, whatever plans they may have, my sweet, watch them get nipped in the bud. Guess who's coming. Ella!" He swept away from her, not needing to remain in her company any longer, having seen her chin drop before.

"I wouldn't take any bets on it," Seth said to Adam.

"Any bets on what?" asked Pharoah, as he and Ada joined Seth and Adam.

"Adam says Ella's coming."

"Well, well, well," mused Pharoah. "The cat herself." Then grinning from ear to ear, he ordered a fresh drink. Seth eyed him steadily, trying to signal him away from the group, but Pharoah was lost in thought.

"Seth," squealed Ada, "you haven't danced with me yet!"

Pharoah got his drink and turned to Seth. "Go ahead, cat. You're in for a treat. Her people have such rhythm." Seth couldn't understand why Ada was blushing as he danced her onto the floor, nor could he fully understand why he felt Ella's possible appearance might ruin his and Pharoah's plan.

"You know what I think, Adam cat?" Pharoah said, swishing the ice around in his drink. "I think Ella cat's got a line on who killed Ben cat. I hope she gets here soon. Before Murderer cat tries to get his claws into her. My Seth baby tried to get hold of her yesterday, but no luck. You don't know by any chance if Brother cat's heard from her?"

"Yes," said Adam, "he's heard from her. When she told him she was coming."

"Uh-huh."

Mrs. Howard sat in the love seat with Herbee and held his hand, delighted and flattered to be surrounded by half a dozen handsome young men and to be the center of their attention.

"So my poor Herbee," she continued with the story, "got up late last Tuesday. He looked out the window to test the weather and there was all the flags at half-mast. He let out such a yell and started crying. He didn't know it was Memorial Day. He thought Barbra Streisand was dead."

"Hullo, baby." Veronica stiffened as Audrey appeared from behind the peony bush. "Stop running, baby. I don't do my flying tackles in public. I just want a little advice."

Veronica conjured up a smile and tried to hold it in position. "Such as?"

"Such as you deal in books, right, baby?"

"Right."

"Then you know how I could go about getting the musical-comedy rights to a book."

"Why, Audrey," said Veronica, genuinely surprised, "are you planning to produce on Broadway?"

"You hear me, baby." She opened a little tin box on a gold chain around her neck and took a pinch of snuff.

"What book are you trying to get?"

Audrey sneezed, pulled a square of red bandana from her sweater sleeve, and blew into it. *"The Well of Loneliness."*

Veronica bit her lip.

"Got a great title for it. *Seven Brides for Seven Brides.* Like it?"

"It really swings, Audrey."

"Thought you'd go for it, baby."

Ruthelma finished her third dance with Mr. Rachel and he led her to the bar.

"You put Fonteyn to shame," he whispered in her ear.

"Oh, *heavens!*" she gasped.

"Is something wrong?"

"I don't *think* you'd *understand.* It's *just* that I'm *feeling* one of my *tingles.*" Mr. Rachel squeezed her hand, and Ruthelma was positive she wouldn't have to waste money on a cruise and gamble on finding a lonely widower.

Adam staggered into their path and clutched Mr. Rachel by the lapels. "Where's Jamie?" he asked thickly, his breath reeking. Mr. Rachel pulled away and averted his head to avoid asphyxiation.

"Upstairs. He said something about a visitor."

"Christ . . . Christ," Adam muttered, and weaved toward the hall and the staircase.

Over one hundred people were now jammed into the lower part of the house. A few spilled out into the garden, and Seth could find no private corner in which to speak to Pharoah. They were in the hallway under the stairs.

"What's your rush?" asked Pharoah. "Let's wait till Ella cat gets here."

"But then it might not work. He's drunk now. Look!

There he goes up the stairs." Pharoah turned and saw Adam push past people on the staircase, stumble, right himself, and continue unsteadily.

"Don't worry, cat," said Pharoah, squeezing Seth's arm. "We can't miss now. It's where I told you it would be. In the bag."

"Well, do forgive me! Am I disturbing your tête-à-tête?" She held a glass of champagne in her right hand, her left propped against the wall. "I've been hearing all *sorts* of things about you two. Must the wife *always* be the last to know?"

"A little louder," said Seth angrily, "and we can waltz to it."

"Why, Mr. Love," continued Veronica, hoping her words would impale them against the wall, "I'll bet Seth plans to dedicate the book to you. He dedicated one to *me* once, you know. That was shortly before he walked out on me for the hustler. You really have to keep an eye on him, Mr. Love. Make the mistake of leaving a door ajar, and Seth takes a walk!"

"Now, Pharoah," cried Seth, "for God's sake, now!"

17

ADAM LUNGED into Hurst's room, tripped on the rug, and fell face down on the floor.

"Dear boy!" piped the all too familiar voice. "Dear, dear boy! Did you hurt yourself?"

Adam twisted his head around and stared at Ella as she slammed the door shut and stood leaning against it. The heavily veiled head had a rose pinned in the hair. Adam grabbed the chaise longue and pulled himself to his feet. "You're not going down there," he said. "I won't let you go down there."

"Why, dear boy? Are you afraid? Isn't it better to have it over and done with?"

"You're not going down there." He advanced on her slowly.

"I shall do as I please. Seth and Mr. Love want their murderer, and they shall have their murderer. And then Jamie will be free. And that shall be my last act on his behalf."

"You're not going down there."

He rushed at Ella, but the fat old woman side-stepped him

with surprising agility. He fell against the door and remained leaning against it, gasping for breath. He couldn't understand the sharp pain that tore through his back. It was as sudden as a summer storm. He clawed at the door, eyes closed, face contorted in agony.

"Oh my Jesus," cried Adam, "oh my Jesus! Why me?"

Seth's hand shot out and caught Veronica across the face. *"Seth!"* cried Ruthelma as she entered the hall.

"Cut that, cat!" shouted Pharoah, as he rushed forward and pinned Seth's arms behind him.

"You stinking queen!" screamed Veronica. "You stinking queen! I'll smear you across every front page in this town!"

"I'll kill her!" yelled Seth. "I'll kill her!" He struggled vainly to free himself, but Pharoah's grip was unbreakable. Ada stood dumfounded in the archway between hall and living room. She watched the scene at the end of the hallway with disgust. She wanted to go home. She wanted to be out of here. Away from these revolting people. Away from these sickening creatures who have gone against nature.

"Shit," said the fat woman standing next to her. "Shit." She was staring up at the head of the stairway where Adam stood clawing vainly at his back.

"Seth!" cried Ida. "Seth!" A sudden silence descended over the area as Seth and Pharoah stopped struggling and stared up at Adam.

"Dear Jesus!" gasped Adam, tears streaming down his face. "Dear Jesus, help me!" He coughed violently and blood was streaming down his chin. Ada heard a woman shrieking hysterically and, until the fat woman started shaking her, didn't realize it was herself. Veronica's hands flew to her mouth as Adam stood on the top stair, arms outstretched, looking into some distant void where possibly he saw Him. He looked like an Olympic champion poised to dive, and he disappointed no one. Ruthelma yelped and buried her head in Mr. Rachel's inadequate chest as Adam plunged down the staircase atop several guests who squealed and yelped in an effort to avoid being struck by his body.

He lay crumpled on the staircase, the bread knife sticking out of his back. Pharoah and Seth rushed to his side.

"There's your murderer," piped the all too familiar voice from the head of the stairs. They stared up at Ella, the front of her dress smeared with blood, rubbing her hands together nervously.

"There's your murderer, Seth. Not Jamie. I knew you thought it was Jamie. Jamie was there that morning. He knows now that you saw him. But I believe Jamie. He didn't kill Ben. He loved Ben. This foul creature did it. He tried to prevent my coming here tonight."

"Who's *that?*" someone whispered. "Is that the crazy sister?"

"Shut your hole!" someone snapped.

"It's a lie!" shouted Seth.

"Shut up!" snapped Pharoah. "Let her talk. You shut up!"

"Why did you kill him?" cried Seth. "Why did you kill Adam? This poor sweet guy! You fucking monster!"

"Seth," cried Ella, agonized, "I did it for *you!* I did it for *you!* I did it . . . I . . . I . . ."

Ella emitted a hideous rattle. She suddenly stiffened, and her arms shot forward as though a charge of electricity had been sent coursing through her aged veins. Seth, Pharoah, and the others stared at her in horror.

243

"It can't be," Pharoah heard Seth whisper. "It can't be! It can't! It can't! I didn't figure this!"

"Catch her!" he heard Veronica shriek. "Catch her! She's falling over the railing!"

The mass of humanity that was Ella Hurst lost its balance and, in the grip of an epileptic fit, fell over the railing and plunged to the ground floor. The veiling around her face unwound as she fell and made beautiful spirals as it untwisted. The body landed on its back, and the sickening snap Pharoah heard told him the neck was broken. He pushed his way to the body's side, Seth following dumbly, but Veronica was there ahead of them.

"I'll be damned," she guffawed. "Oh baby! I'll be damned!" She couldn't control the hysterical laughter that shook her body as she pointed down at Jameson Hurst.

18

PHAROAH'S FIST shot out and caught Seth smack
in the face. He crumpled to the floor where his hysterical
tears subsided into a groan. He lay there, blood trickling
from his nose onto the living-room floor of his apartment.

"Now will you listen, cat?"

"Don't hit me again," Seth whimpered. "Don't hit me
again."

Pharoah knelt beside him and turned him on his back.
"Are you listening to me, cat?"

"Yes . . . yes!" gasped Seth. "Yes, I'm listening."

"No more hysterics now." His voice was softer.

"No more. No more. I promise. No more."

"Adam cat is dead. Jameson-Ella cat is dead. Nothing you
say or do is going to bring them back. You saw them
strapped to the stretchers and carted away. They're on ice
now, cat, with little tags around their big toes. Tomorrow
they'll be headlines and the day after they'll be forgotten. As
far as everybody else is concerned, this case is closed. It is
finished. Our little ploy would have worked, Seth baby,

245

lovely cat." He took a handkerchief from his pocket and held it to Seth's nose. "I didn't want to hurt you, baby cat. But I had to make you listen."

"I'm listening," whispered Seth, staring at the ceiling. "Don't hit me again, Pharoah. I'm listening. I'll do whatever you say."

"Sure you will, baby cat. Because I love you and I know what's best."

"I know you do. I know you do." He took the handkerchief, feeling the stickiness of the blood it absorbed.

He chuckled. "You sure had it pegged right in your notes."

"You read them."

"You knew I did, cat. Who else but me could break in here and get at them? I had to make sure you weren't gumming it up for yourself. I had to make sure I didn't lose you, cat."

Seth struggled and sat up and stared at the blood-stained handkerchief. "It's Adam. I didn't think he'd kill Adam. Oh God. How can I live with that?"

"You'll be surprised what you can learn to live with," said Pharoah, helping him to his feet, guiding him to the couch and sitting him down. He sat next to him and held up the glass of Scotch. Seth took it and sipped. Then he leaned back with a sigh.

"Your chief bought the story."

"Why not, baby cat? It all falls into place nice and sweet and easy. I'll get a citation for this."

"Will you?"

"Yeah, cat. Now I'm up there with the rest of them snotty ofay detective cats."

"And supposing someday they uncover the truth?"

"They never will, baby cat. Not as long as you and me sticks together."

"We're together, Pharoah cat." Seth groped for Pharoah's hand, found it, and held it tightly. "We're together."

"Poor old Jameson cat. Living that double life since he was a kid. Pushing Mama out the window because the old lady probably said to him that morning, 'No more Ella, Jamie. It's not normal for a little boy to make believe he's his own sister.' Cat—" he chuckled—"won't that be something to tell your psychiatrist?"

"I'm never going to see him again. I don't dare."

"That's right, cat. I knew you'd figure that soon enough. See how easy it all is? Hurst must have figured you saw him going into Ben cat's apartment that morning. He knew a jealous man would hang around to see who his ex-boyfriend was expecting. And Adam cat thought all along Hurst cat threw that radio into the bathtub because Ben cat was going to tell the whole world the truth about Ella. They were too dumb to figure the truth because you played it real cool and real smart."

(Don't kid yourself, Pharoah cat. I'm still playing it real cool and real smart. Just give me time.)

"Tell me, baby cat, did Ben cat get you angry? Is that why you killed him?"

Seth reached for the Scotch and took a deep swig.

"The truth, Pharoah cat, is that I asked him to come back to me because I couldn't stand it without him. And he told me he wouldn't come back to me because he doesn't stick with losers. Do you hear' me, Pharoah cat?"

"I hear you."

"I had no intention of killing him when I went there. It

wasn't even in my mind. I just went there to plead. He sat in that tub soaping himself, the radio going full blast, telling me to get off his back and stay off his back. He didn't want me calling him any more at all hours of the night and trailing him to see who he was doing it with. He didn't want me sending him notes and little gifts. He thought I was going to be rich, but I turned out to be a flop."

"You ain't no flop, baby cat. You're going to write that book and make your million. Didn't Ben cat buy the idea?"

Seth stared at Pharoah. "Buy what idea?"

"You writing a book about him." Pharoah winked. "Takes at least three weeks to get an Author's Query into the Sunday *Times Book Review*." Pharoah spoke very softly. "You knew three weeks ago you were going to write the book."

The ice in the glass tinkled as Seth's hand shook, but his voice was steady when he spoke. "He didn't like it at all. He . . ." His voice rose. "He said I wasn't good enough to write it! He shouldn't have said that to me. He knows my temper. He knows it comes over me in a rush and then I can't control myself." The glass slipped from his hand and crashed onto the floor, but neither of them seemed to notice.

"He just went on and on, insulting me, castigating me, and I picked the frigging radio up and threw it at him. And he yelled and got all stiff and clawed at the air and I ran out! I ran out! I ran down the stairs and into the street and crossed to the other side and hid in a doorway when I saw the cab pulling up and Jameson getting out. And if he had seen me . . ."

"I know, baby cat, I know. Even if he did, Ella wouldn't have let him turn you in." He chuckled. "Ella liked you. She did all she could to pin the rap on Adam, didn't she? She even killed him to help make the rap stick." He stroked Seth's head. "I think Hurst knew he was dying. He didn't give a damn any more. He sure made one hell of an exit. What did you do with the negatives, baby cat?"

"Down the incinerator in a box marked 'Rejections.'"

"What were they like?" he asked with a sly smile.

"I don't know," Seth said in a tired voice. "I didn't look."

Pharoah stared at him in disbelief. "Weren't you curious?"

Seth stared back at him. "I was afraid of what I might find. I wanted to preserve one last illusion about Ben. Can you understand that?"

"Sure, Seth cat," said Pharoah. "Sure I can." *I got illusions too, cat. And I mean to keep them preserved for a long, long time.*

Pharoah rose. "Okay, baby cat, you need some sleep now. I'll go fix your bed. Fix yourself another Scotch." He left the room and Seth stared down at the shattered glass and the obscene stain on the carpet.

Okay, Pharoah cat. You have won. You have won your citation and you have won Seth baby cat. But one day you'll be sitting in the bathtub soaping yourself, and the radio will be going full blast. You will call to me from the bathroom, 'Hey, baby cat! Come sit in here and talk to me.' And I will go into the bathroom and see you soaping yourself, and I will suddenly hate myself all over again for what I am and for what I did and for having been edged out of the driver's seat and for no longer being my own man, and I will look at you and accuse you with my eyes and hatred will come boiling up in me, and I will suddenly reach for that radio and . . .

GEORGE BAXT
His Life and Hard Times

On a Monday afternoon, June 11, 1923, George Baxt was born on a kitchen table in Brooklyn.

He was nine when his first published work appeared in the Brooklyn *Times-Union*. He received between two and five dollars for each little story or poem the paper used.

His first play was produced when he was eighteen. It lasted one night.

Mr. Baxt has been a propagandist for Voice of America, a press agent, and an actor's agent. He has written extensively for stage, screen, and television. During stays in England in the fifites, he wrote a number of films *(Circus of Horrors; Horror Hotel; Burn, Witch, Burn)* which are now staples of late night television.

His first novel, A QUEER KIND OF DEATH, was published in 1966. His other novels include SWING LOW, SWEET HARRIET; A PARADE OF COCKEYED CREATURES; TOPSY AND EVIL; "I!" SAID THE DEMON; PROCESS OF ELIMINATION; THE DOROTHY PARKER MURDER CASE; and most recently THE ALFRED HITCHCOCK MURDER CASE.

Mr. Baxt lives in New York, is a bachelor, and is devoted to his VCR.

THE LIBRARY OF CRIME CLASSICS®

Victoria Lincoln
A PRIVATE DISGRACE
LIZZIE BORDEN BY DAYLIGHT
0-930330-35-8   320pp $5.95

Barry N. Malzberg
UNDERLAY
0-930330-41-2   256pp $4.95

Margaret Millar
AN AIR THAT KILLS
0-930330-23-4   247pp $4.95

ASK FOR ME TOMORROW
0-930330-15-3   179pp $4.95

BANSHEE
0-930330-14-5   202pp $4.95

BEAST IN VIEW
0-930330-07-2   251pp $4.95

BEYOND THIS POINT
ARE MONSTERS
0-930330-31-5   213pp $4.95

THE CANNIBAL HEART
0-930330-32-3   207pp $4.95

THE FIEND
0-930330-10-2   245pp $4.95

HOW LIKE AN ANGEL
0-930330-04-8   279pp $4.95

THE LISTENING WALLS
0-930330-52-8   250pp $4.95

A STRANGER IN MY GRAVE
0-930330-06-4   311pp $4.95

ROSE'S LAST SUMMER
0-930330-26-9   223pp $4.95

WALLS OF EYES
0-930330-42-0   224pp $4.95

William F. Nolan
SPACE FOR HIRE
0-930330-19-6   200pp $4.95

LOOK OUT FOR SPACE
0-930330-20-X   192pp $4.95

Ellery Queen
THE TRAGEDY OF X
0-930330-43-9   256pp $4.95

THE TRAGEDY OF Y
0-930330-53-6   244pp $4.95

Clayton Rawson
DEATH FROM A TOP HAT
0-930330-44-7   288pp $4.95

S.S. Rafferty
CORK OF THE COLONIES
0-930330-11-0   314pp $4.95

DIE LAUGHING
0-930330-16-1   200pp $4.95

John Sherwood
A SHOT IN THE ARM
0-930330-25-0   172pp $4.95

Hake Talbot
RIM OF THE PIT
0-930330-30-7   278pp $4.95

Darwin L. Teilhet
THE TALKING SPARROW
MURDERS
0-930330-29-3   301pp $4.95